A month ago, Calvin company of vampires, ha a witch to summon a den his life. In the time since, Sal. He knows entering a but to save his brother, demon might be worth the risk.

Sal is a duke among demons. An immortal being, more powerful than a vampire, but who has one admitted weakness, a fondness for humans. When Calvin comes to him to make a deal, he's hesitant, but can't deny his need to be closer to him. He also knows if he doesn't help him, Calvin will summon another demon, and he knows all too well the treachery of his own kind.

Desire and trust builds between Calvin and Sal. Their relationship grows, but so does a hidden threat, and it might take power greater than a demon duke to save them. It might take that of a witch.

MLR Press Authors

Featuring a roll call of some of the best writers of gay erotica and mysteries today!

Derek Adams	Kyle Adams	Vicktor Alexander
Simone Anderson	Victor J. Banis	Laura Baumbach
Ally Blue	J.P. Bowie	Barry Brennessel
James Buchanan	TA Chase	Charlie Cochrane
Karenna Colcroft	Ethan Day	Diana DeRicci
Taylor V. Donovan	S.J. Frost	Kimberly Gardner
Kaje Harper	Stephani Hecht	Alex Ironrod
Jambrea Jo Jones	DC Juris	AC Katt
Kiernan Kelly	K-lee Klein	Geoffrey Knight
J.L. Langley	Vincent Lardo	Cameron Lawton
Anna Lee	Elizabeth Lister	William Maltese
Timothy McGivney	Kendall McKenna	AKM Miles
Robert Moore	Jet Mykles	Jackie Nacht
N.J. Nielsen	Cherie Noel	Gregory L. Norris
Erica Pike	Neil S. Plakcy	Rob Rosen
George Seaton	Riley Shane	Richard Stevenson
Christopher Stone	Liz Strange	Lex Valentine
Haley Walsh	Lynley Wayne	Missy Welsh
Ryal Woods	Stevie Woods	Sara York
Lance Zarimba	Mark Zubro	

Check out titles, both available and forthcoming, at
www.mlrpress.com

DEMON DUKE

Paranormal Nobles

S.J. FROST

mlrpress
www.mlrpress.com

This book is a work of fiction. Names, characters, places, and incidents either are products of the author's imagination or are used fictitiously. Any resemblance to actual events or locales or persons, living or dead, is entirely coincidental.

Published by
MLR Press, LLC
3052 Gaines Waterport Rd.
Albion, NY 14411

Visit ManLoveRomance Press, LLC on the Internet:
www.mlrpress.com

Cover Art by Scarlet Tie Designs
Editing by Kris Jacen

Print format: ISBN# 978-1-94477-023-5
ebook format also available

Issued 2016

Chapter One

"Someone you love is sick. Poor baby. I can fix that, you know."

The words replayed through Calvin's mind, as they had so many times in the past month. Were they true? Could the demon who'd spoken them heal his brother? And if Sallos could, how would he do it? And for what price? A demon never gave away anything for free.

Calvin sagged down on the bed, lying on his side, his gaze fixed on the bright, sunlit day beyond his bedroom window. A month ago, when he'd answered a request on a witchcraft forum, he had no idea what he was getting himself into. All he saw was the large sum of money being offered to anyone who could summon a specific demon and jumped at it, figuring he'd work out the details after he got the job.

He didn't know the intention was to bind the demon. He didn't know it was a trap to capture a young man, a former blood slave. He sure as hell didn't know it was vampires behind the ad, not until he'd met them, and what a shock that was. Sure, he'd seen postings online by other witches who claimed to have run into vampires, but who knew what to believe online? With him still learning about his own power, he wasn't about to disregard vampires could exist, but did he have some doubt? Absolutely. That doubt had gotten knocked out of him. And it was in learning vampires were behind it that his instincts blazed with warning and everything started to feel wrong.

It was stupid of him to take the deal. Wrong and insulting to his beliefs, his gifts, his power, but the money…he needed it so damn bad. Ten thousand dollars wouldn't take care of all his brother's medical expenses, but it knocked out a chunk. Except now, it seemed for nothing. Nathan was thinking about stopping his treatments.

His brother told him the day before, he didn't know how much longer he could continue with dialysis, or really, what the point was in doing it. He'd argued with Nathan, telling him if he didn't keep fighting and going to his treatments, his kidneys would fail and he would die. Nathan gave him a smile that told him more than the words he spoke; Nathan had accepted his fate. And as for Nathan's words? *"If God still has work for me here, then I'll recover."*

But for all Nathan's faith and devotion—even going to seminary school—God hadn't helped his brother. Instead, Nathan became sick…and suffered.

Calvin closed his eyes against the burn of tears. He didn't understand Nathan's faith. It seemed it was something his brother had always possessed. Even as teens, when their father died from a sudden heart attack. Even two years ago, as they watched cancer steal the life from their mother. Each time, Nathan would pray and seem to come out of it with a greater sense of peace.

Since it seemed to comfort Nathan, he tried to follow him into that faith. It didn't work for him. He'd recite prayers to the same God and he felt…nothing. No sense of peace or enlightenment. No calm or warmth or love. More than that, he felt odd, out of place, as if he was pretending to be someone he wasn't. He came to the conclusion Nathan's path of faith wasn't meant for him, and maybe no path was.

Until he discovered the faith he was meant to follow, the Craft, the way of being a witch.

He'd been in a park near his home, a few days after his mother passed. He needed solace and comfort that he couldn't find with anyone. As it always had, going to nature, sitting among the trees, cool earth beneath him, the wind whispering around him, he found peace. He found strength. A stick in his hand, he absentmindedly sketched in the dirt, and drew a five-pointed star. It was a symbol he'd drawn often, never knowing why, but thinking it was probably because it was easy to do and his artistic talent wasn't exactly high. Only that day, he caught himself as he drew it. He stared at it, wondered about it, and from the shadows of his mind, a thought rose.

He carried that thought to the library, where he found a green volume in the New Age section with that five-pointed star on the cover. He checked out the book and what began as a pursuit to satisfy his curiosity, became a quest for greater knowledge and to understand himself. To be a witch was to live a spiritual life bonded with nature and those who shared the world, animal and human. Witches were healers and helpers, seekers of knowledge and truth. They could even be warriors, if their path called for them to be.

He still remembered the joy that shone through him when he opened himself up to learning the Craft. He felt uplifted, as if he'd discovered a hidden part of himself. He understood why it was in nature—being surrounded by trees, finding a quiet spot on the beach, gazing at the moon and stars—that he felt more peace than when he'd prayed in Nathan's faith. Why when he touched gemstones, he felt more than the cool stone itself, but also a subtle hum of the power within. In his heart and soul, he'd always been a witch. All he'd needed was for his mind to make the discovery.

But in the two years since that discovery and for all the honing of his skills, he hadn't found a way to save Nathan. Though, he knew and understood that being a witch was a lifelong pursuit in strengthening his skills and gaining knowledge. He just didn't have that much time if he wanted to save his big brother.

Calvin rolled to his back on the bed and pulled in a long, slow breath. Not that Nathan was inclined to let him use spells, incantations, or magic to try and save him. His brother refused to take part in any pagan ritual. His being a witch was the one thing they continuously fought over. When he'd revealed to Nathan the path he was taking, Nathan had argued fiercely with him, to the point where he felt akin to those of old who'd suffered the Inquisition and persecution. It was only when he pointed out to Nathan that the same zealotry had led to the deaths of countless innocent people that Nathan backed off.

For that moment, at least.

They continued to argue about it from time to time, but not as heatedly. Despite each of them lacking faith in each other's beliefs, they loved each other. And he was positive Nathan prayed daily for him to turn his back on the Craft, but same as his prayers hadn't brought him the results he wanted when he'd tried to follow Nathan's faith, Nathan's weren't changing him from being a witch.

He still managed to sneak a few healthy herbs into Nathan's food when he cooked dinner, but it wasn't enough. Nathan was growing weaker. Going in for dialysis three times a week was the only thing keeping Nathan's kidney disease from total kidney failure. Hopes for getting a donated kidney were almost nonexistent, especially since he hadn't been a match.

He couldn't lose him. Nathan had always been there for him, and despite their differences, he knew there was nothing his brother wouldn't do for him. And he was the same toward Nathan. Only, Nathan wouldn't accept his kind of help. Regardless, he wasn't going to let him slip away, not when there was the smallest of chances he could save him. His big brother was the only family he had left.

The tears Calvin had managed to hold back threatened again. He pulled off his silver rim glasses and set them on the nightstand by his bed. He closed his eyes and two tears escaped from the corners of them. They left warm trails over his temples and into his hair.

"I can fix that, you know."

The voice played again through his mind, deep and seductive. Sallos…Sal…manifested behind his closed eyelids in such detail, he could be looking at him in reality. Whether in his human guise or his true form, the demon was beautiful. When in his human form, it seemed at this period in time Sal preferred to have flaming red hair that fell to the tops of his shoulders, layered, sharp angles to it. His body was slender and muscular, his fair skin flawless. Sal's face held so much beauty, he seemed sculpted by a divine hand. And his eyes, the enchanting lavender hue, Calvin had become captivated when he'd looked into them.

He thought Sal couldn't be any more stunning, until Sal shifted into his true form.

Calvin laid a hand over his chest. His heart started racing whenever he thought of him. Sal's hair had grown longer to hang down his back. Horns, thick and curled like a ram's, emerged from the sides of Sal's head. His height increased, his body's frame and muscle thickened. From two smoking slits that opened in Sallos's back, great leathery red wings emerged. Fangs that put to shame any vampire dropped down from Sal's canines. And Sal's eyes…they glowed with that stunning lavender color, the round pupils becoming slits.

Calvin rolled from his back to his stomach, pinning his hardening cock between his body and the bed. Was it completely crazy of him to fantasize about having those wings wrap around him as Sal embraced him? If it was, then he was a certifiable lunatic because he'd thought of it daily since meeting the demon.

He knew, though, his lusting for Sal would never go beyond his thoughts. He couldn't get human men interested in him. No way would a demon as gorgeous as Sal want him. And he wasn't entirely sure *he'd* want Sal to want him.

On the witchcraft forums he hung out at, he'd seen more than one person post about summoning a demon, some even claiming to have had sex with them. It never worked out well. The demon always used the summoner to get a strong hold over their life and use them for their own benefit. While someone might think they had control over the demon, they never did. Ever. A demon would always find a way to get the upper hand and once they did, only pain came from it. It took a lot of powerful magic to banish a demon once they became deeply connected to a person.

In the month since everything went down at the blood house, he realized how much he had to learn about summoning, binding, and compelling demons. He studied his craft for hours each day. If he wasn't working or helping Nathan get to and from his dialysis treatments, then he was striving to gain more knowledge and control with his power. Along with studying evocation, he'd searched for, gathered, and read everything he could on demons, working to not only learn about Sal, but others as well.

He understood their hierarchy now, how the titles weren't a

matter of bloodline or age, but power. The stronger the demon, the greater the title. The counts were at the bottom, followed by the marquises, then earls. Next in line came the dukes, then it moved up to the princes, followed by the kings, to the last and most powerful, the Emperor.

Sal was one of the great nobles. And his true form showed it in his powerful body and massive wings, in his strength and his beauty. Sal may have said his true form wasn't as pretty as his human one, but he'd been awestruck by him.

All of it told him, though, despite how much studying he'd done, he didn't know if he was strong enough to compel a noble demon like Sal. And really, he didn't want to. He'd rather have Sal help him of his own free will than try to bend him to his. The only way that might happen would be to strike a deal with him. He never thought he would be one to consider a deal with a demon, but if Sal could help him, it might be worth any price the demon duke asked for.

Chapter Two

"Beezy, catch!" Sal tossed a red ball toward the little black crocodile.

The ball bounced lightly over the patio cobbles…and off the tip Beezle's snout. The crocodile opened his yellow eyes to slits, peering at Sal with an unappreciative look. He closed his eyes again, returning to soaking up the sun.

A snort and a snicker came from behind Sal. "Do they have entity obedience classes in DemonLand? Because if they do, you should really consider signing Beezle up."

Sal glanced over his shoulder at Sebastian floating in the in-ground pool, his arms folded over the edge as he watched him and Beezle. Sebastian was such a lovely young human. Brilliant blue eyes, golden blond hair, delicate and pretty facial features. It was no wonder Sebastian had broken down the barriers his dear vampy friend, Valentin, had built around himself. And though Sebastian didn't know it, he was grateful to him for bringing Valentin back to his old self. After Malcolm's betrayal, Valentin had become somber and guarded. Now, Valentin's smiles came easily again.

Sal arched an eyebrow as he met Sebastian's gaze. "*DemonLand?*"

"Since it's not really Hell with all the brimstone and burning souls, what else would you call it?"

"We demons just call it our realm, same as we call this one the human realm."

"I think DemonLand sounds better than Demon Realm."

Sal sat on the patio, leaning back on his hands, his legs stretched out in front of him. "It does, actually. Kind of touristy."

Sebastian laughed softly. "Yeah, but instead of people in cute cartoon character costumes running around, you've got little horned minions and flesh-eating entities."

Sal pointed at him. "Don't forget the orgies! Those would be our main attraction. Man, this is a billion dollar idea waiting to happen. Why didn't I ever think of setting up a resort there?"

Laughter came from the mansion.

Sal tossed his head back to look through the open sliding door, where Valentin and Basil sat within the shadows.

Valentin stood and stepped close to the shadow's edge, leaning a forearm up on the doorframe. Long, silken black hair fell past Valentin's shoulders, and his eyes of light frosted blue were quite the lure themselves, especially combined with his face of flawless beauty. As he spoke, Valentin's voice rolled with an elegant English accent. "I'm not so certain. I think there are quite a few humans who wouldn't be too comfortable at the idea of having sex with a demon."

Sal let a smirk rise to his lips. "None that I've ever fucked have complained."

Basil moved to Valentin's side. "But how many of them have known you were a demon?"

Sal focused on Basil. The two vampires were true blood cousins from their human life. They both had similarities in the slender builds and pretty features, but they were opposites in many other ways. Basil wore his wavy, dark blond hair shorter, often bound in a loose ponytail at the nape of his neck. And while Valentin's eyes were icy and cool in color, Basil's were warm, honey-brown.

"I'm sure they had to have some suspicions of me being an otherworldly being since I can fuck better than any human."

"Hey!" Sebastian said. "Those are fighting words! Or fucking words. One or the other."

Sal turned a smirk toward Sebastian. "Only one way to prove me wrong. You two will have to let me watch you at it, and I'll tell you if you're better than me."

"I think you'd be a rather biased judge," Valentin said. "And, no, we're not letting you watch us fuck."

Chuckling, Sebastian pushed out of the pool. He walked by Sal toward Valentin and stepped into the embrace of his vampire prince. "I'll agree on that 'no'."

Valentin wrapped Sebastian in his arms, not the least deterred by Sebastian's wet body pressing against his clothes. Sal couldn't blame the vampire. He wouldn't mind getting a little wet to have a hot human pressed against him either. With his final thought, a human, a name, floated to the front of Sal's mind…one he'd been trying to forget about for the past month—Calvin.

Damn witch. If he didn't know better, he'd swear Calvin had cast an enchantment on him. In fact, he would've preferred it if Calvin had. It would be a hell of a lot less disturbing of a reason as to why he couldn't get the human out of his head.

If he had one admitted weakness, it was for humans. Their intoxicating energy. Their bodies so warm and delightful to touch, caress, have his dick buried deep inside. And Calvin was a *very* lovely human, though, he felt certain Calvin didn't realize it. The witch was on the smaller side in build and height, but he imagined Calvin had quite the tight body beneath his clothes. Calvin's black hair didn't have any kind of style to it, seeming perpetually tousled, giving him a look like he was just getting out of bed…or ready to climb into it.

He liked that last thought, especially with adding himself to the bed. The innocence he sensed from the witch told him Calvin wasn't the most experienced in the erotic arts, but his intuition sensed Calvin was a man filled with lust and passion waiting to be unleashed. And he would love to be the one doing the unleashing.

Behind the silver-rimmed glasses Calvin wore were intelligent, thoughtful, and sad blue eyes. The sadness was tied to Calvin's sick loved one, whoever that was. When he'd viewed Calvin's aura, he saw a man of deep compassion and love, things his little black heart were drawn to. But with those, he also saw power, raw and potent, not completely trained or even the depth of it realized. If Calvin fully honed his skills, he'd be a wicked force to reckon with.

But even if Calvin did reach his full potential, Sal doubted that the witch would ever use his magic to harm anyone. He'd seen the distress in Calvin when he'd learned of the vampires' intention with him, to lock him away forever. And who was it that came to his rescue at the first opportunity? Why, none other than Witchy Poo. He could count the times a human had come to his aid on not only one hand, but on one finger. Well, two fingers. He'd give one to Sebastian, since he'd been part of the rescue too. Sure his life might not have been in true jeopardy, the vampires couldn't kill him, but that didn't mean he wasn't trapped in a sticky situation until Calvin came through for him.

For that alone, he'd like to know the witch better…and get closer to him. Not that it mattered. Unless Calvin summoned him again, he'd never see him. After they'd left the burning remains of the blood house, Basil had taken Calvin close to Savannah and dropped him off, the sunlight and its toll on Basil not letting him take Calvin further. None of them knew where Calvin lived and they hadn't pried enough to get any information on him. Now he wished they had.

It was really annoying that humans, with the right knowledge, could summon a demon at will, but a demon couldn't track down a human unless they had a strong connection to the human or something personal of the human's. Shit like that was one of many reasons why so many demons were bitter against mortals. So unless Witchy Poo wanted to see him, chances were they'd never meet again.

Sal let out a sigh at the thought and caught Basil speaking to him again.

"Aww, darling, there's no need to pout that your pet won't play with you. Shall I call the Savannah Humane Society and see if they're open after dark? We could go get you a puppy."

"Yes!" Sebastian blurted out. "Call them!"

Valentin startled back. "You can't be serious."

Sebastian gave him a sweet smile. "Wouldn't it be fun to get a dog?"

Valentin slowly turned to Basil. "See what you've started?"

Basil clasped his hands behind his back, his posture far too innocent for the mischief in his eyes. "The only reason you're opposed to it is because you don't want dog hair to get on your suits."

Valentin flung his hand out in the direction of Beezle. "And that's why I like Beezle. He doesn't shed." He took Sebastian's hand and walked backward, drawing Sebastian with him. "Let's get you inside, out of that wet swimsuit, and see if I can't redirect your thoughts elsewhere."

Basil watched them disappear inside, then smiled at Sal. "Sorry. It doesn't look as though you'll be getting a puppy today."

Sal chuckled. "That's all right. Too much responsibility for me. It's a damn good thing Beezy's an entity or I probably would've accidentally killed him by now."

"I'm not going to say responsibility isn't exactly a strong suit of yours, but…well, yes, actually I am going to say that."

Sal laughed and brandished a middle finger at Basil.

Grinning, Basil turned on his heel into the mansion. "And on that note, I'm going lie down for the day. It's far too late in the morning for me."

"Have a good sleep," Sal called.

Basil lifted his hand in thanks before disappearing into the darkness inside.

Sal turned back to Beezle, stretching across the distance between them and picking up the ball. "Okay. Let's try this again."

A growl rumbled from the little croc. He swung around, waddling toward the pool.

"Hey! Don't you go in that pool! You know how Baz and Valentin don't like it when…" His voice trailed off as Beezle slipped into the water with hardly a ripple.

Sal tossed the ball into the air and caught it as it came down. "Maybe I should get a dog. I could get Sebastian do all the dirty work."

He tossed the ball again…and it bounced to the ground. Sal gasped, one hand on his chest, one on his abdomen. The pull, it was as if someone had hooked him on the inside and was reeling him to them. He was being summoned. And the presence calling for him was familiar, but far more controlled, confident, and stronger than the last time the summoner had evoked him.

A grin slid onto Sal's lips. Speak of the devil…or witch, in this case. He wouldn't fight this summoning. This was what he'd been waiting for.

Sal took a breath, calling to Beezle. "I've got to go for a little while, Beezy. Be a good boy."

Closing his eyes, Sal willed his body to dematerialize, using his power to do the same with his clothes. As he descended into the gray haze between dimensional planes, he felt happier than he had in ages at being summoned, and that itself troubled him.

Chapter Three

The temperature in the room cooled, the chill moving deeper than flesh to reach Calvin's soul. Tall black pillar candles lined a circle of salt, their flames blazing higher. In the center of the circle, he'd drawn Sal's demon sigil in white chalk on the hardwood floor. He didn't know if it was the candlelight reflecting on the chalk or the rising energy, but the lines, curves, and circles of the sigil glowed with faint luminescence. Something told him it was the latter, energy and power coursing through the symbol.

He was coming.

Calvin swallowed hard. His heart pounded fast and beyond his control to slow. It took all his concentration to not tremble with anticipation and excitement. He'd tried to deny how badly he wanted to see Sal again. Now that the demon was coming, he couldn't deny it any longer.

In his hand, he clutched a smooth, silver pentacle that he used to help focus his energy. The amulet was warm in his hand, more so than from his body's heat. He pulled the amulet's black leather cord over his head to wear it about his neck.

A blast of icy air rushed over him and through the room, tinted with an intoxicating scent; a blend of spice, wood, and earth. All things deeply connected to the world. Demons may have their own realm, but they'd inhabited this world far longer than humans. He knew from studying them, their resentment toward humans came in part from humans spreading and taking over this world. The demons wanted this mortal realm for themselves and believed with their power, they should be the rulers of it.

While humans may be weaker in many ways to a demon, they had one great strength, and it was the other part of demons resenting them. Humans had the power to summon demons, to banish them, to compel them. *If* they honed that power. At this moment, he was really hoping he had, though, he had no intention to banish or compel Sal.

Mist appeared in the center of the circle over the sigil, low near the floor, rolling across it, rising higher and thickening. In the center, a figure manifested. The masculine silhouette was slender, tall, long hair falling just below his shoulders. Slowly, he lifted his head. The mist dissipated, and Calvin met the lavender gaze of Duke Sallos.

His racing heartbeat stumbled. Calvin had barely enough sense left to seal the circle with salt, but it took the last shred of his concentration. How could any being be so incredibly beautiful? At that moment, Sal was in his human form, his body muscled and formed to perfection, but in Calvin's mind, he also saw Sal's true form as a demon. This one demon encompassed so much beauty and sensuality.

And deception. He needed to keep that in mind. He'd watch Sal spin words and throw them at the vampires, Malcolm in particular, to raise their emotions and anger and as he did, Sal had gained more control over them. Demons were great talkers. As much as he wanted to put his trust in Sal, he needed to stay guarded.

A smirk curved one corner of Sal's lips. "Well, hey there, witchy poo. Long time, no see." He looked around the room, his gaze lingering for a moment on the bed. "I like this a lot better than where you summoned me the last time." He brought his gaze back to Calvin, his voice deepening to a sex-filled, huskier timbre. "How nice of you to call me to your bedroom."

The heat of a blush crept up Calvin's neck, spreading over his cheeks.

Sal sauntered toward him, drawing closer until only the line of salt separated them. "Now that you have me here, what do you want to do with me?"

Calvin stared into Sal's eyes, then realizing what he was doing, he dropped his gaze. It was never good to hold eye contact with a demon. The eyes were a passageway to allow the demon to take greater control over the mind, to build a connection before it could even be realized.

Keeping his gaze on the floor, Calvin pushed his glasses up on his nose. "I'm sorry for summoning you. I didn't have any other way to reach you and I needed to see you."

"Did you, now? Well, here I am for you to see as much of me as you want, and if you sweep away this pesky salt, I'll show you *all* of me."

Calvin dropped his mouth open, nothing but a stutter leaving him. The heat of his previous blush turned to a full burn. No doubt about it, Sal knew he was attracted to him. Demons were nothing if not astute, not that he wasn't making it obvious on his own. Still, it didn't change the reason he summoned Sal. He needed to get control over himself, or Sal was going to control him and the situation. "I didn't mean I needed to see you in *that* way."

Sal arched an eyebrow. "No? Are you sure about that?"

Calvin let out a single laugh. "No, I'm not. But it's not as important as why I summoned you."

Sal folded his arms across his chest. "Something more important than wanting my dick? I can't think of anything that could possibly be, but you've piqued my curiosity. What is it?"

Calvin couldn't hold back his smile and mentally cursed himself for it. Damn it. He knew he needed to be cautious, but he couldn't help it if he found Sal charming. Granted, it was a debauched, twisted kind of charm, but charming nonetheless. He took a breath, trying to fortify himself against Sal's wiles. Before he could speak, Sal started talking again.

"Mmm…this room, there's a delicious scent lingering in the air. Faint. Your human sense of smell probably can't detect it any longer, but I can." Sal breathed deep through his nose. "Light sweat, masculine musk, slight bitterness, a hint of saltiness…the good kind, not like the pure shit you've got on the floor." Sal locked his gaze with Calvin's. "You jerked off before summoning me, didn't you?" His smirk took on a wicked edge. "I'm not sure I believe you about not wanting my dick. Let me guess. You were hoping by shooting off a load before summoning me, you'd have more control around me."

Calvin could do nothing but gape and stare at Sal, and be hopelessly aware of how fast his cock was hardening in his jeans…again…as if he hadn't just jerked off…exactly like Sal said. He was losing control fast, if he still had any at all. He needed to get Sal focused on something else, and himself too. Since the truth was out, he might as well fess up. Getting it out of the way might even help so they could move on to what he needed to ask him.

Calvin shrugged and held up his hands in a gesture of surrender. "You got me. I did think it'd help me have a clearer mind for dealing with you. Sadly, I was wrong."

Sal's eyes and expression brightened. "That's nothing to be sad about. I'm pretty damn happy to hear it, myself."

Sal's words sent Calvin back into being speechless. Was Sal really happy about him confessing his attraction? As in, genuinely? Not for some devious reason? Calvin gave the questions a mental push aside. He'd go over them later. Right now, they were nothing but another distraction. "Well, I'm glad you're happy. But I need to ask you something important, so can you try to behave? For a few minutes?"

Sal clasped his hands in front of him, seeming to attempt a look of innocence. Too bad for him, the wicked shine in his eyes gave him away. "All right, all right. I'll behave. But keep it short. Restraining myself for too long hurts."

A smile threatened to break onto Calvin's lips, but he fought it down. He needed to be serious to get through to Sal. "I *might* want to make a deal with you."

Sal nodded slowly, a shadow of skepticism moving into his lavender eyes. "Okay, you've got my interest. What is it that you think I can do for you?"

Calvin took a step closer to the salt line, no longer averting his gaze from Sal's. "When we met, you knew someone I love was sick and you said you could fix that. Is that true? The powers of demons aren't fully known, so I don't have any other choice but to ask and please, answer truthfully. If you can't heal someone, fine. But if you can…" He left his words hanging.

"Well, we demons aren't exactly the most forthcoming with revealing about our powers, so it's not surprising you couldn't find out if we really can heal or not. But the quick answer is yes… and no. Not all demons have that power, or are very good at using it. Now me, I do have that power and I'm damn good with it. And no, I'm not bullshitting you."

A breath of relief rushed from Calvin. He took yet another step closer to the salt line. "If I were to ask you to heal someone for me, what would you want in return?"

Sal paced away from Calvin. "That's a complicated question. Maybe you should clear the salt so we can talk."

"I don't think that's such a good idea."

Keeping his back to him, Sal let out a loud sigh and hung his head, shaking it. "If you want me to help you, you're going to have to put some trust in me."

"I'll consider it after I hear what you want in return for your help."

Sal glanced back at him and flicked his hand toward the salt. "You realize that shit burns, don't you? It's hard for me to concentrate."

Calvin allowed a smirk of his own to rise to his lips. "Oh, I'm sure a big, strong demon like you can handle a little salt stinging you."

A laugh slipped from Sal. "There's that tough guy side to you I saw back at the blood house. I like that in a human."

"I'm not tough." Calvin motioned toward himself. "Look at me. A strong wind knocks me off balance."

The smile on Sal's lips shifted to having a warmer edge. "Being tough isn't about being big or having physical strength, dear witch. It's about strength here." He pointed to his head. "And here." He laid a hand over his heart. "And rising to an occasion and doing the right thing, like you did when you ran through a horde of vampires to set me free. And I've got a little feeling that the reason you summoned me is because you're trying to do something good again."

Sal's expression shifted to his playful grin. "And it must be something very good and honorable since you claim to not want this." He drifted his fingers down his chest, his abdomen, nearing his crotch. "Which blows my fucking mind."

"I didn't say I didn't want it. I said—"

"So you do want me. Well, now we're getting somewhere. If you'd clear the salt away, or at least break the circle, we could start having a good time."

Calvin opened his mouth to respond, then stopped. He did it again. Sal had taken control of the conversation and looped it back around to sex and trying to get out of the salt circle. He needed to stop following Sal whenever he took the conversation somewhere else.

Calvin lifted his hand, pointing at him. "Stop it. You promised to behave."

"And you were taking too long. I told you to keep it short."

"It hasn't even been five minutes."

"Three is about my top end for good behavior."

"Then we're starting over with a fresh three minutes. Now…" He stopped at a scratching sound outside his bedroom door.

Calvin turned as a small black nose pushed the door open, the scruffy brown and white head of his dog poking through. He sighed. The door never did latch tight. He turned toward the dog. "Buster, you can't be in here right now."

"I love dogs! What is he, a terrier mix? He's cute." Sal dropped to one knee, locking his gaze with the dog's. "Hey, poochy! Here, boy. Come here."

Tongue lolling out of his mouth, the little dog bounded toward Sal.

Calvin dove at the dog. "Buster, no!"

Buster crossed the salt line, his paws scuffing it and breaking the circle. Within himself, Calvin felt the "snap" of his energy breaking that he'd poured into the circle to seal it. The barrier was broken.

Sal lunged forward, snatching the dog and hopping over the salt line.

Calvin stumbled back, trying to put more distance between them. Sal stood only an arm's length away, nothing separating them. The demon was free.

Calvin dropped his gaze to Buster. He'd been so careful with planning everything for the summoning, but never had it crossed his mind about the dog coming in. He'd read it was easy for a demon to control an animal's mind. Even with the salt weakening Sal's power, he was able to bring Buster to him. Or maybe his goofy, overly friendly dog went on his own. It didn't matter either way. Sal was loose and he had Buster.

Calvin lifted his hands out toward the dog. "Please, don't hurt him."

"Hurt him? What kind of monster do you think I am? I just told you, I love dogs. I admire a creature who can possess such loyalty and faithfulness. Plus, they're fun to play fetch with." Sal held the small dog out in front of him and up to his face. His voice shifted to a babying tone. "He thinks I'm going to hurt you. Isn't he silly? Yes, he is."

Buster's tail hit a frantic pace, his tongue flicking out in attempts to lick Sal's face.

Sal brought the dog to his chest, stroking him on the head, and carried him to the door. He placed Buster on the outside of it. "You be good while I have some alone time with your master." He closed the door and a click sounded, revealing it was shut tight. He turned to Calvin. "Now, isn't this better?" He took a step toward him.

Calvin stepped back.

"Nothing between us." Sal moved forward another step.

Calvin retreated the same distance.

"We can talk, man to man. Or demon to witch. Whatever. And without that nasty salt blocking me, I can even touch your mind and see what you want from me, if that's easier for you than expressing yourself with words."

A flicker of unease passed through Calvin. "Demons can do that? Like vampires?"

One corner of Sal's lips curved up.

Cool energy washed through Calvin, bringing a refreshing and pleasant tingle. Sal's voice, deep and smooth, rolled through his mind. *Anything a vampire can do, a demon can do better.*

The truth behind Sal's words hit Calvin. Vampires could be dangerous and deadly, their strength and speed much greater than humans. They healed quickly, moved fast, jumped incredible heights. They could read thoughts, use persuasion to bend a human to their will, even leave a haze on a human's mind so a person didn't realize they were being fed from. While a demon didn't take blood from a human, Calvin knew many of them were drawn to other things mortals possessed, the richness of emotions, the warmth of life essence, and simply being able to create havoc in a person's life was satisfying for them.

Sal advanced toward him, and the reality that he was dealing with a being stronger than a vampire, hit Calvin and overwhelmed him, and also sent a sense of awe washing through him at Sal's power.

"I gotta say," Sal continued, "you're a damn good witch, powerful as hell, but you've still got a lot to learn about casting, such as having a completely secure environment. Since it's worked out to my advantage, I'm not complaining. I'm just saying in case you ever summon a different demon, you need to be more careful. But why would you ever want to call a different demon when you can have me?"

The way Sal moved, each step, every motion of his hand, the smirk on his lips, exuded sex and lust. Simply being in the same close space as him, sensing it, practically feeling phantom caresses over his skin, was enough to give Calvin a heady rush. He bumped into the wall and flattened his back against it.

Sal stopped close to him. One hand on his hip, he braced his other on the wall near Calvin's head and leaned toward him. "But seriously, you can stop acting as if I'm about to rip out your heart and have it for a snack. I might be a demon, but I'm not a bad guy."

Calvin took what he swore was his first breath since Sal broke free. "I just figured you'd be pissed at me summoning you and trapping you again."

"Believe it or not, it takes a lot to piss me off."

"I believe you. I saw it at the blood house. You were so calm through everything. The only time you got really pissed was when the vampires hurt your entity companion. Beezle, right?"

Sal gave a single affirmative nod. "He's kind of my baby and I'm a little protective of him."

"Considering he was the size of a dinosaur with a mouth full of razor sharp teeth and his blood looked like molten lava, I can understand you feeling as if you need to protect him."

Sal laughed. "Oh, look who's got some jokes now. I like it." He waved his hand between them, motioning to himself and Calvin. "See? Isn't this better? Us able to talk with nothing between us."

Calvin rested on the wall, relaxing under Sal's calm tone. "Actually, it is. I guess it was a bit extreme of me to use the salt again."

"No, it's always best to err on the side of caution when it comes to demons." Sal touched his own chest. "Except with me, of course."

Calvin let out a snort. "Of course."

He took in the smile resting on Sal's lips. So close. Sal was so close to him. All he would have to do was lift his hand and he would touch him. And he wanted to. So damn bad, he wanted to touch him. And Sal's lips, they were only inches away. He couldn't stop his gaze from drifting to them, admiring how full and finely shaped they were, just a little bit wet, perfect for a kiss…

Calvin snapped his gaze up. Staring at Sal's lips had been a bad idea, but now he found himself trapped in that stunning lavender gaze. He couldn't look away. He needed to, but the willpower wasn't there to make him. Only a whisper of why he'd summoned Sal remained in his mind. He grabbed hold of it, clung to it. "So, what we were talking about, the reason I summoned you. Is there a chance of us making a deal?"

"Maybe. You know, you have really pretty eyes."

Calvin's heart galloped in his chest. His cock strained against his jeans with how full it was. His balls ached as if it'd been days since he'd come, not an hour ago. "Thanks, but I really need to know, will you help me and heal my brother?"

"Possibly. You have no idea how beautiful you are, do you?"

"Stop trying to change the subject."

"I'm not."

"You are. You're not answering my questions."

"Yes I am. I'm just not giving you the answers you want."

Calvin sighed in exasperation. "You're really difficult to deal with."

Sal held up one hand, shifting his voice to a singsong tone as he said one word, "Demon."

A laugh broke from Calvin. Sal had him on that. Still, he was laying out making a deal with him. For a human to want to make a deal, that was the kind of thing a demon thrived on. So why wasn't Sal jumping all over it?

Space. He needed to get more space between them. This closeness…it was too much.

"You need to back up…" Calvin placed his hands on Sal's chest to push him away and paused. The muscle, the strength. He shouldn't have put his hands on Sal. The single small touch of Sal's body felt so damn good. Beneath the thin red T-shirt Sal wore, he could feel the coolness of the Sal's skin.

Sal dipped his head low, bringing his lips close to Calvin's ear. His voice left in him a rumbling whisper. "What were you saying?"

Calvin swallowed, hoping to loosen his tight throat. "You… you need to back up."

"You're sure that's what you want?"

No. It wasn't what he wanted. But it was what he needed.

Sal brought his body even closer. "You're very aroused right now."

Calvin forced his thoughts through his roaring desire. "Please, I need a favor from you."

"You need more than that from me. You want me. It's okay to admit it. I want to hear you say it."

Calvin dropped his head back on the wall. Sal's closeness, he couldn't concentrate from how good it felt. He moved one hand, resting it on Sal's waist.

A moan of approval rumbled in Sal's throat. "There you go. Touch me anywhere you want."

As Sal lowered his head, his breath tickling over Calvin's neck, Calvin blurted out, "Horns. Your horns. And your wings. I want to see them."

Sal paused. Slowly, he lifted his head. "What?"

"Your demon form. I want to see you in your true form again."

Sal shook his head. "No, really, you don't."

"Yes, really, I do."

Sal stared at him, silent.

Calvin could see in his eyes Sal was confused, trying to figure out if he was up to something. It seemed the trust wasn't there for either of them yet. "I'm not up to anything. I just…I want to see your true form again."

Sal shifted back the slightest bit. He straightened his arm against the wall, putting more space between him and Calvin. "Yeah, that's not going to happen."

"Why?"

"Because it's not."

"It's not like I'm going to get scared or shocked. I was standing beside you when you shifted at the blood house."

"Yeah, well, it'd be different now. Whatever you thought you felt when you saw me in my true form was deluded because of me saving the day from the blood suckers. If I shift now, you wouldn't think I was so—how did you put it?—*beautiful*, this time around."

Calvin allowed a smirk of his own to rise to his lips, challenging Sal. "Only one way for us to find out."

Sal's stance relaxed, his grin returning as he leaned close to Calvin again. "You're an odd one, even for a witch."

"I get that a lot."

A knock on the door startled Calvin. He snapped out of his arousal, peeking over Sal's shoulder as the door swung open, his brother standing in the doorway.

Nathan stared back at him. Slowly, his brother looked away, taking in the room, the broken salt circle, the black candles, the chalk sigil on the floor, then back to Sal. His gaze widened, horror filling his face. "What have you done?" He took a step back. "What have you done?!" He repeated, his voice louder, frantic.

"Nathan, it's not…"

His brother turned, darting out of the room.

"Shit!" Calvin ducked around Sal, hastening toward the door. "This wasn't how it was supposed to go."

Sal turned toward him. "Don't worry. Most people freak out when they see a demon in their house."

Calvin shot him an unappreciative look. "He wasn't supposed to know you're a demon."

"Well, the salt circle, black candles, witchy items, my sigil, and me appearing out of nowhere instead of knocking on the door were probably a dead giveaway." Sal pointed toward the door. "So I'm assuming Mister Cock Blocker is who you want me to heal. I'm can smell the sickness in him. I'm feeling a little less inclined toward doing that at the moment."

"Yes, he is, but don't judge him. He's my older brother and the only family I have left. The problem is—"

"Demon!"

Nathan stood in the doorway, a crucifix in one hand, a vial of clear water in the other.

Sal's eyes shone with faint light. He snapped his head toward Calvin. "Your brother is a priest? Are you fucking kidding me?!"

"You can tell that from looking at him?"

"Now that I'm getting a chance to look at him, hell yes, I can! It's shining through his goddamn aura that he's worked with that power, and that's no trinket in his hand like what you brought to the blood house. That damn thing is blessed! I can't believe you summoned me to help a priest!"

"Does it help that he's not officially a priest? He was never ordained."

A shocked cough slipped from Sal. "No, it really doesn't."

Nathan stepped into the room, holding the crucifix out before him. "Calvin! Stop talking to it and step away from it."

Calvin turned an exasperated look on his brother. "He's not an *it*. I know this all looks…disturbing to you, but let me explain." He motioned toward Sal. "He's here to help you. His name is—"

"No!" Sal grabbed Calvin's arm. "Holy shit, don't tell him my name!"

Nathan rushed forward. "Release him, demon!" He slashed with the hand holding the vial. Water sprayed out, landing across Sal's arm.

Sal's skin hissed, smoke rose from a red welt as if he'd been lashed by a whip. He jerked his hand back from Calvin. "Fucking hell, that stings!"

Nathan advanced on him. "It's supposed to, demon. Leave this home! Now!" With a flick of his hand, he sent more water spraying from the bottle.

It landed in a strip across Sal's shirt. As it seeped through, Sal's skin burned, leaving a hole in the shirt.

Sal winced and slapped a hand over his chest, pointing at Nathan with his other. "Knock it off! I didn't even come here out of my own free will!"

Calvin jumped between Sal and Nathan. "Stop it! You're hurting him!"

Nathan shoved Calvin aside. "Get out of the way!"

Calvin stumbled back and into one of the candles. He lost his balance, reeling backward, falling toward the floor.

Sal jumped forward, catching him from behind and putting him back on his feet. "Are you…ow! Motherfuck!" A thin strip of his jeans burned away to a welt of red skin beneath.

Sal spun toward Nathan. Swinging with speed too great for Calvin's eyes to fully catch, Sal knocked the back of his hand into Nathan's. The vial flew from Nathan's hand and across the room, shattering against the wall.

Sal's eyes had shifted, his round pupils becoming vertical slits. His voice deeper, guttural with anger, he shouted, "I told you to knock it off! It's a damn good thing you're just a baby priest and not fully grown into your power or else that shit would leave some serious marks! So drop the holier than thou act and cool it! You want me gone? I'm outta here!"

Calvin rushed toward Sal. "No, please don't go."

"Sorry, witchy poo, but I can't hang around someone like him and that blessed water is in the air now. I have to go. And since he's the one you wanted me to help, there's no way I'll make that deal." Sal aimed his index finger toward the wall. His fingertip smoldered red and he moved his hand in quick slashes, a number burning black onto the wall as he did. "The next time you want to hang out, try giving me a call instead."

Calvin took a breath, wanting to ask again for Sal to stay, but those seconds were too long of a delay. Sal met his gaze a final time, then closed his eyes and vanished, only mist remaining in his place.

His held breath rushed out of Calvin. It felt as if his strength was draining from him, disappointment stealing it away. It all went so terribly wrong. He not only didn't get Sal's help, but now he was positive Sal wouldn't want to see him ever again. Sal probably believed he'd tricked him into coming to where there was a priest. He supposed, in a way, he had. But he thought if he could talk to Sal, explain everything to him, it would be okay and also, he didn't know if it would matter since Nathan wasn't ordained.

Something clattered to the floor.

Calvin spun, his gaze going to the crucifix lying at Nathan's feet. A light sweat covered Nathan's face, and his brother sagged toward the floor. "Nathan!" He jumped toward him, sliding down to his knees and grabbing hold of Nathan's arms. "You did too much."

A humorless snort left Nathan. "What else was I supposed to do when my little brother decided to summon a demon for a date?"

Calvin met Nathan's gaze. They both had their mother's black hair, but where he'd inherited their mother's blue eyes, Nathan had their father's green ones.

"I knew you were up to something," Nathan continued. "I could smell the candles burning and I heard you chanting. I thought you were just playing at your witchcraft again…then I heard two voices. I've seen those websites you go on, reading about demons, even though you try to close the pages when you know I'm around. How could you do it? Summon a creature like that?"

"He's not a creature. He might be a demon, but he's good

and…he helped me before. There are things I never told you, *couldn't* tell you. I thought I could get him to help you."

Nathan pushed back from him. "Help me how?"

"I was going to ask him to heal you."

Nathan stared at him, his mouth dropped open. He slowly closed it, but while his shock faded, anger replaced it. "How could you ever think I would accept the help of a beast like that?"

"Stop calling him things like that. If you would talk to him—"

"His kind doesn't belong here! You know that. And all of this…" Nathan waved his hand at the candles, the salt, the silver pentacle resting outside Calvin's shirt on his chest. "It needs to go. You need to stop before you get hurt. We've argued, we've talked, we've debated about it. You know it's not safe. Not for your soul and now, not for you physically."

Calvin clamped his lips shut. Having gone through so many past arguments with Nathan, he knew anything he said would spark a fresh one. It was the same old topic, just a new day.

Nathan hung his head, closing his eyes. "Maybe when I'm gone, you'll understand how important it is for you to direct your faith where it belongs."

"Don't say that. You're not going to die."

That same soft smile rose to Nathan's lips. He hated it when his brother got that smile. It made him feel that Nathan knew things he didn't, and maybe his brother did.

Nathan pushed off Calvin as he struggled to his feet. Calvin bounced up, helping him.

"I'm going to lie down. Put out the candles and try to not summon any more evil beings into the house."

Walking Nathan to the door, Calvin muttered, "He's not evil."

Nathan stopped and pointed to the wall. "Look what he did. Think of how his body burned when the holy water touched him. Now tell me again he's not evil."

Calvin looked into Nathan's eyes. "He's not evil."

Nathan held Calvin's gaze for a long moment. He lowered his head with a sigh. "Just promise me you'll never summon him again."

Calvin's chest tightened, but he forced the words out. "I promise."

Nathan gave single nod and shuffled down the hall. "After I rest, we'll go get some paint for the wall."

Calvin watched Nathan move down the hall and disappear into his bedroom, as if sixty extra years were on top of his natural twenty-six. He glanced down the opposite end of the hall. Buster peeked around the corner at him. He pointed at the dog. "You. You started it all rolling downhill."

As if sensing he wasn't really angry at him, the little dog bounded toward him.

Calvin picked him up. Sal had been so gentle with the dog. His gaze drifted to the wall and the numbers. If Sal was truly mad at him, he wouldn't have left his number…burned into the wall. He grinned and shook his head. Sal certainly had his own way of doing things. Nathan might not want Sal's help, but he did, and with the promise he'd made to his brother, it was a good thing Sal had left a way for him to get in touch without having to summon him.

Chapter Four

Sal manifested with a burst of energy. Instant relief rushed through him. He breathed deep the hot, dry air of the demon realm and opened his eyes.

The tall black spires of his castle rose to the gray sky streaked with rusty colored clouds. The walls of the castle, sleek and smooth, shone like black glass. He stood in the center of a bridge made from the same ebony stone, arcing over the inky waters of the broad moat. Tendrils of steam rose from the water and dissipated into the air. In the far distance, sharp peaks of mountains cut through the clouds.

Behind him, the land sloped down to the village where many of his lesser demons resided. The homes and buildings were solidly built from brown rock, trimmed in gray stone, many of them carved with designs similar to human Celtic knotwork, but sharper in the points and lines, like blades or thorns. Some had carvings of faces, human and demon, animals and entities. Over the years, he'd brought back several books written by humans and had a library built, placing those volumes and demon texts inside it. He also brought over instruments from the human realm that complimented the demon ones. He encouraged his demons to read, to learn, to create. He wanted them to have hobbies, enrichments, to do more with their lives than fuck or fight.

And his demons thrived under it. Certainly, fucking was still their favorite pastime—his too—but educating and growing themselves in other ways had drastically cut down on the inner fighting within his lands. To the rest of the demon realm and nobles, his duchy was known as a center of peace and culture. He liked that reputation. Not only because it meant he'd accomplished some good in this world and with his demons, but it also made him appear less of a threat to those who cultivated their demons to learn nothing other than fighting.

He looked over the lands, rolling with grass, though it was patchy, revealing many spaces of barren ground and cracked dirt. Great boulders dotted the area, along with a few scraggly trees and brush. The grand orchard and vineyard he'd tried to establish was wilted and sickly. He would need to purify the ground waters again from the looks of it and make sure his demons assigned to tending it were doing their jobs, not slacking off with him having been gone.

He'd poured his power into his lands over the years, trying to bring it back from the devastation the Great Wars had caused, but the burning energy of the battles had left this world scarred. It was recovering, bit by bit, with himself and other nobles trying to bring it back, but it would be a long time before it came back to full health…if it ever could.

The best and surest way to bring it back would be for all the nobles to come together and use their power for the good of their world, and that sure as fuck would never happen. Demons could still live and thrive here. Making it pretty was a waste of time and energy, many thought.

"Home sweet home," he grumbled.

He didn't particularly care for his homeland. He far preferred the human realm. It was vibrant with color and energy and human essence. Here, it was little more than a wasteland, thanks to the wars and battles of demons vying for power. Not that he could completely criticize them for it. He'd taken part too, winning himself the title of duke. But he remembered the lands before the wars, when it'd been as beautiful as the human realm with trees and valleys, clear streams and lakes. A lot of demons preferred the land the way it was now. They found beauty in the desolation. Him? Not so much. Though, it did suit his mood at the moment.

He sent out a mental summons and an instant later, Beezle manifested around his shoulders with a pop of black smoke. Sal drew him off his shoulders and kissed him on the tip of his snout. "I thought you might enjoy stretching out and going for a swim in familiar waters."

He placed Beezle on the ground. The little crocodile wandered toward the edge of the bridge and slipped between two carved posts. He dropped into the water with a plop, vanishing into the black depths for an instant. He surfaced, his head and body already the length of Sal's height, the water rippling out from him as Beezle continued to grow.

Sal watched Beezle swim away, gaining some happiness from his entity's joy at swimming in his moat. He turned toward the castle and marched forward. The double black doors towered above him, meeting in a sharp point. With nothing more than a thought, he sent both doors bursting open. Sal stopped in the doorway, hands on his hips, surveying the great hall.

Massive pillars of gray stone ran the length of the great hall, carved with humans, demons, vampires, shifters, all engaged in sexual acts; males with males, females with females, males and females, all combinations imaginable were graphically detailed in the throes of pleasure. And scattered across the floor, many of his lesser demons doing several of those acts.

Not uncommon. His castle was an endless orgy, and he was more than good with that. It was as much for his pleasure as for his demons'. But at this moment, it annoyed him. His unsatisfied lust for Calvin raged inside him. Normally, he'd grab one of his demons and fuck until he was sated. He had a feeling no matter how much he fucked, if it wasn't with Calvin, that satisfaction wouldn't come. A growl rumbled in his throat. Maybe the witch *had* cast an enchantment on him.

Sal stormed down the center of the hall. As he did, word spread like a wave to the lesser demons that their master had returned. They disentangled from each other and prostrated themselves before him. He passed by without sparing any of them a glance. Reaching the other end of the hall, he climbed the stairs to his ebony throne. He spun around and tore his shirt over his head, throwing it out into the hall. He kicked off his shoes and started unbuttoning his jeans. "Elek! Where are you?"

"Here! I'm here, my lord!"

Sal glanced to the side. Elek ran toward him carrying a bundle of black cloth. A little more of Sal's bad mood slipped away.

Sweet Elek, always so willing to please him…and he was very easy to look at. Elek's long white hair flowed out behind him as he ran. Two horns, about the length of his hand, protruded from the top of Elek's head, spiraling back. His bluish-tinted wings were clamped tight to his body as he ran, and like many lesser demons, they were too small to lift him into flight. Some of the lessers didn't have wings at all, but Elek was high in rank and power among them. He could glide if he jumped from a tall height, but Elek had a bit of a fear of heights. His white skin was radiant against the darkness of the room. He didn't doubt Elek picked up he was in a mood, but still, Elek's crystal blue eyes shone with happiness at the sight of him.

Sal shoved off his jeans as Elek climbed the stairs.

Elek dropped to his knees before him, holding up a wrap of silken black cloth. Sal looked down at him. For as much as Elek was playing at being the good little minion, he saw Elek's gaze was focused on his cock, still hard and aching for Calvin.

The last of Sal's bad mood vanished. He caught Elek lightly under the chin, tipping his head back and smiling at him. He scolded him with soft tsking. "Not this time, my lovely. I didn't come back for that."

Disappointment crossed Elek's face, but the lesser demon gave him a smile. "I'm happy for your return, no matter the reason." He wrapped Sal's hips in the cloth, then took a step back.

Sal closed his eyes and began to shed his human form. His height grew and body thickened. His horns emerged, curling off the sides of his head. As his wings grew out from his back, comfort filled him. It always felt good to stretch out his wings. His hair lengthened, claws took over his fingernails, his fangs dropped down from his upper jaw in place of his canines.

He sighed in relief. Now, he was feeling better. He eased down in his throne, leaning back to one corner and hanging a leg over one of the throne's arms.

"My lord!" Elek cried, pointing to Sal's chest and the red welt still across it. "What happened to you?"

Sal rubbed the welt, pain rising as he touched it. "I had a run-in with a priest. Not fully into his powers, though, so this should heal soon enough."

Elek reached toward him, pausing before touching him. "May I?"

Sal nodded.

Elek brushed his fingers over the mark. His touch stole the heat of the wound. Elek may not have the power to heal, but same as many lesser demons, he had elemental power, that of ice. He could freeze water, create frost, and as he was doing now, take the heat out of a wound. And there were other more… erotic uses Elek could use his power for. Sal was well familiar with those. Of all his lesser demons, Elek was the only one he took to his bed regularly.

But now, not even lovely Elek could capture his interest. He was focused on Calvin. When he'd been close to Calvin, he could feel the heat of Calvin's arousal. A few more minutes and he would've had the witch in bed, as they both wanted.

Then the priest came in. A priest! He'd had his share of shitty luck, but that was up there. Talk about a mood breaker. He didn't know what Calvin had been thinking to want him to heal a priest. Regardless of being Calvin's brother, the witch had to know demons and boys of the cloth didn't play well together.

Was Calvin that desperate to help his brother? He could tell with a glance that Nathan was gravely ill. If human means to heal Nathan had failed, then what other choice did Calvin have but to call upon otherworldly means?

Sal tapped a slow beat on the arm of his throne with one clawed fingertip. A deal…

A human offering to make a deal. A favor given, a favor returned. It was the kind of thing demons dreamed of. An open door to getting an upper hand on a human. Only problem was, that wasn't something he wanted.

He'd never been the type to lord over humans. He enjoyed them and all their warmth and passion and irrationality. They were endlessly amusing. He even had respect for them. Resilient little buggers, humans. He couldn't help but admire the indomitable spirit they'd displayed since their rise in the mortal realm. Admittedly, his demon nature whispered to him about the things he could get in return for helping Calvin, but really, all he wanted was to enjoy the witch's body. He felt pretty damn confident he could get that without making a deal.

Maybe. If his little outburst of not wanting to help Nathan hadn't blown his shot. He suppressed a growl of frustration. Why did humans have to make shit so complicated? Sometimes they needed to put those annoying emotions aside and just have a good time.

Thinking on that, Sal glanced out to the great hall and noticed none of his demons had resumed to their activities. He snapped his fingers, the sound sharp and resounding through the hall. "At ease, my darlings. Go back to what you were doing." He looked at Elek, lingering near his throne. "You too. Or at least go clean the dried cum off your chin."

Elek rubbed at his chin with the back of his hand. "I'm sorry, my lord."

Sal grinned at him. "You should be, since it looks like you were having a much better time than me a little while ago."

Elek laughed softly. "From what you've said, I'd have to agree." He rested a clawed hand over Sal's. "Are you certain there's nothing I can do for you?"

Sal gave him a warm smile and squeezed his hand. "I'm positive."

Elek inclined in a bow and turned to leave.

Sal watched him go, but his thoughts returned to Calvin. He would go back to the human realm soon. He needed to stay here for a few hours, where he was strongest, let his wounds heal. A typical wound from a human healed almost instantaneously, but these weren't typical wounds. It was another game when blessed items and magic came into play. When he did return, he would track down Calvin. Once he manifested somewhere, even when summoned, he could always find that place again, so it wouldn't be a problem to locate Calvin's home. What could be the problem would be Calvin's reaction to him when he showed up and hadn't been summoned.

Chapter Five

The heavier atmosphere of the mortal realm warned Sal to prepare to manifest. As he did, with Beezle around his shoulders, he heard a loud sigh, followed by Valentin's refined voice.

"And here I thought we had a moment alone."

Sal glanced to the side. Valentin laid on the leather couch, Sebastian on top of him, chest to chest. He could smell the lust emanating from them and see it without needing to shift his sight to view their auras. It was slightly obvious with Sebastian's jeans pushed halfway off his ass and one of Valentin's hands shoved in the back of them. Blood seeped from two punctures in Sebastian's right wrist, another sign they were *playing* together.

"As if you two don't get plenty of moments alone." Sal motioned to Sebastian's ass. "Are your hands ever not down his pants?"

"Yes, of course." Valentin smirked at Sal as he drew his tongue over his bite marks on Sebastian's wrist. "When he has them off, I can't very well have my hands down them."

Sal nodded his approval at the comment. "You got me on that one."

Sebastian met Valentin in a passionate kiss before easing back and looking again to Sal. "You seem to be in a mood."

Sal turned for a plush leather chair, pulling Beezle off his shoulders. He set the entity on the floor and dropped into the chair. "Just a bad case of blue balls. That's all."

"*You* have a case of blue balls," Basil said, walking into the room, a glass of red wine in his hand. "Has the great demon lover, Sallos, finally met his match in someone who can resist him? Except, of course, for myself, Valentin, and Sebastian."

Sal lifted his chin with an arrogant tilt. "That's only because I've never really tried with you guys."

Valentin turned a smirk on Sal. "No, I think it's that we've all gotten to know you and that's killed and gutted any attraction."

Sal grinned as everyone laughed. Returning to the demon dimension hadn't done much for improving his mood, but being around Basil, Valentin, and Sebastian was lifting it in only a few moments. He moved his gaze to Basil again. "And as far as your little comment goes, Valentin's right on how he calls you a master of exaggeration."

Basil sat in another leather chair opposite of Sal's. "I was being polite when I said you were a great lover. I didn't realize it was an exaggeration."

"Not that part! The half about someone who can resist me."

Basil tipped his glass toward him. "But you said that yourself, in having blue balls."

"Listen, if we wouldn't have gotten interrupted, *by a priest*, I would've been balls deep in his cute little ass."

Basil winced in sympathy. "A priest? That's a load of bad luck." He paused. "Wait. What were you doing trying to have sex where there was a priest in the vicinity? Were you trying to have sex in a church again? You know how hallowed ground weakens you. I can only imagine what it'd do to other things." He held up his hand, his index finger pointed straight up, then slowly curled it down as though it was wilting.

"No! I wasn't trying to have sex in a church…again. And not even hallowed ground does *that* to me." Sal sagged back in the chair. "It's a complicated story."

"I know the story," Sebastian said, grinning.

Sal glanced toward him. "How do you know?"

"Because someone was blowing up your phone this afternoon. Valentin and Baz were still asleep, but it was driving me nuts hearing it go off, so I answered it. I had a nice little chat with Calvin."

"The witch from the blood house?" Valentin asked.

Sebastian nodded. "That's the one. I was about to tell you

when you woke up, then you came down here and found me and well, you know…" He held up his bitten wrist to indicate how they'd gotten distracted.

Sal leaned forward in the chair, not wanting them to get distracted again. "What'd he say?"

Sebastian slowly turned his gaze from looking into Valentin's eyes to Sal. "Lots. We talked for quite a while. His last name is Blackwood. He's twenty-three. He works doing stock at a grocery store in Savannah not far from his house. His brother, Nathan, is three years older than him. He wears glasses because he's near-sighted and he doesn't like contacts, sliding them over his eyeballs weirds him out. He only really started to understand his power and calling as a witch about two years ago after his mother passed away." He tipped his gaze upward in a thoughtful look. "Hmm, what else…oh! His favorite color is purple, which works out great for you with those eyes of yours."

Sal breathed out an exasperated sigh and rubbed his forehead. "That's not what I meant. What did he say about *me*?"

"You know, if you're going to be in a relationship, you should take some time to learn about the other person. Not be so focused on yourself."

Sal opened his eyes, trying to lock Sebastian in a glare. Sebastian countered with a mocking grin. A few soft chuckles broke from Sal. "Come on! Just tell me what he said."

"Alright, alright. He said he was worried about you and told me what happened. Then we talked about that day at the blood house. It was really good to talk to him, and I think he was happy about it, too. It's probably been hard for him, trying to deal with everything that happened that day and not having anyone to talk to about vampires, a giant crocodile entity, and in his words, a beautiful demon." Sebastian let out an exaggerated sigh as if lovesick.

"What *did* happen today?" Basil asked.

Sal reclined in the chair. "After you guys went to bed this morning, I was summoned by him." He told them what'd happened with Calvin. As he reached the part of breaking through the salt line, his memory rose strong of standing so close to Calvin, feeling his body's heat, breathing in Calvin's scent tinted with the fragrance of the candles…and his dick started to rise again.

"So I went to the demon realm for a while to cool down and heal before coming back," Sal finished.

Basil rested his cheek on his fist. "Interesting. Two brothers gifted with *other* power, but one chooses the path of the witch, one the path of God."

"What I don't get," Sebastian said, "is you've said before and it goes with what I've read about demons, that you guys aren't fallen angels or anything like that. You're creatures that have been around as long as the Earth has. Your realm isn't Hell, no sinful souls or pointy tailed demons with pitchforks. So how is it that a priest can still hurt you with religious…uh, tools, I guess I'll call them. Crucifixes and holy water and stuff?"

Sal waved a hand, as if to stop Sebastian's thoughts from going down that path. "No, no, no. It's not about religion, that's got nothing to do with it. It's the evocation of a greater power, whether spiritual or natural. Any human, no matter their religious faith or lack thereof, can do that. Though, some have a greater capacity for it than others and can channel more. But what they need is to know how to tap into that power, bring it to them, and have true belief in what they're doing. That's how people of different faiths or who have no religious path can summon or banish a demon. With the ones who've studied it more, they've got a better handle on how to channel that power, and a lot of religious sects provide that education in some form.

"Take Calvin and his brother for instance. Calvin has no trouble summoning me because he's studied the Craft and knows the ritual. Same as I'm sure he'd have no trouble banishing me. His brother has studied the banishment half under the Catholic rituals. They both accomplish the same thing, but in a different way."

Sebastian nodded, a thoughtful look coming over him that Sal had seen many times when Sebastian was absorbing and learning something. "Then, in a way, religious practices aren't that much different than magical ones."

Sal winked at him. "You got it. But you better keep that between us in this room. You wouldn't want to be called out for blasphemy and put to the stake."

Valentin moved into the conversation. "As Baz and I remember quite clearly, it used to be their way or no way when it came to those of the Church. For some sects, it still is, but there have been a few steps forward in acceptance."

"Such as not holding inquisitions, torturing, and burning people any longer," Basil added.

Sal stretched his arms over his head. His human form was feeling much better after staying in his homeland for a while. "Never a dull moment in those days. You humans provided endless entertainment, but you always do."

"Seems to me, you were providing some pretty good entertainment for Calvin today," Sebastian said. "He was worried that his brother had hurt you. He said he wanted to make sure you're okay and see you again, so I told him he could come over. He's going to stop by later tonight, about eight, which works out since Valentin and I are going out."

Valentin gazed up at him, amusement shining in his eyes. "We are?"

"Yep. And Basil's going with us."

Basil lowered his glass before taking a drink. "I am?"

"Yes. Soooooo…" Sebastian said, drawing the word out as he moved his gaze to Sal again, "you'll have the house to yourself."

A smile pulled at Sal's lips as he realized what Sebastian was doing. "Thanks, sweetheart."

Basil swirled his wine in the glass. "I suppose it works out for me to go into town. I'm due to feed and I'd like to get your opinions on a couple of buildings."

Valentin glanced back to Basil. "Buildings? What for?"

"You know me, how I like to dabble in business here and there. I'm not saying that I've been mainly responsible for growing our fortunes, but we both know I have been."

Valentin rolled his eyes. "As you've endlessly reminded me with every new business venture you set out upon. And yes, you've always had highly successfully returns. I admit it. Are you pleased, now?"

Flashing a bright smile, Basil said, "I am. Thank you."

"Now what's your latest endeavor?"

"Since we settled here, I've been giving some thought to what I'd like my next venture to be and I've decided to open a blood house."

"What?!" Gently moving Sebastian back, Valentin sat up, turning to face Basil. "Have you gone completely mad? How could you even consider doing that?"

"How could I not? Savannah doesn't have a blood house any more. Not that the previous one was much. We'd have the full market to ourselves."

"*We*? What makes you think I'd lend any support to such a thing? And that's not what I meant. You know how I feel about blood houses. The same as you feel about them! And most of all, what about 'Bastian? After what he went through, to have to stand by and watch you open a blood house."

"I don't intend to have him stand by. I'd like his help, actually." Basil looked at Sebastian. "Because of your experience, I think you'd make a fabulous manager of the donors for me. And, of course, you'd be a partner in the business getting a share of the profits."

Valentin stood, glaring down at Basil. "You *have* gone mad!"

Basil held up a placating hand. "You need to hear me out before making that judgment. It'll be blood house finer than either of us have ever known. The donors will truly be donors, not simply slapped with that title for correctness. It'll be more of a club, where membership will be required to enter. Obviously only vampires will be members, and I'll screen every vampire before granting them membership. I'll not have any fools like those who frequented that poor excuse for a vampire, Wesley's, house.

"As for the donors themselves, they'll be screened as well, to ensure their trustworthiness because they'll not be living in the club. They can if they choose, I'll have quarters there, but they'll still be able to live their lives. It'll be nothing more than a night job, so to speak. And with the pay I intend to give them, that alone should be enough to ensure loyalty and discretion, but I plan to be a fly on the wall, so to speak, in their minds while interviewing them to know their true thoughts, with them none the wiser of me being there."

Valentin shook his head at him. "It'll never work. Someone would go to the authorities."

"And tell them what? That they're getting paid to give their blood to vampires? They'll be locked in a cell until they're presumed to have sobered off whatever they're on. There are hundreds of blood houses across the world, some of which give their donors a fair amount of freedom. I'm simply going to give ours more."

Valentin folded his arms across his chest. "And the vampires? How are you going to ensure the ones you're giving memberships to aren't scum-sucking leeches, same as the ones who abused 'Bastian? And, how are you going to stop a vampire who's crazed with bloodlust? And, how are you going to keep vampires who aren't members from entering the club?"

Basil took a sip of wine. "All valid questions, to which I have answers. As for the first, after more than three hundred years of existence, you and I have seen proof enough that like attracts like. Wesley was a vile little troll of a vampire and as such, attracted other uncouth types to frequent his blood house, many of whom fled this region when their lead leech was destroyed. I, however, am a vampire of high sophistication, so it stands to reason those will be the same types of vampires who'll come to my blood house."

Sal snickered. "If you can attract so many sophisticated vampires, why are you still single?"

Basil pointed at Sal. "I'm answering Valentin's questions. Not yours."

Valentin grinned at him. "I do like Sal's question, though. Regardless, your point has minor validity since it's based on ego, not fact. But continue with your others."

"Your second question about stopping a blood-crazed vampire and keeping unwanted vampires out are tied together, I think. I believe simply having us running the house will be enough to deter most unwanted behavior. Not too many out there who would be fool enough to get on the bad side of two vampire princes. But in the rare instance of someone being so stupid…" Basil turned to Sal. "That's where you have the solution to my problem."

Sal folded his arms behind his head. "Do I, now? And what's that?"

Basil tossed up both hands, the wine nearly sloshing over the rim of the glass. "Demons! You can bring over some of your lesser demons to be guards in the club. Even a lesser demon would have greater strength than a vampire, and I'm sure your lesser demons would jump at the chance to come into the human realm for any purpose."

Sal laughed and brought his hands together in a loud clap. "You *have* lost your mind, and I love it!"

"What's so mad about having demons as guards?"

"Everything! You've got to understand, lesser demons don't get to come to the human realm unless a noble brings them over. And when a noble has done that, I guarantee you it's never been for a good cause. It's to create chaos and trouble. And lesser demons don't have the same grasp on adapting to human society like nobles do. They'll have to learn to how to act human, how to control their impulses, how to basically have some damn manners."

"I will say my demons are probably the best suited for such

a task as opposed to those under any other noble, because I've exposed them to many human items and books, so most of them have at least a cursory knowledge of this realm. If you really want to try it, I can bring some of my more trusted demons over. I'll tell them to behave and they'll listen…while I'm watching. But I can't watch them every minute of the day, so I can't promise they won't get into some mischief."

Basil waved the concern away. "I'm fine with mischief. So long as they don't harm anyone or affect my profits."

"Fair enough. I'm sure too, the threat alone that if they step too far out of line, I'll take them back to our realm will be enough to keep them on their best behavior."

"And what of the people to be donors?" Valentin asked. "Where will you find them?"

Basil shrugged. "I haven't fully worked that out yet. Perhaps I'll cruise clubs or wander the city looking for prospects. Or maybe I'll put an ad on Craigslist. I've certainly seen stranger things listed there, so it wouldn't stand out or seem so unusual."

Valentin stared at the both Sal and Basil. "A new blood house. Bringing lesser demons into the human world. It's all madness."

Sebastian leaned forward. "I think it sounds like a cool idea."

Valentin spun toward him. "You can't seriously approve."

"From all I'm hearing, I do. It's totally different from the blood house I was a prisoner in. In Baz's house, the blood slaves would have freedom, something I never had. I mean, to be able to leave, have a life, only show up to spend a night giving blood and get paid for doing it, they really would be donors. Plus, I like the idea of being a manager to the donors. I could take care of them, be there for them, give them support and guidance. Not to mention, being a partner and getting paid, too. You know I've been having trouble finding a job. The money would help out a lot with my upcoming tuition."

Valentin's mouth hung slightly agape as he stared at Sebastian. "I'm going to pay your tuition."

"But if I can make money to help pay some of it myself, wouldn't that be good? We can all be partners in it, working together, helping each other, making it an awesome success."

Sal watched Valentin's expression soften. And with that statement, Sebastian won Valentin's support. He hoped Basil was going to give Sebastian a hell of a cut, because getting Valentin's support wasn't going in Basil's favor until Sebastian spoke up. But he knew that Sebastian did want to help pay for his school.

The week before, Sebastian came running into the mansion after getting the mail, waving his acceptance letter to Armstrong State University, where he was going to study music. Sebastian had been so happy, but sobered quickly when he realized how much tuition would be. Valentin assured him it wasn't a concern and really, it wasn't. Valentin didn't exactly have small bank accounts.

But from the moment he'd been freed, Sebastian didn't want to be dependent on Valentin. He had worked hard to earn his GED, then to get accepted into college. He'd also been trying to find a job—part-time, full-time, anytime—but it was a struggle for him with no solid work history for three years. Being a partner in Basil's club could be a good option for Sebastian.

Valentin exhaled a sigh of relent and extended his hand to Sebastian. "If you accept his idea and he has your support, then I'll give mine. My main worry was you, anyhow. I didn't want you upset at having a blood house opened by someone so close to you."

Sebastian took Valentin's hand and drew him closer. "I know, and I appreciate that. But his idea does sound like how a blood house should be run and…it's Basil. I know he'll be good to his donors."

Basil saluted Sebastian with his glass. "That I will. And with your help, it'll make it even more so that they're getting what they need. So then, Sebastian will be the donors' manager. Sal will manage security. I wouldn't mind taking on another partner to assist with the general operations and management…if only there was someone else I trusted…"

Valentin turned to him. "Just how much profit do you believe this blood house will bring in?"

"*A lot.* Think about it, dear cousin. We know firsthand the cost of visiting a blood house. And as I said, there are no blood houses here or anywhere within the vicinity. The nearest I've been able to uncover is in Atlanta, and I've heard it's rather unsavory, as well. While many vampires left when we killed Wesley and his cronies, there're still many here and in neighboring areas. I'm positive the *good* vampires, the ones with class and manners, weren't going to Wesley's vile establishment. Those are customers waiting to be catered to. Those are also the ones with money."

"And again it comes back to your old friend."

Basil let out a happy sigh as he gazed at his wine. "Money and I have always gotten along. The only time I've argued with it has been when I feel it needs to multiply more quickly." He focused again on Valentin. "But really, to open a blood house would be a service to the vampire community. Without a safe haven for vampires to feed, they run the streets, taking blood from any human who happens by. Eventually the word will spread and humans will live in panic and fear. Then the humans will start attacking and killing anyone they think is a vampire. It'll be chaos. Complete and utter chaos. So by opening a blood house, we'll stop those dreadful things from happening and hence, save both societies of human and vampire."

Sal stood, clapping his hands in enthusiastic applause. "And that, my bitey little friend, is why you're the master of exaggeration."

Valentin chuckled. "Indeed. When he puts his skills to work, he can give quite the resounding oratory…overblown though it may be."

"It could happen!" Basil said.

Valentin gave a single nod of assent. "It could. It's about as likely as one of us getting staked through the heart with a wooden spoon, but it could happen."

Basil huffed and mumbled into his glass. "We'll see how

snarky you are when the cash flow starts coming in. *If* you're interested in helping."

"Well, it'll be something to occupy the time, if nothing else."

Basil hopped up, a bright smile on his face. "Then let's get ready to go. The sun'll be setting soon and I've got a list of buildings we can visit."

Sebastian got to his feet, holding Valentin's hand. "And then Sal can start getting ready for his evening, too." He turned a knowing smile at Sal.

Sal clapped him on the shoulder. "I do need to go to the store to get some things. I think this calls for a cake."

Basil glanced back at him as he stepped through the doorway. "Be sure to save me some."

"There'll be leftovers, since I'm planning on giving him plenty of distraction."

Valentin rubbed his hand across Sebastian's lower back. "We'll be sure to make it a late night, then."

"Doesn't matter. We've heard each other at it enough over the years where there's no point in being shy or restrained about it." Sal gave Basil a light shove on the back. "Except I haven't heard you fuck in a long, *long* time."

"Maybe I'm fucking outside your hearing range. Did you ever consider that?"

"Are you?"

Basil hung his head slightly. "Not for a while."

"How the hell does a vampire have so much trouble getting laid?"

Basil stopped and spun toward him. "I don't have trouble getting laid. I simply don't like to sleep with people after I've put them in the persuasion haze to have their blood. It feels… creepy."

Sebastian looked back toward Sal. "And if something's creepy to a vampire, then you know it's really creepy." He looped one arm through Valentin's, then slipped his other through Basil's, walking with the vampire princes on either side of him. "And speaking as someone who's been on the receiving end of persuasion and being compelled, I think it's awesome of you to not do that. And that's why I know you'll take good care of your donors."

"Yeah, yeah, yeah," Sal interrupted. "But going back to what I was saying, you wouldn't have to compel anyone. Just go to one of those cute little Goth clubs and pretend to be a fake vampire. You'll get laid like that." He snapped his fingers.

Basil stopped at the base of the stairs, fixing Sal with an unamused look. "I'm absolutely *not* doing that."

Valentin placed one foot on the stairs. "The problem is, he wants a relationship. He's tired of meaningless nights of passion."

"But those are the best!" Sal said. "No emotions, no connections. Get in, get out, go home happy. I swear, you silly bloodsuckers never lose all your humanness. You still complicate things."

A half-smile rose to Basil's lips. "Love is often complicated."

Sal turned a playful glare on Sebastian. "You see what you've done? You've made my vampires mushy."

"Hey, I couldn't have done anything that wasn't already in them. Their inner mushiness has probably been waiting to come out for decades."

Sal grumbled low in his throat. "I suppose I've seen a few warning signs over the years." He turned to Basil. "Well, if that's really what you want, then pick out a guy and I'll use my power to make him fall in love with you. There. Problem solved. Don't ever say I never gave you anything."

Basil looked away from him and started up the stairs with Sebastian and Valentin. "I'll pass. Thanks."

"You know what would be awesome?" Sebastian paused and pointed back to Sal. "If *you* fell in love."

Sal pointed back at him. "Don't you threaten me like that."

He listened to Sebastian's, Valentin's, and Basil's laughter as they climbed the stairs. When they disappeared down the hallway, he headed across the grand entrance hall to the access door leading to the garage. He snatched the keys for his Viper ACR off the key ring and stepped out to the garage, walking toward the sleek red and black car.

He opened the door and slid behind the steering wheel. The car rumbled to life as he pushed the start button, and he tapped the remote to open the garage door. Sebastian's words played through his mind. Love? Nope. Not on his agenda. He'd been there, done that, and knew it never ended well. At least, not for him it didn't.

Chapter Six

Calvin drew in a deep breath, held it, and blew it out slowly. He'd hoped it would help calm his nerves and pounding heartbeat. It didn't. He couldn't believe he was standing on the porch of the house that belonged to a demon duke, two vampire princes, and a former blood slave.

It had been nice to talk to Sebastian. During their conversation, he'd found Sebastian to be someone he could speak freely to. Probably because Sebastian didn't think he was crazy when he mentioned things such as summoning, demons, or vampires. And he was grateful to Sebastian for inviting him over to see Sal. Sebastian had said he wasn't sure if Sal would be back, because he hadn't known where Sal was when Calvin had called. Now that he was here, he hoped Sal had returned from wherever he'd gone.

Calvin gazed at the large wooden door, ornately carved with heavy dark metalwork bolted onto it, reminiscent of Gothic style. On either side of the door, were large and stunning stained glass windows. The door and windows seemed touches added by the vampires, because they certainly weren't original to the period of the two-story white colonial mansion, but the blend of European and American made for a beautiful contrast. Admittedly, he'd been surprised when he turned down the long driveway, lined in willow trees, to see the mansion at the end. He'd checked the address Sebastian gave him to make sure he hadn't made a wrong turn.

White columns lined the wrap-around porch, more lining the balcony that ran along the second story. The lawn and shrubbery were finely manicured. He may have only met Valentin and Basil briefly, but now thinking of them, it made sense they'd live comfortably. Calvin glanced back at his old, white Honda Civic with its red passenger door, a replacement from a junkyard after the window of the previous one had gotten smashed a couple of months ago. He never found out who did it, but he had his suspicions. Getting the whole door from the junkyard was cheaper than having the window replaced. If only he could've found a white one, or afforded to have it painted. Either way, it wasn't exactly adding to the ambiance here.

He faced the door and took another breath. Same as his car, he didn't fit in, but it didn't stop him from wanting to see Sal, and hoping…

Calvin stopped the thought. There were so many things he was hoping for, he didn't know which one to put first. If he was selfish, to have Sal press close to him again and more would be his first hope. But he couldn't be selfish. He needed to put his hope on securing help from Sal. Or if not help, then advice, at the very least.

His determination fortified, Calvin lifted his hand and knocked on the door. It swung open almost before he lowered his hand. His gaze locked on Sal's.

Shit. Oh shit. How was he supposed to not be selfish now, with Sal standing there looking gorgeous? Sal wore a tight, black V-neck T-shirt, black leather pants, and was barefoot. The dark color accentuated his fair skin, made his hair seem an even more fiery red, and pulled out the lavender hue of his eyes. And the tightness of the clothes hugged his body to show off the fine definition of muscle…and the front of the leather pants looked extremely well-filled in the crotch.

Sal stretched one arm up, bracing his forearm on the doorframe. "Now isn't this a nicer way to get together, rather than summoning me through the dimensional planes and forcing me to stand in a circle of salt?"

Calvin opened his mouth. Words. He needed some. But damn it, standing in that position, his body stretched, the shirt rising up to reveal a hint of skin and muscled abs, Sal emanated sex and sensuality. And the little quirk to the demon's lips told him Sal knew exactly how he was affecting him.

Calvin wet his lips, seeming suddenly too dry, and caught Sal's gaze droping to watch. "I…yeah, it is." He took a breath. "I'm glad you're okay."

Sal shrugged one shoulder. "I've gone through worse."

"I'm sure, but I'm sorry, *so* sorry, you had to suffer any pain because of me. I didn't mean for that to happen."

Sal offered him a warm smile. "I know you didn't. Sometimes the best plans can go wrong." He swept to the side. "Coming in?"

Calvin nodded. He shifted the strap of his backpack on his shoulder and crossed the threshold. "I'm also happy you don't seem pissed at me."

Sal closed the door. "I told you, it takes a lot to piss me off."

"Well, if me summoning you and trapping you in a salt circle didn't do it, I kinda figured getting burned with holy water would push you over the edge."

Sal leaned toward him. "But you weren't the one doing the burning."

Instant heat and desire rushed through Calvin. There was that closeness again…what he had hoped for. A single half step to the side and he'd bump into him…feel Sal's hard body again… touch his cool skin.

Sal laid his hand on Calvin's lower back. "This way. I was putting the finishing touches on a cake I made."

Calvin moved only from the pressure of Sal's hand on his back. He didn't understand how a single, non-sexual touch could feel so good. Then again, this was a demon. And it was Duke Sallos, a demon noble. Power flowed around him like air and it was natural for him. And he had a feeling most of what Sal did had sexual intention behind it. He tried to focus his thoughts away from Sal's touch. "This is a beautiful house."

"I'll pass that on to Baz and Valentin. They picked it out and did the decorating."

"You don't have a place of your own?"

"In this realm, no. I just live wherever they are. They're good with that and so am I since they have great taste."

Calvin walked into the kitchen of dark wood cabinetry, stainless steel appliances, and stone and granite accents. He stopped as Sal did.

Sal sighed. "Really, Beezle? I left the room for five minutes."

Calvin followed Sal's gaze to the kitchen counter and laughed. Only the body of the little black crocodile was visible. His head was stuck in a nearly empty container of frosting. Beezle waved his head back and forth, the container moving with him.

Sal crossed the kitchen and pulled the container off Beezle's head. "It's a good thing I bought two. You've got about as bad of a sweet tooth as me."

He flicked on the faucet and picked up Beezle, holding him under the water and washing away the frosting on the crocodile's head. Beezle draped across Sal's forearm, blinking his brilliant yellow eyes through the water. If Calvin didn't know better, he swore the croc had a reptilian grin of satisfaction over getting into the frosting. Once cleaned, Sal patted Beezle dry with a paper towel and placed him on the floor.

Beezle ambled toward Calvin. He stopped at Calvin's feet, peering up at him.

Calvin gazed down at the crocodile. "Is it okay to touch him?"

Wiping away tracks of frosting off the counter, Sal nodded. "Yeah, he seems to like you."

Calvin lowered to one knee, stroking Beezle on the head. "It's so strange seeing him like this after having my first look at him being gigantic and terrifying vampires."

"Beezy likes to terrify vampires, but who doesn't? The shitty ones, I mean. Not the good ones like Baz and Valentin."

Calvin walked to the center island. He slid his backpack off his shoulder, placing it on the countertop, and hopped up on a stool. "After dealing with those shitty vampires, I can understand that." He watched as Sal pulled the foil seal off another container of frosting. On the counter near Sal, a round chocolate cake sat on a porcelain cake stand. "Did you make that?"

"Yeah. Usually I make the frosting too, but I was running short on time. I have to make the cakes from scratch because the mixes never have enough chocolate in them."

Calvin grinned at him. "A chocolate loving demon. And you said I was odd, even for a witch. You know, when I was talking to Sebastian, he said *you* were an odd demon. I'm starting to think he was right."

Sal pointed a frosting laden spatula at Calvin. "First off, Sebastian hasn't met enough demons to make that call. Second, if you came from my crappy ass dimension, you'd love chocolate, too. Third…Sebastian probably does have a point. But that's beside the point, which were my first two points."

Calvin couldn't help but laugh again. As he did, a smile rose to Sal's lips. Once again, where he should feel nervous and guarded, he instead felt comfortable and drawn to Sal.

Sal turned back to frosting the cake. "So, now that you know your brother didn't banish me to one of the nine circles of Hell, is there anything else I can do for you?"

Calvin tried to not let the many things he'd love for Sal to do for him dominate his mind, but Sal's voice, how it had dropped to a lower register, becoming huskier, seemed to imply all of those things. "Well, I was wondering if, maybe, you would reconsider my proposition for a deal."

"Sure I will."

"Really?"

"Yeah."

"And?"

Sal tipped his head back, tapping his index finger on his chin in a thoughtful expression. "No." He turned back to frosting the cake.

Calvin's breath left him in a rush of disappointment. "I know things went bad, *really* bad, and that my brother studied to be a priest, but you haven't even heard my half of the deal."

"Doesn't matter. The answer will still be no."

Calvin stared at Sal's back. Hurt weighed down his heart, made his stomach feel heavy and upset.

His voice soft, his back to him, Sal said, "The problem isn't you, witchy poo. It's your brother and what he is. Ordained or not, he's been touched by that power and it responds when he calls for it. For centuries, his kind were trained to be warriors against my kind. It's not talked about much in this age, hell even the Church doesn't like talking about it, but that doesn't stop them from keeping that education of exorcisms going and passing it on to those who have a proclivity toward it."

Calvin nodded, knowing the truth far too well of Sal's words. When Nathan was in seminary school, he'd studied exorcisms. He remembered one day, leaning over Nathan's shoulder as he sat at a table with a book from the seminary library on the subject. When he'd asked Nathan why he was reading it, his brother had responded, "Because it terrifies me and fascinates me at the same time."

Knowing what he did, hearing it from Sal's perspective, he understood why Sal didn't want to help Nathan. Calvin glanced at his backpack. Since Sal wouldn't help him, he only had one option left. He unzipped his bag and pulled out a thick book.

Sal glanced back at him. "What's that?"

"An encyclopedia of demons."

Sal turned fully around. "You've got to be shitting me."

Calvin shook his head. "It even has you in it. Gives all the forms of your true name, mentions how you ride a crocodile, that you're a duke among demons, and control several legions."

Sal snorted and turned back to the cake. "All stuff it stole from the *Lesser Key of Solomon* and *Ars Goetia*. So glad to know there's one more pain in the ass for every demon. What're you going to do with that?"

"Ask your opinion on another demon to summon who'll be more inclined to help me."

Sal whipped around again. "Now I know you're screwing with me. You can't ask me to help you find another demon. That's like going to your boyfriend and asking his opinion on other men you should fuck."

Calvin let a smirk curve his lips. "I didn't realize our relationship was so serious that I couldn't see other demons."

Sal let out a rough snort. "Remember when I said I liked that you were showing me your cocky side?"

"Yeah."

"I take it back."

Calvin laughed softly, not sensing Sal's words were fully true. He opened the book. "So then, what do you think about Duke Agris?"

A low growl came from Sal. "Do you want to be possessed? Have your sanity chewed up and spit out?"

"Uh, no."

"Then don't summon that old bastard."

Calvin pulled a pencil from his bag and wrote a big "NO" beside Agris's name. He flipped a few pages in the book. "How about Marquis Leraj?"

Sal paused, seeming hesitant to answer. "I think since he's great at spreading pestilence, probably not the right demon for healing someone. Could he do it? Possibly. Will he tell you he'll do it? Absolutely. Will he actually even try to do it? Fuck no."

Calvin jotted "no" beside Leraj's name in the book. He skimmed over other names. "What about Prince Sytri?"

"No!"

Calvin startled at the sharpness of Sal's voice. He glanced up at him. Sal stood with his arms spread, gripping the counter. Even across the distance, he could see how tense Sal's muscles were.

Sal tipped his head back, pulling in a long, slow breath. "Not Sytri. And don't say his true name. Even from here, in the mortal realm, repeatedly saying a demon's true name can catch their attention. Call him Sy, if you have to bring him up at all, which you don't. He's nothing but a deceiver."

Calvin picked up the emotion in Sal's softer tone. "There's something between you and him."

"No, there's not. Not anymore." Sal spun around, a few quick strides bringing him to the island. He closed the book and pulled it away from Calvin. "I think that's enough for now. Do you want some cake?"

Calvin glanced up at him. Sal was avoiding talking about Sy. He wondered why mentioning Sytri's name had upset Sal, but he didn't want to push him too hard on it. He nodded. "Sure."

Sal turned back to the counter with the cake…taking the book with him. He set it down and cut a large slice from the cake, sliding it on a plate and taking it to Calvin. "Careful when you eat this. People have been known to fall in love with me for my cakes."

In the smirk playing on Sal's lips, Calvin saw he'd gotten control over himself. He picked up the fork. "I'm not sure if I should take that as a joke or not, considering you do have that power."

Sal laughed softly as he went to get a piece of cake for himself. "Take it as a joke. I don't use that power much these days, and I'm certainly not stupid enough to use it on anyone toward me."

Calvin opened his mouth, but wasn't sure what to say. He was too stunned that Sal wouldn't want anyone to fall in love with him. Or, was it that Sal didn't want to fall in love back?

He pushed the questions away, not knowing where to begin with answering them or how to answer them. He dipped the fork into the cake and took a bite. Strong cocoa sweetened with sugar filled his mouth. One bite and all he could think was to eat more. "This is the best cake I've ever had."

Sal leaned back on the counter, holding a plate with a piece of cake on it. "Better eat in moderation or else you'll be proposing to me before you finish that."

Calvin took another bite. "I wouldn't want to scare you off. I've got a feeling if there's one thing you're afraid of, it's commitment."

"It does tend to make me feel as if a noose is slowly tightening around my neck."

Silence spread between them. Calvin couldn't help but think there was truth in Sal's jokes. His appetite started to fade, despite the deliciousness of the cake. He didn't know why he felt disappointed. He should've known that not only wouldn't Sal help him, but that Sal didn't want him. Not that he was asking for Sal's love, way too soon for something like that, but he'd take some care and affection.

He almost snorted aloud with his final thought. He wanted care and affection from a demon? He knew it'd been a long time since he was in anything close to a relationship, but damn, talk about looking for love in all the wrong places.

Still, if he could have it from Sal…

Sal poked at his piece of cake with the fork, but didn't take a bite. "You're really going to try to summon another demon to heal your brother, aren't you?"

Calvin set his fork down and pushed the plate away. "I don't see what other options I have."

Sal nodded, his gaze focused down on his plate. His voice left him, low and deep. "Your side of the deal. What is it?"

Calvin snapped his head up. "What?"

"What're you putting up in return for the favor?"

Even though Sal wasn't looking at him, Calvin locked his gaze on him. "Me."

His head tipped down, Sal lifted his gaze, peering at Calvin.

Calvin paused in breathing, his heart jumped into frantic beating. Sal's eyes…the heat, the lust, it made them smolder. As he gazed into Sal's eyes, he realized that for as cool as he'd tried to play things, Sal had also been restraining himself.

"That's a dangerous deal to make with a demon," Sal said.

Calvin swallowed hard. "I know. But I don't have anything else to offer. I'm barely making ends meet as it is, working full-time hours at a part-time job with no benefits. So I don't have money or any kind of wealth to offer. Even if I did, I know that's not what a demon would want."

Sal set his plate aside. He moved toward the island, his strides slow, stalking. "That's pretty much throwing the door wide open and welcoming a demon to take control of your mind, your body, your life."

Calvin nodded, words becoming evasive to him.

Sal stepped around the island, his hand sliding across the countertop. "Demons exist for a moment like this, to be able to own a human. Resentment of humans having control of this realm, of your ability to control us, they'd see this opportunity as one small step toward revenge. Or even, justification, since many demons feel with our greater strength, weaker creatures such as you mortals shouldn't be able to call upon us, request favors, bend us to your will.

"They would take over your life, slowly destroy it, what you care for, and finally, they'd destroy you. And all the while they would revel in the chaos and heartache they'd bring as if it were the greatest game since time began. And for many of them, it is."

Sal drew closer, and Calvin could hardly concentrate. His focus turned to how aroused he was, triggered by the rumbling timbre of Sal's voice, his graceful movements, the heat and dominance in Sal's eyes.

Sal stopped behind him.

Calvin could feel Sal's presence around him, pressing against him as much as a physical touch.

Sal leaned forward, bracing a hand on either side of Calvin on the counter. He dipped his head toward Calvin's ear. "Lucky for you, all I want is to fuck you."

Calvin's breath rushed out of him. He slowly turned on the

stool. He met Sal's gaze, and he didn't know how much longer he could resist throwing himself at the beautiful demon. But he had to secure Sal's word first. "Then, you're going to help me and heal my brother?"

"Yes." A wicked smirk curved Sal's lips. "With conditions, of course."

"Like what?"

"Well," Sal touched his middle fingertip to the hollow of Calvin's throat. He drew it down the center of Calvin's chest, traveling lower. "You'll have to convince your brother to accept my help. As they say, can't help those who won't help themselves. And it'd be far too dangerous for me to try and heal him without his consent. If he won't accept my help, well…" he shrugged, "that doesn't change anything between us and what you're putting up for the deal."

The last half seemed fair enough to him. The first, convincing his brother? Not an easy task. His plan had been to have Sal slip into Nathan's room while he was sleeping and heal him. Not the most honest thing on his part, but he knew Nathan would never accept a demon's help. But if this was the only way to get Sal's help, then he didn't have a choice but to convince Nathan. "All right. Is that all?"

Sal curled his fingers over the top of Calvin's jeans. "Do I need to spell out the sex half?"

Calvin shook his head. "No."

"You accept my conditions?"

Calvin stared into Sal's eyes. There was nothing he wouldn't agree to in that moment. "Yes, I do."

Sal grabbed Calvin by the hips and pulled him off the stool. He caught him around the waist and pressed Calvin tight against him. "Then congratulations on making a deal with a demon."

Gripping a handful of Calvin's ebony hair, Sal pulled Calvin's head back and brought their lips together in a rough kiss. Calvin opened his mouth, accepting Sal's tongue as he thrust it deep inside. The force of Sal's passion ignited Calvin's. Never in his life had he been kissed like this. The energy behind Sal's kiss, the power, the desire, it made him desperate to give himself to Sal and to feel all of what Sal could give him in return.

Calvin tossed his arms around Sal's neck, burying his fingers in Sal's hair. He pushed against him, needing to be as close to him as possible. Feeling the strength, the firmness of Sal's body only made Calvin want more of him. A high, wanton moan sounded from his throat. For as tightly pressed to Sal as he was, it still wasn't enough. He'd been with men. He'd had relationships, short though they were. But never had he felt desire this powerful.

Was it demon magic? Was Sal already controlling him?

No. He had full control over his thoughts and body. This passion, this desire, as strange as it may feel to him, was all him.

Calvin sucked on Sal's tongue and took his turn to enter Sal's mouth. He rubbed his tongue along Sal's, earning a moan from him. The sound, deep and gravelly, was pure sex vocalized. He melted against Sal. If Sal moaned again, he would come from nothing more than that sound.

Sal ran his hands down Calvin's body. He cupped Calvin's ass and hoisted him up. Calvin broke the kiss with a gasp, and he slung his legs around Sal's waist. He looked into Sal's eyes and smiled. "This is new for me."

Sal grinned. "I'm going to show you a lot of new things."

Calvin met Sal's lips in a smiling kiss. He didn't doubt Sal's words, or that in giving himself to the demon duke, his life would never be the same.

Sal carried him to the stairs and started up them, his steps as light and graceful as if Calvin's weight wasn't a burden. And Calvin knew, he probably wasn't. Vampires had strength far superior to a human's, and a demon's surpassed a vampire. In the arms of a demon should be the last place to feel safe and yet, he did.

Sal hopped up the last step, moving his lips to Calvin's neck. He sucked at the tender skin, grazed his teeth along it and nipped. The bite went through Calvin, a shock of pleasure. His cock ached even more, straining in his jeans. Lost in his pleasure, Calvin only caught a peek of his surroundings, the dark wood floor with a deep burgundy rug running down the center, the walls of polished panels matching the floor in color.

Sal swung through an open door on his left, giving it a backward kick to close it. A few quick strides brought them to the center of the room and the bed. Sal bent over it, laying Calvin on his back. Calvin loosened his hold on him, sinking into the plush red satin jacquard comforter. Sal straightened and pulled his shirt over his head, tossing it behind him.

That body…Calvin had seen Sal in only underwear before, but he felt that his mind hadn't fully captured how stunning Sal was. He dropped his gaze to the black leather pants, and he was eager for them to come down. The vision of the long, thick hard line pushing against Sal's boxer-briefs that day at the blood house filled Calvin's mind. The image had replayed itself to him every day since, bringing fantasies and yearning with it. Now, his fantasy stood before him.

Sal unbuttoned the leather pants and pushed them down, slowly. The broad head of his cock emerged over the top of the pants.

Calvin's breathing quickened as Sal took the pants lower. The foreskin half-covered the head, the slit wet with pre-cum. The shaft, lined in thick veins, had such girth, he knew he would be stretched more than he ever had. Sal shoved the pants all the way down and stepped out of them. Trimmed curls, the same brilliant red as Sal's hair, framed the cock's base, though the sac was smooth, and Sal's balls hung large and low.

Calvin's mouth already filled with saliva for wanting to lick, suck, and taste him.

Sal caught Calvin's foot and tugged off the shoe and sock. He grabbed Calvin's other leg and did the same. "I got you started. Want to help me with the rest?"

Calvin almost missed Sal taking off the shoes and socks since he could focus only on the beautiful cock inches from him. But now Sal wanted him to strip, too. He thought of his body and glanced again at Sal. Self-consciousness crept through him. He sat up, inching his shirt higher. "I don't look anything like you."

"Which is a good thing. I mean, I know I'm fine as fuck, but I'm not so narcissistic to want to fuck myself. Most of the time. When I'm having a really good hair day, then I wish I had a double."

Laughter broke from Calvin, taking away his inhibitions, and the gentle smile on Sal's lips encouraged him more. He took off his glasses, stretching to put them on the nightstand, then lifted his shirt over his head…and felt it pulled off the rest of the way.

Sal threw the shirt behind him and pushed Calvin lightly on the center of the chest, sending him to his back. Braced on one hand over him, he trailed his fingers down Calvin's torso. "Silly, witchy poo. My first assumption of you not knowing how beautiful you are is now a proven fact. Look at this body, so lean and tight." His fingers brushed across Calvin's flat, firm abdomen. "I think you underestimate yourself. In many ways."

Calvin closed his eyes in a long blink. Sal's soft and light touch sparked pleasure over his skin. "I'm feeling pretty good about myself right now."

Sal reached Calvin's jeans and opened the button. He drew the zipper down. "As you should with me." He lowered to him, meeting Calvin in a softer kiss.

Feeling Sal tug at the jeans, Calvin lifted his hips off the bed. Sal ended the kiss, moving his lips to Calvin's neck. His fingers hooked over the jeans and briefs, drawing both down as he drifted his kisses to Calvin's chest.

Cool air touched Calvin's cock, followed by the touch of Sal's skin. Sal pressed his body between Calvin's legs, letting Calvin's dick rub against his abdomen, then his chest as he went lower on him. Calvin sucked in a breath. The friction, skin on skin, it was so damn arousing. He rocked his hips up toward Sal, needing more contact. Sal's breath blew over Calvin's abdomen as he exhaled a moan. Heat rushed through Calvin. Pre-cum seeped from his cock and smeared over Sal's skin.

Sal buried his nose where Calvin's leg met his body, his lips at Calvin's sac. "Your scent…your warmth…your essence radiating from you…" He touched his tongue to Calvin's sac, drawing it up in a long, slow lick, "Your taste…it's intoxicating."

Calvin grabbed his cock, as if the action would stop him from coming. Nothing was going to stop that if Sal touched him much more. "You've already got me feeling I could come."

Sal slipped a finger in his mouth, wetting it with saliva. "Go ahead. I'll make you come again."

Calvin could only reply with a hushed moan.

The wet tip of Sal's finger touched his hole. Calvin spread his legs wider, shifted his ass closer to the bed's edge.

"Now there's a good witch. I like you asking for it."

"Sal…"

Sal rubbed the outside of Calvin's hole. "It's been a while, hasn't it?"

Calvin managed a nod. "I don't do so well with men."

"Maybe because you were meant for a demon." On his final word, Sal pushed his finger into him.

Calvin pressed his head back on the bed, a loud groan leaving him. Sal moved his finger deep into him, sliding it nearly out, back in again, repeating the motion again and again. He withdrew it briefly, only to enter Calvin with two fingers.

Calvin held a fistful of the comforter in one hand, still gripped his cock in the other. It took every bit of his control to not pump it. A few strokes and he'd come, he knew it. He wanted it to last a little longer to enjoy, savor, revel in the pleasure Sal gave him…

Ecstasy jolted through his body, shocked his mind out of any thoughts. Sal massaged Calvin's gland and at the same moment, took the cock's head into his mouth. The wet heat of Sal's mouth, the demanding sucks pulling at his cock, Sal's skilled fingers working his gland, any semblance of control Calvin thought he had, shattered. He cried out, jerking his hips up, driving his dick deeper into Sal's mouth as he came. Sal pushed further down the hard rod, his throat working as he swallowed Calvin's cum. Through his ecstasy, Calvin felt the vibration of Sal's voice, moaning around his cock.

His pleasure slowly began to fade with his climax ending, and Sal released him from his mouth. He pulled his fingers out of Calvin's hole and stood. His thick cock in hand, Sal pumped it hard and fast. Sal tossed his head back, breathing out a long moan. Calvin drank in the sight of him, Sal's muscles tense, his beautiful face filled with ecstasy, his strong hand working to bring himself to release.

Knowing Sal was about to climax, Calvin pushed himself up. He caught Sal by the wrist, stopping his from stroking his cock, and closed his lips around the head. He moved his head forward, taking in as much as he could. Sal grabbed Calvin's hair in two fists, thrusting into his mouth. Sal's assertiveness, his dominance, taking control to have his pleasure, sparked fresh desire in Calvin. Never had he known a lover so confident or skilled.

"Calvin…" Sal's voice rumbled. "I'm about to come."

He finished his last word, and the first shot of cum filled Calvin's mouth. He swallowed, more followed, and though he swallowed again, from Sal's thrusting, some still escaped from the corners of his mouth. Sal slowed his thrusts to a stop. Calvin let the hard cock slip from his mouth, but stayed with his head bowed toward it. He panted for breath, his head dizzy and light from his release, then the rush of taking down Sal's. The taste of Sal's cum lingered in his mouth, the scent of it keeping him aroused.

Sal touched him gently under the chin and tipped Calvin's head back. He bent down to him, whispering against Calvin's lips, "You had me wanting that from you all day." He smiled, and drew his thumb across Calvin's bottom lips, wiping the cum away. "But now that I've had some of you, I want all of you."

Calvin brushed his lips over Sal's in a tease of a kiss and

leaned back, meeting Sal's gaze for before he rolled to his left. He slipped off the bed, standing with his legs spread, and leaned over it. He looked back to Sal. "I'm all yours."

Lust smoldered in Sal's lavender eyes. He took the single step to put himself behind Calvin and dropped to his knees. A hand on each ass cheek, Sal parted them wide and pushed his face between.

Calvin's breath left him with a high moan. Warm and soft, Sal's wet tongue licked over his hole. Every nerve of pleasure around his hole ignited as Sal teased and licked him. Sal cupped Calvin's balls, and a cool tingle moved through them, up his shaft, through his groin, making him feel as though he hadn't climaxed moments before.

Pressing his hard cock to the bed, Calvin ground against it. Fierce hunger and passion came through in each thrust of Sal's tongue, in every lick over his hole, how he sucked it, lightly bit his ass cheeks. And Calvin felt the same abandon taking hold of him. He heard his own moans filling the room. Sal had him desperate to come again.

Seeming to sense Calvin's fraying control, Sal drew back and stood.

Calvin twisted at the waist to see him. Sal closed his hand and opened it again, his palm filled with thick, clear fluid. Calvin grinned in amazement. "You manifested lube."

Sal gripped his dick, pumping it from base to tip as he slicked it. "Neat trick, huh? But I didn't make it appear from nowhere. I borrowed it from my bottle in the drawer. Since I knew where it was, I could take from it and bring it to me."

"That's handy."

"Yeah, especially when I'm running a few bucks short at the grocery store."

Calvin gave him a confused look. "Where do you manifest money from?"

"Well, the cash register's right there."

"That's stealing!"

Sal leaned over Calvin's back, slipping two slicked fingers into Calvin's tight hole. "Shhh, morals don't belong in the bedroom."

Calvin struggled to hold onto his thoughts beyond how good Sal's fingers felt inside him. "I'll…I'll need to have…a chat with you about that…later."

Sal sucked on Calvin's earlobe, giving it a nip. "Then I better make sure I fuck you good enough that you forget about it." He pulled his fingers out of Calvin's hole and pressed the head of his cock to it. "I'm sure you know, I can't catch diseases or sickness from humans, or transmit them."

Feeling the pressure of Sal's cock on his hole, knowing Sal was about to enter him, stole Calvin's voice for a moment. He forced it out between his quick breaths. "You wouldn't catch anything from me, anyhow."

"I know." With Calvin braced up on his hands, his arms locked, Sal pressed the center of his back to get him to dip it more and push his ass out. "You ready for me, witchy poo?"

Calvin nodded. "I've been ready since the first time I saw you." He didn't need to look at Sal to know the demon was smiling. Probably because Sal knew his words were true.

Calvin kept his body relaxed, waiting for the push…then lost his breath as it came. His rim stretched around Sal's wide cock head, the thick shaft following. Calvin panted out each breath, trying to keep his body relaxed against the burn and slight pain. Sal had prepped him well, but fuck, he was hung. Sal touched his fingertip to Calvin's tailbone and caressed down, tracing around Calvin's hole. Cool tingling spread over and through Calvin at Sal's touch. His pain vanished, leaving only pleasure in its place.

Emotion rose within him. Sal was so in tune with his body, he'd sensed his pain and took it away. To Sal, it was probably a small thing. To him, the consideration meant so much.

Sal buried his full length into him, his balls resting on Calvin's ass. A low, growling moan left him. "Goddamn, this ass of yours…" He drew his hips back, pushed deep into Calvin again, "is so fucking incredible."

Sal's words and movements sent arousal roaring through Calvin. He dropped to his elbows, pushing his ass against Sal. "And your dick is filling me better than I've ever had."

Sal ran his hand up Calvin's back. He rubbed Calvin's shoulder, then gripped it. "If you like my cock in this form, you should try it in my true form."

Calvin rested his hand on Sal's holding his shoulder. "I want to."

Sal let out a deep laugh. "Do you, now? What a brave man you are."

Before Calvin could respond, Sal thrust forward…hard. The force of the thrust jolted Calvin, but it was the ecstasy it gave him that stole his voice. He gripped the bed, bracing himself against Sal's quick, strong thrusts and also, working to push into them. He heard Sal's breathing deepen, the growling moans leaving him on each exhale. Sal's pleasure was peaking fast. He knew it and it made his own rise faster.

Sal tightened his grip on Calvin's shoulder and took him by the hip. On his next thrust, the yanked Calvin back to meet him.

A sharp, high moan left Calvin. He gave full control of his body to Sal, surrendered himself to the ecstasy taking him over. Sal's thrusts rocked him against the bed. His cock slid over the satin comforter and with each move, it became more and more sensitive until his pleasure couldn't be held back.

Calvin moaned hard and loud, sweet bliss gripping his mind and body as he came again. Sal continued to thrust into him, every stroke of the thick cock inside him drawing out Calvin's pleasure. He pounded into him harder, faster. He tossed his head back, a rough groan leaving him, and he slammed into Calvin a final time.

Calvin closed his eyes, knowing Sal had come. Satisfaction deeper than he'd ever known hummed through him. Without a doubt, Sal had given him the best sex of his life, but the satisfaction was more. It was from forging a stronger connection with Sal. He wondered if Sal felt the same way, then decided he'd rather not know. Demons didn't deal in emotions the same way humans did. Satisfaction. Gratification. Power. Those were the things that mattered to a demon.

Except, Sal had power. He was a demon duke, after all. Helping him wouldn't bring Sal any greater power. Satisfaction, gratification…he supposed Sal was getting those things from him through sex, but Sal could sleep with anyone and have men a lot more attractive than the oddball of a witch that he was. So Sal must be getting something more out of agreeing to help him. But what?

Sal blew out a hard breath and shifted back, easing his cock out of Calvin. He patted Calvin on the ass. "Climb up on the bed and get comfortable. I'll give you a little bit of a rest."

Calvin pulled himself onto the bed and moved to the head. He slipped beneath the covers, his gaze on Sal walking toward the adjoining bathroom and his tight, muscled ass. Looking at Sal's back, he couldn't help but think of how it had slit open near his shoulder blades for the wings to emerge. Those wings…he'd meant what he said, he did want Sal in his demon form.

As Sal disappeared into the bathroom, Calvin lifted his voice. "Only a little bit of a rest? I might need more than that after the way you made me come twice."

Sal returned, a towel in his hands. He wiped himself clean as he walked. "I told you, don't worry about that. I'll handle making you come."

Calvin smiled up at him as Sal handed him the towel. "That's one more thing I believe you about."

"You should. As far as demons go, I'm pretty honest." Sal leaned down to him, bringing his lips close to Calvin's. "So believe me when I say… your ass, your body, *you*…are the finest I've had in a long, long time."

Calvin smiled and brushed his lips across Sal's. "And you're the finest I've ever had."

"Yeah, that's a given."

Calvin laughed and gave Sal a shove back.

Chuckling softly, Sal took the towel, giving it a toss toward the bathroom. He stepped around the bed and climbed in on the other side. He held out his arm toward Calvin.

Understanding the invitation, Calvin slid close to him. He rested his head on Sal's chest and draped an arm over him. "Who would've guessed you're a snuggly demon."

Sal kissed him on the top of the head. "I can't help it. I've got this thing for a human's body, the warmth and softness, feeling the energy of it. And yours in particular feels amazing with your natural power coursing through it."

"I'm glad for that."

"And right now, I'm glad for our deal."

Calvin tipped his head forward, placing a soft kiss on the center of Sal's chest. "So am I."

Fatigue from the pleasure and exertion pulled at him, and Calvin closed his eyes. Resting on Sal's chest and held by him, he felt more comfortable than he had in longer than he could remember. Once again, that sense of safety moved through him. Ridiculous though he knew it was, he couldn't help or change what he felt. Thoughts whispered through his mind…he needed to stay guarded…needed to protect himself…needed to not fall for Sal…but those thoughts faded as he succumbed to sleep.

Chapter Seven

Sal stood at the window of his bedroom. Though the sky was deep in darkness, he could sense the sun's approach. Another couple of hours and the world would start to turn gray with the breaking light of morning. He glanced back to his bed where Calvin slept.

He would be the first to admit he had a weakness for humans, especially when it came to sleeping with them. Their warmth, emotions, and essence drew him in. What he *didn't* want to admit was, things were different with Calvin. Everything with Calvin felt stronger, more intense. It had to be because of Calvin being a witch and a powerful one at that. Sure, he'd slept with a few witches in his day and it hadn't felt the way it did with Calvin, but that was probably because Calvin was stronger in his power.

It was nothing else making him feel this way. Nothing.

What bothered him the most right now was he thought once he had slept with Calvin, he'd feel settled. He wouldn't keep wanting him. Wouldn't be thinking of him even when Calvin was lying beside him. He could count on one hand all the times in his existence these kind of…*feelings*, for lack of a better word, had hit him, but it meant nothing. Except maybe he was hornier over Calvin than he'd realized. That's all, and that was an easy fix.

Sal moved toward the bed. He almost wanted to laugh at himself. Obviously, he'd spent too much time around humans, and even around Valentin and Basil. Those two might be vampires, but they'd retained much of their humanness. All those damn emotions had rubbed off on him, and if there was one thing not becoming to a demon, it was feelings.

He stopped at the bedside, gazing down at Calvin. A smile pulled at Sal's lips. Okay, so he did feel one thing other than horny when he looked at Calvin. He felt good. He enjoyed Calvin's company. And so what if he did? It still didn't mean anything else. And there was another feeling he couldn't deny that was humming beneath the surface—protectiveness. That one was a little more disturbing, because it was one lock undone to opening the Door of Mushiness, but regardless, it didn't mean anything.

Sal shook the thoughts away and went to the other side of the bed. He slipped in, sliding close behind Calvin. A light push to Calvin's back was all it took to get him to roll to his stomach, though he sensed Calvin was in a light sleep. He eased on top of him, resting his cock along the crack of Calvin's ass. He nuzzled into Calvin's tousled hair and whispered, "Wake up. I want you again."

Calvin groaned and shifted beneath him. The darkness had no effect on Sal's vision, and he saw the smile rise to Calvin's lips.

Calvin rested his hand over Sal's. "What time is it?"

"About four thirty.

"I should get back home. Nathan doesn't like it when I stay out all night and I have to get to work at eight."

Sal kissed Calvin near his ear. "I hate to break it to you, but you've already been out all night. And you've got a few hours before you need to be at work."

Calvin lifted his ass, pressing against Sal's cock. "You do make a convincing argument."

"Silver-tongued, that's what I am."

"I'll go with that. Especially since I know just how good you are with that tongue." Calvin pushed up slightly and rolled to his back. He looped his arms around Sal's neck and lifted off the bed to bring their lips together.

Shock mingled with Sal's arousal. He didn't fuck face to face much, not with humans anyway. Usually, he'd bend the human over and take them. Of course, he also didn't stick around long after he had someone, normally waiting until the human fell asleep, then he'd take off. He couldn't very well do that since they were in his bedroom. Another thing he didn't do. He never brought humans to where he resided, in this realm or his.

Everything with Calvin was different.

These thoughts. Why the fuck was he thinking when he had a hard-on and a hot man under him? He needed to stop! Feelings, thoughts, all of it needed to go.

Sal pushed his tongue into Calvin's mouth. As Calvin moaned around it, Sal's thoughts began to fade. Lust filled his mind and needs. He slipped a hand beneath the covers to his dick. With a thought, he drew lube from the bottle in his drawer and manifested it into his palm. He slicked his cock, then rubbed the extra on Calvin's hole. It hadn't been long since he'd last taken him, and he felt in Calvin's body he didn't need further prepping. Keeping a hand on his cock, he guided the head into him.

Sal broke the kiss, tipping his head down, closing his eyes. Calvin's warmth, it was the most exquisite sensation. He felt it spreading through his body and carrying pleasure with it. He sank deeper into him. He stopped, his dick pressed deep into Calvin, wanting to take a moment to savor Calvin's warmth and energy.

Calvin tangled his fingers in Sal's hair, holding some of the silken strands in a tight grip. "Having you like this…your dick… it's so good. You're…"

Sal eased his hips back and thrust forward.

A high moan slipped from Calvin's throat. "Right on my gland." He released Sal's hair and ran his hands down Sal's back. He gripped Sal's hips. "Let's go slow. I'll lose it if we don't."

Sal nodded. He was all for going slow and enjoying him. He kept his pace easy and gentle, sliding his cock in and out of Calvin in long thrusts. On each move, he lost more of himself to the pleasure of Calvin's body. He touched their lips together in a tender kiss, drifted his lips lower to kiss Calvin's neck. Everywhere he could reach on Calvin, he showered with kisses, hardly aware of what he was doing, consumed with the closeness he was sharing with Calvin and how amazing it felt to have Calvin's arms and legs wrapped around him.

Soft moans left Calvin. He rubbed his hands along Sal's ass and back. Embracing him tight, he buried his nose into the curve of Sal's neck. "Sallos."

Sal nearly lost his rhythm. His true name. Humans didn't say his true name during sex. He avoided sleeping with those who summoned him, so no human he slept with knew it. Even the witches he had slept with, while they might sense he was otherworldly, they didn't know exactly what he was, who he was.

But Calvin did.

Being with him was more than meeting his end of the deal for Calvin. Attraction radiated off him before proposing the deal. And Calvin knew exactly what Sal was, had seen his true form. With that knowledge, Calvin still wanted him.

Sal groaned low in his throat. The realization sent his arousal soaring, intensified his pleasure. He quickened his pace, put more force into his thrusts. Calvin's breath washed against his neck in a rush. Sal felt it in Calvin's muscles constricting, smelled it in the pre-cum leaking from Calvin's cock, he was about to come.

Sal concentrated his energy and extended his power out to touch Calvin. He shifted his sight to see both their auras, blending together, growing brighter with rising emotions and pleasure. The swirls of colors, his of darker shades, Calvin's of brighter, were dazzling. He never opened himself up to anyone in such a way anymore, but he wanted to with Calvin.

Pure bliss shone through Calvin. His moans came louder, more desperate. He rocked his hips up to Sal, grinding against him as he came.

Sal reveled in not only his own pleasure, but Calvin's as well. Calvin's hot fluid coated Sal's abdomen. Breathing in the scent, Sal couldn't help but want a taste. He slipped a hand between them, drawing his fingers through the thick cum and caressed the length of Calvin's cock. He sucked on the tips of his index and middle fingers. Calvin's succulent taste, the energy in his cum, pushed Sal over the edge.

He drove his cock deep into him, a growl of pleasure leaving him as he released. He continued to thrust, sending aftershocks of ecstasy through his body. He came to a slow stop and took

Calvin's lips in a passion-filled kiss.

As the kiss came to an end, Sal rested his forehead on Calvin's. He slipped his cock out of him and rolled off him and to his back. Sal tossed an arm over his head. Pleasure swirled through him, but so did less pleasant sensations. He should've kept fucking longer to keep the thoughts, the emotions at bay. Except, he had a suspicion it was the fucking that was bringing it all out, because this had been more than getting off. He'd connected with Calvin.

Calvin slid across the bed toward him, snuggling into Sal's side. "That was incredible. It wasn't like anything I've ever felt."

Sal cleared his throat. "Yeah. It was damn good."

He listened to Calvin's breathing deepen as sleep took him. What was he doing? Connecting with Calvin. Transposing his emotions for Calvin to feel. That sure as hell was more than fucking.

Distance. He needed to distance himself, for both of them. It wouldn't do Calvin any good to get attached to him more than he already was. If there was one thing he knew never worked out, it was a relationship between a human and a demon.

Chapter Eight

Calvin listened to the other line ring. Sal wasn't going to pick up. It would go to his voicemail…again. As he finished the thought, the automated message for Sal's voicemail started to talk. Calvin lowered his phone and ended the call. No point in leaving a message. He'd left two over the past three days since spending the night with Sal and tried texting him once. He didn't get a response on any of it. What he should do was summon Sal's demon ass and tell him that leaving someone hanging was considered rude by human standards.

A heavy sigh left him. No, he wouldn't do that. It would be an abuse to his craft and even more, to Sal. He might have the power to call upon Sal at a whim, but that didn't mean he should. And he was positive Sal wouldn't appreciate it.

Really, he didn't know what he'd expected. So things between them had felt amazing, incredible, the most intimate and connected he'd ever been to anyone. It obviously wasn't that way for Sal. The demon was an eternal being. Throughout his existence, the number of lovers Sal must have had would be staggering. And how many of those beings—human and demon—had Sal developed true emotions for? If it was one percent, he'd be surprised.

It didn't mean Sal wasn't caring, compassionate, or even loving. It meant he was a demon. Simple as that. Demon nature was demon nature, and from what he knew about them, demons didn't give away their emotions lightly.

Calvin glanced at his half-eaten peanut butter and jelly sandwich. It might be an econo-lunch, but it was also one of his favorites. Too bad he had no appetite for it. He leaned back on the grocery store's brick building. Rather than eat in the break-room with everyone around him and no one to talk to, he'd taken to eating outside by himself, as long as the weather was decent. He tried to time his break so he would miss the other guys who worked stock and trucks, but…

"Hey, bitch!"

Calvin closed his eyes and pulled the earbuds out of his ears to better hear any threats, though his music continued to play. Obviously, his timing was off today. Frankie. The asshole made his life hell at work, and he suspected him as the one who busted his car window. He didn't need to look to know three other guys from the truck crew were with Frankie. The guy was the leader of their pathetic pack and he always put on a show for them… whenever they were out of sight and earshot of the supervisors, of course.

One of the other guys laughed. "He's a witch, man. Not a bitch."

Calvin sighed. When he first started working at the store, he'd made the mistake of sharing too much information about himself in the attempts of building camaraderie with his co-workers, and when he was asked about his pentacle, he'd answered honestly as to why he wore it; he was a witch.

It was a bad move. Not for the first time, others labeled him as a Satanist, whispering "devil worshipper" when he walked by. He tried to explain how wrong their misconceptions of witches were and about the symbolism of the five-pointed star, that each point had meaning; earth, fire, water, air, spirit. It was about having the elements of life brought together in harmony. No one heard him over their own ignorance. Now he wished he would've kept it all to himself.

But then, why should he? Why was it fine for other people to talk about going to church on Sunday, but his beliefs were considered weird, wrong, even sinful? It wasn't right and it wasn't fair. He shouldn't have to adjust who he was for the comfort level of others, when no one gave the same consideration to him and his beliefs as a pagan and a witch.

Frankie stopped near Calvin, standing over him. "Seems about the same thing to me."

Calvin didn't bother to look up at him. And standing wouldn't put him in much better of a position since Frankie had about six inches over his five foot eight. He'd been shoved, knocked down, slammed into enough to know Frankie had more body strength, too.

What the fuck was it with some people? It was as if high school never ended for them. They stayed the same immature asses they'd always been. Never hit a higher level of emotional maturity and still got their giggles off by running in a little gang and playing at being a badass.

Frankie spoke, his tone indicating he was directing his words to one of his gang members. "Guess he's going to pretend he can't hear us. Let me see if I can get his attention." He hovered his foot over Calvin's sandwich and stepped down. He spoke through his snickering. "Whoops. Didn't see that there. Sorry."

Calvin glanced at his ruined sandwich. Immature stupid ass bullshit. He shook his head and pushed to his feet, grabbing his water bottle off the ground. "I don't know why you have to be like this." He moved to walk past him.

Frankie stopped him by slamming him on the chest, knocking Calvin back a step. "Because I don't like you, that's why."

Calvin lifted his gaze to meet Frankie's. "I don't like you either, but you don't see me constantly bothering you. Just leave me alone." He sidestepped to go around Frankie, but the larger guy blocked him.

Frankie leaned toward Calvin's face. "Or what? You gonna turn me into a frog? Why don't you try it? C'mon. Do a little magic trick for us."

Calvin glared into Frankie's eyes. He would love to. At that moment, he'd love nothing more than to summon Sal. "That's not how it works."

"So what you're saying is, it doesn't work at all."

Calvin tried to step to the other side, only to have one of the other three fill the space. He took a deep breath, trying to collect his patience. Yelling, shouting, losing his cool, would only fuel Frankie more. "Get out of my way, Frankie. I want to go in."

"Too fucking bad, because you know what I want? For you to quit and never come back."

"I—"

"Damn it, Sebastian. I knew I shouldn't have let you drive. Trying to get us into Savannah and you brought us to Doucheville judging by those four over there pestering the hottie."

Calvin's heart jumped at the sound of the voice, one that he already knew well. He peeked around Frankie. Sal and Sebastian walked toward them from the front of the store. Sebastian had told him he'd recently turned twenty-one. It was hard for him to believe Sebastian was two years younger than him, seeing the way Sebastian carried himself with confidence he wished he could have. He hadn't seen Sebastian since the attack at the blood house and the former blood slave looked even more beautiful.

But Sal, he was radiant. His fiery red hair captured the sunlight and shone. His lavender eyes seemed all the more brilliant in natural light.

An ache tightened in Calvin's chest. Why did three days feel so much longer now that he was looking at Sal? He'd known he missed him, but he didn't fully understand how much until that moment.

"I'm pretty sure I brought us exactly where we need to be." Sebastian lifted his hand in a wave. "Hey, Calvin. How's it going?"

"A lot better now." Calvin moved his gaze off Sebastian to Sal, finding Sal's gaze already focused on him.

The others in the group faded back at Sal's and Sebastian's approach. Frankie stepped back, but his gaze remained locked on Sal.

Sal stopped in front of Calvin. A soft smile on his lips, he looked into Calvin's eyes and cupped him under the jaw, brushing his thumb along Calvin's cheek. "It's good to see you."

Calvin could only stare at Sal for an instant before his brain kicked in to give him a response. Sal had him swooning with nothing more than appearing and saying a handful of words.

"You too."

"What the fuck?" Frankie blurted out. "Is this your boyfriend?"

Sal's smile shifted into a smirk with a wicked edge. Slowly, he turned away from Calvin. He flicked his hand at the other three young men in a shooing motion. "Off with you now, you little ankle biters. I need to talk to your pack leader in private."

The three young men started to walk away, one bumped into another, throwing nervous glances back at Sal. Sal's tone hadn't wavered beyond congenial, but Calvin sensed a shift in the air around them. It all but crackled with Sal emanating his otherworldly dominance. His co-workers wouldn't understand that, though. All they knew was their instincts and that inexplicable sixth sense was warning them away from danger.

Frankie moved to follow them.

Sal lashed his arm out, slapping his palm on the building and cutting off Frankie's escape. "Now, didn't I just say I wanted to talk to you?"

Frankie nodded toward the front of the building, where his friends had already disappeared inside. "My break's over. I gotta go in."

"Do you? Funny, you didn't seem in such a hurry before." Sal touched the center of Frankie's chest with his index finger and pushed.

Frankie fell back against the wall. He jumped to straighten his posture and glared at Sal. "You need to back off me, man."

Sal let out an amused snort. "Another funny thing, since I believe Calvin asked you to leave him alone, but you didn't want to listen to him. Now here you are, in the same position. Amazing how things come full circle, isn't it? And since you didn't want to listen to him, I'm telling you, *leave him alone.*"

"And if I don't, what're you gonna do about it?"

"Things you won't like."

The temperature in the space around them chilled.

"You see, Frankie," Sal continued, "it's bad enough that you're hard for him and that you're ashamed about it, so you're making his life hell and trying to drive him away from working here."

Frankie lurched forward. "That's a fucking lie!"

"Shh, we both know that's not true. I can smell it coming off of you. You blame him for making you feel things you don't want to. As I was saying, that's bad enough. But there's another hitch to the problem. He's mine." Sal's voice deepened, became rougher, guttural. "I don't like it when people mess with what's mine."

A sharp breeze rushed around them. The sunlight faded. Calvin glanced toward the sky. A large cloud had moved to block the sun.

Frankie's gaze darted to the left, to the right, up at the sky. He lunged to the right.

Sal caught him by the throat and slammed him back into the wall. His fingernails shifted to claws, digging into Frankie's skin short of drawing blood. "I'm not done talking yet."

Fear filled Frankie's voice, pitching it high. "What the fuck are you?"

Sal closed his eyes and as he opened them again, his round pupils had become slits. He dropped his voice to a whisper and yet it resounded around them. "I'm everything your nightmares are made of."

Frankie's eyes widened in fear. He opened his mouth, but seemed unable to cry out.

"So, from now on, you leave Calvin alone. Don't touch him. Don't talk to him. Don't even breathe air that could be his. If you happen to look at him, immediately take your eyes off him. You understand, yes?"

Frankie bobbed his head in frantic nods.

"Good. I'll take your word, but I'll know if you break it. And if you do, I'll be pissed. I don't think you'd want to see me when I'm pissed. You got me?"

Frankie managed more nods.

Sal released him. He took a step back, clasping his hands lightly behind his back. His pupils rounded and he flashed Frankie a bright smile. His voice returned to its normal rich baritone. "Okay, then. You run along now. It was nice meeting you."

Frankie launched forward. He stumbled hard, his feet moving faster than his body could keep up. He regained his balance and sprinted, disappearing around the front corner of the building.

Sal laughed as he watched Frankie run. "Now that was fun." He turned a smile to Calvin, shaking his head at him. "You and trouble, witchy poo. You're like this." He held up his index and middle fingers crossed over each other.

Calvin stared at him. What he'd just seen, it was Sal's demon nature at work; the dominance, the taunting, taking control of a situation and turning the advantage to him. He'd seen Sal in this mode before, but on a much grander scale at the blood house. Same as then, he found himself enamored by Sal. How messed up was that? Getting turned on by a demon being all…demony.

He should have had the same reaction as his co-workers. His primal drive for survival should warn him away from Sal. And yet, he was drawn to him. Still, it didn't change the fact that Sal had seemed to be doing perfectly fine away from him, going by the lack of returned calls. But then, Sal said he was *his*…

Not knowing where to begin with that thought, Calvin focused on the immediate moment. "I think me getting in trouble coincides with you being around. But I'm glad you guys showed up when you did. Frankie's always an ass to me, but he was really upping his game today." He paused. "Is what you said true? About him being attracted to me?"

Sal nodded and moved toward him. "His aura was charged with it when he was close to you."

Sebastian let out a snort. "He probably doesn't know how to handle being attracted to another man and he's taking it out on you, as if it's your fault. Lucky for you, you've got a badass demon watching your back."

Sal flung up both hands. "Now I get the badass title?"

Sebastian rolled his eyes. "You got it back when I saw you grow big horns and wings and throw vampires around. And that was pretty cool how you blocked out the sun with that cloud."

"Yeah," Sal said, drawing the word out. "I didn't actually do that. It was just a happy coincidence."

Sebastian shook his head at him. "You just dropped a couple notches on the badass scale." Sal opened his mouth to protest, but before he could, Sebastian looked to Calvin again. "Hey, it's nice to see you, by the way. You're looking good."

"You too, on both things. I couldn't believe it when I saw you guys coming to help me."

"Yeah, I thought we'd swing by and see if you were here, since we were heading into town for lunch. He and I hang out a lot during the day if he's not in DemonLand."

Calvin gazed at Sebastian for a moment. "It sounds as though you brought him here, then. Not that he wanted to come." He slowly moved his gaze to Sal.

Sal held up an index finger in protest. "Not true. I *have* wanted to see you."

Sebastian laid a hand on Sal's shoulder, but kept his attention on Calvin. "He's been going through some issues the past few days. See, you've given him a bad case of emotions and it's kind of freaked him out."

Sal shoved Sebastian on the shoulder. "Hey! You know what? Your help? I don't need it. Thanks."

Snickering softly, Sebastian started walking toward the front of the store. "I think you do, but I'm going to let you guys chat while I go in for a pint of ice cream. Want anything?"

"No," Sal grumbled.

Silence stretched between them. Calvin wanted to ask if what Sebastian said was true. Sal's words to Frankie rang through Calvin's mind again, stronger than they had when Sal had spoken them.

...he's mine. I don't like it when people mess with what's mine.

Did Sal mean those words? Or did he say them because they strengthened his threat toward Frankie? Calvin lowered his gaze. He'd love to ask those questions, but didn't know how to get them out.

Sal's voice broke the silence and through Calvin's thoughts.

"You're listening to Imagine Dragons." Sal pointed at the earbuds. "Their song, 'Demons', is one of my favorites. For more than the obvious reason."

"It's one of mine, too."

Other than the faint hum of music from the earbuds, the silence returned, drawing on...and on.

Calvin tried to think of more to say, but everything he wanted to ask would lead around to what he was sure Sal didn't want to talk about.

Sal cleared his throat. "So, I've been a kind of a dick. Obviously. And..." He took a deep breath, held it, then let his words come out in a rush on the exhale. "I'm sorry."

A grin pulled at the corners of Calvin's lips. "That must've really hurt."

Sal sagged against the building as if his strength was drained. "You have no idea how much."

Calvin laughed softly. He stepped closer to him. "Well, I appreciate you putting yourself through so much pain to make an apology. I want to ask why you weren't calling me back these past few days, but I have a feeling you might disintegrate trying to explain. So I'll just ask, is what Sebastian said true? You can nod, if it'll hurt too much to say yes."

Sal drummed his fingers on the wall as he contemplated Calvin. "Yes. And by you being almost as much of a smartass as me, I'm feeling a relapse coming on."

Calvin laughed harder. He rested his hands on Sal's chest. "Then I guess I should apologize too, for giving you such a bad case of emotions."

Sal placed his hands on Calvin's hips. "You should. I didn't think it was possible for a demon to catch anything from a human."

Calvin pressed against him. "It's probably really rare."

Sal slipped his hand behind Calvin's head, cupping the base. "Exceptionally rare."

Calvin followed the gentle pull from Sal and brought their lips together. He parted his lips, a moan rising up in him as Sal's tongue rubbed over his own and filled his mouth. Heated desire slammed through him. His cock, already half-up from watching Sal flaunt his demon dominance, finished filling. Having his body against Sal, kissing him, feeling Sal's hand roaming over his ass, made the need he'd kept stamping down in the past three days come roaring to life.

If only he wasn't at work. And late to return from his lunch break.

Calvin gathered every bit of willpower and eased back from the kiss. "I have to go back in."

Sal leaned forward to kiss him again. "No, you don't."

Calvin swallowed a laugh and placed a light kiss on Sal's lips. "Yes, I do."

"You don't want to. I can tell."

"You're right, I don't. But my bills wouldn't be too happy with me if I don't."

Sal tugged him closer again, pushing the hard line of his cock against Calvin's. "I won't be happy if you do."

Calvin tipped his head to the side. "You sure you want to go there? Talking about me doing something that won't make you happy, after you've *finally* decided to grace me with your presence after three days?"

"That's not fair. I was sick."

"You weren't sick!"

"I was! I was having an allergic reaction after being infected with mushiness."

Calvin rolled his eyes. "I'm going in."

Sal trailed after him. "Witchy poo, don't walk away like that."

"It's for the best. I wouldn't want to expose you to me for too long and risk you having another reaction." Calvin slowed his pace as Sebastian rounded the corner.

A pint of ice cream in his hand and a bag hooked over his fingers, Sebastian pulled a plastic spoon out of his mouth. "Aww, look at you, Sal. You're following him like a puppy. Is that how it works with witches and demons? He summons you a couple of times, and then you're smitten and follow him around?"

Sal pointed at Sebastian. "Again, your help? Not needed."

"Someone's in a mood." Sebastian scooped some ice cream onto the spoon and held it out to Sal. "Here. It'll make you feel better."

Sal scrunched up his nose in distaste. "Strawberry. Ew. No."

"What's wrong with strawberries?"

"They're fruit. I don't do fruit."

Sebastian took the bite of ice cream. "You should. It'll make your cum less bitter."

"Hold up." Sal tipped his gaze up to the sky, thoughtful. "Hmm…strange. I don't seem to have any memories of you drinking my cum, and since I don't forget anything, ever, that would mean you don't know what it tastes like."

"I'm assuming, since all I ever see you eat is red meat and chocolate." Sebastian nudged Calvin with his elbow. "Am I right, though?"

Calvin nodded, answering Sebastian as he turned a grin on Sal. "It is a little on the bitter side. But I like it." With his words, he saw the lust return to Sal's gaze.

Sebastian spoke around a mouthful of ice cream. "Well, that's all that matters. And it's a good thing, because from the way Sal's been acting, he could do with a blowjob to settle him down."

"He could've been getting blowjobs and more for the past three days if he would've picked up the phone." Calvin glanced at Sal. "Think about that. *Hard.*"

Sal frowned, but kept his lips closed.

Sebastian laughed. "You've totally got his number, man."

Sal turned on Sebastian. "Why do you keep insisting on offering your help?!"

"Because I'm a kind-hearted guy."

Calvin smiled at Sebastian and started walking again. "I get off work at four thirty, Sal. If you want, give me a call then."

Sal laid his hand over his heart. "You're hurting me, witchy poo. I thought the witch's creed was 'harm none'."

"It is. But there's another line you don't know about. The full creed is, harm none, but take no bullshit."

A loud sigh left Sal. "Witches and your mysteries. Complicated buggers, you are."

Calvin glanced back, letting a flirtatious grin rise to his lips. Sal's gaze was locked on him and he swore at first glance, Sal looked worried, but it faded as Sal returned the smile. He also heard soft chuckling from Sebastian. Calvin faced forward and stepped around the corner of the building. He had a strong suspicion his phone would be ringing at four thirty.

Chapter Nine

Calvin stepped out of his bedroom, his backpack slung over his shoulder. True to his hunch, as soon as he was clocking out at work, his phone was ringing. Sal wanted to see him. Asked him out to dinner even. A real date. He didn't know where the night would lead, but he thought it'd be best if he packed an overnight bag.

He walked into the family room. Nathan laid on the couch under a blanket, Buster curled in front of him. The TV was on, but Nathan's eyes were closed.

Worry pulled down Calvin's mood and guilt spread through him. He shouldn't be going out. He should stay home with Nathan, be here if his brother needed anything. And, he also needed to talk to Nathan. He still hadn't tried to convince him to accept Sal's help, since he didn't know where to begin in broaching that subject. They hadn't talked about him summoning Sal since that day. Nathan didn't know he'd spent the night with him, only that he'd been with "a guy" he was seeing. Not a full lie, and he was positive his brother would be a lot more comfortable thinking he was having sex with "a guy" than a demon.

But he needed to bring up Sal. Each day that passed was a day closer to Nathan's life ending. Somehow, he needed to convince his brother he was better off living…and only a demon could help.

Calvin went to the couch and kneeled down. Buster popped up his head, his tail beating against Nathan's arm in happy wags. Calvin petted the dog on the head, his gaze on Nathan.

His eyes still closed, Nathan said, "What time is this man of yours picking you up?"

"I'm meeting him in about fifteen minutes. I wasn't sure if you'd be comfortable with him coming here." An all out lie. He knew Nathan would go ballistic if Sal walked up to the door, so he told Sal he'd meet him up the road at the small park near his home.

Nathan opened his eyes. "This is the same man you saw over the weekend?"

"Yeah, he is. But I think I'm going to cancel tonight to stay home with you."

Nathan rested his hand on Calvin's head. "You've stayed home with me too many nights. You deserve to have fun."

Calvin managed a small nod, fighting back the thought that he didn't know how many more nights he would have with Nathan.

"I hope I'll get to meet him," Nathan said.

"Yeah," Calvin mumbled.

Nathan ruffled Calvin's hair. "What's wrong?"

Should he go there now? Bring up Sal healing Nathan? The door was open for him to do it. But he also didn't want to get into a fight, then leave with tension between him and Nathan. Still, maybe if he tread gently…

"It's about a few days ago."

Nathan's hand slipped off Calvin's head. "What about it?"

Calvin took a deep breath. "I wish you'd open your mind to accepting Sal's help."

"*Sal*? That's its name?"

Calvin pushed up his glasses and rubbed his eyes. Patience. He could do this. "He's not an *it*. And he could help you."

Nathan sat up, taking Buster in his arms and holding the dog. "There's nothing that thing could offer that would be worth the price. *Nothing*."

Anger rushed through Calvin, but he reined it back. Yelling at Nathan wouldn't help open his brother's mind. He hadn't expected Nathan to react any differently, but maybe if he kept gently pushing him, Nathan would eventually be more willing to hear him out.

Calvin stood and adjusted his backpack on his shoulder. "I

knew that's what you were going to say and because I know you, I understand. Same as I know the price you think it would be, some kind of eternal damnation. Which is wrong. You're putting your religious ideology where it doesn't belong. I can tell you that from now until the world ends and you won't believe me. But you always told me, everything happens for a reason.

"There's a reason even I don't understand for why I'm a witch. There's a reason you were guided toward your faith. Maybe, for as strange as it might sound, I was given my gifts as a witch to help you when the time came. Life isn't always about conflict. It's certainly not about one way being the only way. But it might be about finding a balance in the world, and that even the most different people can unite and work in harmony for common goals."

Nathan sagged back against the couch. "So what's our common goal?"

Calvin bent down to him and softly kissed the top of Nathan's head. "Love. Compassion. Kindness." He drew back and looked into Nathan's eyes, widened with surprise. He turned toward the front door. "You and I have both said, the world needs more of those three things. And you have all of those things to offer. And in *my* faith, they're things I want to spread through the world, too." He walked toward the door and stopped, glancing back. "You sure you don't want me to stay home?"

Nathan moved his head in a single nod. "Yeah. Have fun. Be safe."

Calvin gazed at him for a moment longer. His words had stirred something inside Nathan. He knew that distracted tone, the concentrated look on Nathan's face. His brother was going deep into thought. Nathan could shut out and disregard any ideas that didn't fall in line with what he felt was right, but his brother was also the smartest person he'd ever known.

Sharp. Intellectual. Scholarly. Nathan had always seemed to have knowledge on everything and anything. When he was growing up and stumped by homework, any question he came to Nathan with, his big brother could answer. When Nathan went into these modes, it was because he was trying to rationalize and comprehend something. So while Nathan's mind might be closed to Sal now, the hope was there of it opening. It'd happened before.

Calvin opened the door and lifted his hand in a wave. "Have a good night."

Nathan nodded, but said nothing more. His hand moved in absentminded strokes over a dozing Buster.

Calvin stepped outside and closed the door, using his key to lock it behind him. He headed down the short walk through the small front lawn and turned right. Knowing the way to the park, he let his feet carry him while his mind stayed occupied, his thoughts slowly shifting from his talk with Nathan to Sal.

His heart pounded harder. His steps quickened with his eagerness to get to him. He glanced toward the sky, filled with the gray and purple hues of dusk. Shadows lengthened over the ground, beginning to meld with the growing darkness. Calvin veered to the right and through the wide gated entrance to the park.

And there he was. Sal paced slowly, moving in and out of the shadows. He stopped and glanced toward him. Electric heat swirled through Calvin's balls, moving up his shaft. The lust in Sal's eyes…the intensity…Calvin swore he could come from nothing more than that look. A slow smirk curved one corner of Sal's lips. Sal knew the exact effect he had on him.

Strong, commanding, Sal's voice floated through Calvin's mind, *Follow me.*

Sal turned away from him and walked up the trail, heading into a small copse of tall and thick trunked oak trees. He stepped under the low and twisted branches, and disappeared into the shadows.

Calvin rushed forward. He passed beyond the first few trees, the darkness thicker, the branches blocking the sky and rising moon. Spanish moss swayed with the light breeze, draping the branches in green veils. He turned in a circle, but didn't see Sal.

He stopped, scanning the space, listening. A presence cooler than the breeze rose behind him. Sal moved in silence, but his energy betrayed him drawing closer. Calvin smiled, but didn't turn around. "I'm glad you called me."

Sal bumped into him from behind. "Well, I did a lot of thinking on what you said, about all that time I wasted when we could've been fucking. I might've existed for eons, but I'm far from a perfect being. I'm aware I make mistakes. I don't intend to make that one again."

Calvin shifted back, pressing his ass into Sal's crotch and hard cock. "I'm glad to hear that."

Sal slipped his arm around Calvin's waist. He drifted his fingers under Calvin's shirt, along his abdomen, and took a step back, drawing Calvin with him. "And I plan to make up for lost time starting now." He pulled the button open on Calvin's jeans.

"Here?"

Sal brushed his lips up Calvin's neck. "Yes."

Calvin rested his hand over Sal's. "I want to be with you as… you. In your true form."

Sal stilled behind him, even his breath halting for a few brief seconds. "No, you don't."

Calvin looked back at him. "Yes, I do. And I want to go home with you. Your true home. I want to see where you come from."

Sal sighed, dropping his hands away from Calvin. He stepped back from him. "Listen, I know when you saw me shift that day in the blood house, it might've seemed cool and impressive. I mean, I know how badass I am. But there was a lot going on that day. A lot of distractions and emotions running high. For fuck's sake, you were about to get eaten by vampires. But now, here, it wouldn't be the same. All those things that you think you feel about my true form, would change. I guarantee it."

Calvin slowly turned around and faced him. Sal stood with his hands on his hips, his shoulders sagging slightly, his gaze averted. Understanding lit through Calvin's mind. "You're afraid of how

I'll react. That I won't want you."

Sal let out a rough snort. "You're putting too much human emotion on it, witchy poo. Thinking I'm worried you'll reject me when you see…" his voice dropped off the slightest bit, "…me."

Sal's denial gave Calvin the truth. He closed the distance between them and placed both hands on either side of Sal's face. "Fuck me in your true form. It's what I want. You as you."

Sal closed his eyes in a long blink. He opened them again, and his pupils had changed to slits. "It's what you really want?"

"Without a doubt. And then I want to go to your true home."

"I'll give into your first request, but not the last."

"Why? Can't you take humans into the demon realm?"

"No, I can. But it's not the safest."

"I'm not worried about that. I know you'll protect me."

Sal moaned low in his throat. "I shouldn't like how it makes me feel, you knowing that and hearing you say it." He started walking backward, drawing Calvin by the hand with him. "I'll think about it…when I *can* think about it. There's one thing dominating my mind right now."

Calvin moved with him through the low brush. Sal guided him where three trees grew close and pushed him back against one. Calvin reclined on the trunk, watching as Sal pulled his shirt over his head, kicked his shoes to the side, and opened his jeans, pushing them down and off with his boxer-briefs.

Faint strips of moonlight passed through the branches, illuminating Sal's fair skin in a soft pearlescent glow. His red hair was already growing out, flowing past his shoulders. His muscles were taut, expanding, becoming larger. His frame thickened, his height towered. He leaned forward, bracing both hands on the tree trunk at either side of Calvin's head. Soft scraping close to his ears made Calvin look to the side. Long claws extended out from Sal's fingernails and dug into the bark.

"You're still sure?" Sal's voice…it'd shifted to his deep, rumbling, rough demon tone.

Calvin's cock throbbed at the sound. He laid a hand over it, squeezing it through his jeans. "Yeah. I'm still sure."

Sal lowered his gaze to Calvin's hand. His lips curved into a smirk, long fangs peeked out from under his upper lip. "So it would appear."

Sal bowed his head toward Calvin. The sharp tips of two horns poked through Sal's hair on the sides of his head. As more of the horns emerged, they grew thicker and curled. Smoke rose from behind him, and over Sal's shoulder, Calvin got a glimpse of wings extending up and out, growing larger. Once fully formed, Sal snapped them open.

The wings were massive. Red skin covered thick outer bones, thinner bones ran through the leathery flesh. Calvin could stretch his arms out on each side, and from the tip of the fingers on his left hand to the tips on his right, he would still fall short of even one wing's span. Certainly they were large enough to carry Sal into the air, as Calvin had seen them do.

He lifted his gaze to Sal's face. Sal's beautiful features were still the same, and to him, seemed all the more stunning with his slit pupils, horns, and longer hair. He cupped Sal's face in both hands and leaned forward, bringing their lips close and whispering, "You're beautiful."

A groan rumbled in Sal's throat. He closed the meager distance between them and pressed his lips to Calvin's.

Calvin opened his mouth and eased his tongue into Sal's. His tongue brushed between the fangs and feeling them pushed his arousal higher. He wrapped his arms around him and his hands bumped the wings where they met Sal's back. He ran his hands up the thick top bones as far as he could reach and down again.

A growl of pleasure passed from Sal's mouth to Calvin's. Against his abdomen, Calvin felt the unyielding hard line of Sal's cock, but it was longer, thicker. He broke the kiss and gripped Sal's hips, pushing him back the slightest bit as he lowered his gaze. "Ho-ly shit."

Sal dipped his head toward him. "Are you *still* sure?"

Calvin opened his mouth, thinking a response would come out, but instead his mouth stayed hanging open for a moment. "I…uh, yeah. I'm sure. I'm just a little…cock shocked, I guess you could say."

Sal's deep laughter filled the space around them. "I can take the size down to what it is in my human form, if you'd prefer."

Calvin touched Sal's cock at the base and drew his fingers up the underside, over the foreskin, and ran his middle fingertip through a large drop of pre-cum. "No." He closed his hand around the shaft. "I want it exactly the way it is." He glanced up at Sal and grinned. "I've seen videos of guys fisting and taking some pretty huge things up their asses. It's amazing what the body can handle."

Sal gripped the bottom of Calvin's shirt and lifted it up. "So fragile in some ways. So resilient in others, the human body." He dropped Calvin's shirt to the ground and moved his hands to Calvin's jeans, opening them the rest of the way and pushing them down with the briefs. "But you have something none of those men have."

Calvin held Sal's gaze as he stepped out of his shoes and kicked off the rest of his clothing. "A demon duke who can make it easier on me?"

"Exactly." Sal covered Calvin's mouth in a rough kiss. Cupping Calvin's ass, he hoisted him up.

Calvin broke the kiss with a gasp. His back scraped along the tree's bark, but it was more than the pain that stole his breath. It was Sal's large and powerful body, and being pinned between him and the tree. He wrapped his arms around Sal's neck, hooked his legs over Sal's hips. He felt the tip of Sal's cock against his hole. A drop of his own pre-cum rolled down the underside of his cock head. He needed Sal's cock, his body, all of him and in this exact way.

Needing only one hand to keep Calvin propped against the tree, Sal rubbed Calvin's hole. Calvin closed his eyes, exhaling a breathless moan. Sal's fingers were slicked. He must've manifested the lube. And there was no scratch or prick of claws, telling him Sal had pulled them in.

Sal pushed two fingers into him. Calvin tossed his head back, moaning louder.

Sal put his lips to Calvin's neck, sucking hard at the tender skin, licking up to Calvin's ear. "I'm not going to be gentle, but I'm not going to hurt you, either."

Calvin dug his fingers into Sal's shoulders. He rocked against Sal's hands, his movements already urgent. "Don't be gentle. It's been too long."

Sal worked a third finger into him. "It seems you can read my mind, as well." He thrust his fingers in and out of Calvin. "Three days of thinking about you." He sucked Calvin's earlobe. "Three days of wanting you." He kissed down Calvin's neck to the curve. "Three days of stroking my dick and coming with the vision of you before me." He pulled his fingers out of Calvin and looked into Calvin's eyes. "You've bewitched me and you don't even realize it."

Calvin's mind spun over Sal's words. He took a breath, but it left him in a sharp moan as Sal jerked him down and thrust up, driving his dick into him.

The burn…even with Sal's cock slicked, the intense burn of having his rim stretched so far stole Calvin's breath. Holding Calvin's ass in both hands, Sal pushed his cock in more. Calvin found his breath, but it left him in quick pants. Sal had him filled beyond anything he ever imagined, ever thought possible. The familiar cool tingle of Sal's energy moved through his hole and deep inside him, leaving only pleasure in its wake.

His arms still around Sal's neck, Calvin pressed his upper back against the tree, letting it brace him, and pushed his ass down the rest of the way on Sal's cock.

Sal moved his hands to Calvin's hips, gazing down at their bodies flush together. "That's good, witchy poo. Take all of me."

Calvin rolled his hips, shifting Sal's cock inside himself. "Now that I have, fuck me."

As Sal lifted his gaze, his eyes glowing with lavender light, Calvin's balls tightened. It wasn't going to take him long and from the tension already in Sal's body, it wouldn't take his demon long, either.

Sal tightened his hold on him. His claws returned, pricking Calvin's skin, but not drawing blood. Sal pushed his hips forward, the force of his thrust jolting Calvin.

Moaning between clenched teeth, Calvin gripped onto Sal's shoulders, digging his short fingernails in. "Like that. Hard. Fast. And don't stop until we both come."

Needing no further encouragement, Sal pumped his cock in and out of him, his pace quick, each thrust rocking Calvin against the tree.

The bark scratched and cut into Calvin's back, but as soon as the pain started, once again, that cool tingle came, traveling up his spine and soothing the sting. Calvin held Sal's gaze, reading the pleasure in the demon's face. Sal was in perfect harmony with him, so in tune with what was happening to his body and ensuring he felt only ecstasy.

And that ecstasy was growing. Calvin's cock strained from his body, bouncing with each hard thrust. Drops of pre-cum splattered across his abdomen. Moans left him on every breath. His body was tight, ready for release. It was building. Not much longer. Sal was driving him closer and closer.

Sal released one of Calvin's hips to slip his arm behind Calvin's lower back, supporting him. He let go of Calvin's other hip and took hold of Calvin's cock.

Calvin snapped his hips up and tossed his head back. "Fuck. I'm there. I'm so close."

The demanding need to come consumed him. The heated pleasure of his rising orgasm moved through his balls. In a single quick move, Calvin released Sal's shoulders and grabbed him by the horns. He arched, heaving and bucking against him. "Sallos!"

His orgasm claimed him, his cock shooting hard. Cum landed high on his chest, on his abdomen, dripped over Sal's hand.

Through his pleasure, Calvin heard Sal's growling moan, and he felt the deep throb of the thick cock releasing inside him.

Sal slowed his thrusts and stopped. He bowed his head toward him, his eyes closed. "You're the most amazing human…Calvin."

Through his lingering pleasure, happiness rushed through Calvin. He angled his head toward Sal's lips, giving him a soft kiss. "And you're the most amazing demon."

"Well, yeah, I already knew that. But I'm pretty sure you don't know how amazing you are, so that's why I figured I should tell you."

Calvin laughed softly. "Thanks."

"I'm nothing if not helpful." Sal kissed Calvin's neck with smiling lips. "And you, when you grabbed me by the horns, that about made me lose it right then."

Calvin ran his hands along Sal's horns. "I've fantasized about these since the first day I saw them." He stretched over Sal's shoulders to touch his wings. "And these."

Sal drew his hips back, slipping his cock out of him. He gently set Calvin on his feet. "You've impressed the hell out of me tonight, witchy poo. And it's not the first time you've done it."

Calvin leaned back on the tree, his legs and body weak and drained from their shared pleasure. "Same goes to you." His gaze roamed over Sal's wings, horns, claws. "You know, I'm pretty sure I just followed in the footsteps of a few of my witch predecessors."

Sal picked up Calvin's briefs and handed them to him. "You mean fucking a demon under the moonlight out in the forest? Not that this is a true forest, but close enough here in suburbia."

Calvin stepped into his underwear and took his jeans as Sal offered them. He pulled them on and collected his shoes to put them on next. "Yeah, all of that. At least I won't get put to the stake for it in this day and age."

"Not literally, but maybe metaphorically. You know surprisingly, we demons weren't behind much of that. Sure, there was the occasional demon/human liaison, but for the most part, you humans did that persecution all on your own. Talk about an intense reality series. We demons couldn't look away. But humans always have been entertaining." Sal lifted Calvin's backpack off the ground and stepped close to him. He curled his fingers under Calvin's chin, keeping his head tipped up. "Do you still want to see my home?"

Calvin's mind stumbled in shock to form a response. He managed one word. "Yes."

"It might be the mind-blowing orgasm I just had that's messing up my normally good sense, but if it's what you want, then I'll take you there." Sal held up a finger, as if to stop Calvin's excitement. "Briefly. And only to my chambers. Not into the rest of my castle."

Calvin stared at him, then finally blinked. "You have a castle?"

Sal laughed and nodded toward Calvin's hands. "Put your shirt on and we'll go."

Calvin glanced down at his cum-smeared torso. He didn't have anything to wipe himself clean, but he did have a couple of shirts in his bag. He could always clean up at Sal's. He pulled on his shirt. He couldn't believe what was about to happen, or stop the excitement from rising inside him. He was going to Sal's true home. It didn't matter how briefly. Sal being willing to open himself up to him more had him ecstatic.

Sal collected his clothes and handed them to Calvin to hold. "Ready?"

Calvin moved his gaze down Sal's nude body. "Um, aren't you forgetting something? Like, clothes?"

"I'm staying in my true form, my clothes won't fit. Besides, my demons have seen me naked plenty of times."

Calvin stared at him with what he hoped appeared to be an expectant look, because he certainly expected an explanation on that.

A knowing grin spread over Sal's lips. "You're not going to

be roaming the halls, so you won't see it, but in my home, sex is freely given. If lust sparks between any of my demons, they have each other then and there and anywhere in the castle, save my chambers, which are off-limits. It's fairly standard among our kind. True relationships are rare. Fully monogamous ones, even rarer. Sex is about pleasure and we don't burden it with emotions."

"Or else you have an allergic reaction, right?"

Sal narrowed his eyes in a glare at Calvin.

Calvin smiled in return.

Sal shook his head, laughing softly. "Smartass." He opened his arms. "You ready?"

Calvin shouldered his backpack and stepped into Sal's embrace. He wrapped his arms around him, laying his head on Sal's chest. "Couldn't be more so."

Sal folded his wings, closing them around Calvin. "It'll be very cold, but only for a moment."

Calvin nodded, giving Sal a squeeze. Held in Sal's arms, closed within his wings, it was what he'd dreamed turning to reality.

Sal tightened his arms around him. "Here we go."

The cool touch of Sal's demon magic spread through Calvin, far more intense than he'd felt before, and it chilled him. The weight of his body—or maybe it was the gravity around him—lightened. Pressed to Sal's body, his great wings enclosing him, he couldn't see around him and then he was falling…and yet, he wasn't. The motion and speed was similar to falling, but he had no fear of crashing. Rather, his body seemed light and simply dropping through space.

And it was over. As quickly as his mind processed it, the heaviness of his body and the atmosphere returned. His feet touched solid ground and crackling told of a fire nearby.

Slowly, Sal unfolded his wings. He loosened his hold on Calvin and bowed his head, kissing him on the cheek. "Welcome to my home."

Chapter Ten

Calvin opened his eyes. He stood in a room with walls and a floor of dark gray stone. Shimmering drapes of red and black silken material hung around tall sharp-peaked windows. A massive fireplace was on one wall, a fire burning strong, yet there were no logs or coals, and the flames had an odd green hue dancing around the outer edges. Black steel sconces lined the walls, the same flames, but smaller, burning in them with no candles.

A large, leathery black skin of…something, lay over the floor in front of the bed. Whatever it was in life, he couldn't identify it in death, but it had been huge. As for the bed, he couldn't decide if it was amazing or intimidating. Much larger than a king-sized bed, it was covered in black silks, and the ebony posts were carved to be beautiful male demons, nude, their arms raised over their heads in a sensual pose, as if they were holding up the great canopy.

"If I may," Sal said, "I'm going to do one small thing as a precaution." He with the tips of both index fingers, he traced the outer edges of Calvin's ears. He rested his thumbs behind the lobes. "I'm going to cast an enchantment so if anything happens and somehow other demons come around, you'll be able to understand our language."

"Is demon language a lot different?"

"Think of it as kind of like the bastard cousin of Latin. Ready?"

Calvin nodded. The cool tingle of Sal's magic moved through his ears.

Sal looked into Calvin's eyes. "Do you understand me?"

Calvin nearly startled at Sal speaking words with a rough and guttural tone to them. True to Sal's description, it did sound similar to a twisted form of Latin. The strangest part was, he understand the words perfectly, the magic translating them into

English. “Yeah, I understood you just now.”

Still speaking in the demon language, Sal said, “Perfect. I don’t expect other demons to come around, but if anything should happen, I’d rather you be able to understand and know anything that’s being said.”

“Sounds like a good idea to me.” Calvin glanced behind him. He took a cautious step away from Sal, then looked back at him.

Sal gave him an encouraging smile. “It’s all right. You can move around.”

Calvin stepped closer to the fireplace, inspecting the flames. Their heat was greater than mortal fire. He could feel it from a much further distance than he’d felt flames in a fireplace back home. Turning from the fireplace, he moved toward one of the windows. His senses told him he was up high, but he didn’t realize how high until he reached the window.

Bracing his hands on the ledge, Calvin leaned out. A castle. Sal hadn’t been exaggerating. He was in a demon castle, in a tower, high above the rolling ground. The ebony stone of the castle was smooth, a broad moat flowed before it. He wished he could see the castle from the outside, but he had a feeling Sal would shoot that down. It didn’t look dangerous. There weren’t demons crawling all over the place, though he could see movement in the village at the bottom of the hill the castle sat upon. Neat rows of trees to the left formed of an orchard, same for the tangled vines planted in straight lines looked to be an vineyard.

Sal stepped up to Calvin’s side, tying a long, black wrap around his hips. “So, what do you think?”

“It looks like it was beautiful once, but the land was burned, or devastated.”

Sal braced his forearm up on the stone molding, leaning into it. “Because it was. In the last of the Great Wars, the amount of sheer power the nobles put out to defeat their enemies in vying for position left a damning effect in this world, and it wasn’t in the best of shape from previous wars. It’s been slowly been coming back, my lands and a few other nobles’ lands from us feeding our power into it, but it'll probably never be the same."

"That's really sad."

"Yeah, it is." Sal nudged him with his elbow, giving him a grin. "Now you know one of the many reasons I hang out in the human realm so much. It's kind of a downer being here."

Calvin laughed softly. "Yeah, I see that now. I almost can't believe I'm here. I feel as if I should be waking up and finding out this was a wild dream."

Sal hooked his fingers over the top of Calvin's jeans and drew him closer. "Should I fuck you hard so you know you're awake?"

Calvin wrapped his arms around Sal's waist. "Don't most people just pinch someone for that?"

"Yeah, but in case the horns and wings didn't give it away, I'm not a people. So here, in this realm, we demons fuck. For everything. All the time."

"I like the sound of that."

Sal dipped his head toward him, pausing as frantic knocking pounded on the door.

The door flew open. A demon, slender and beautiful, his shining white hair flowing behind him with his speed, burst into the room. "My lord! You've returned—" A gasp cut off the demon's words. "A human!" He slapped both hands over his mouth, as though he was trying to stop himself from saying anything more.

Rumbling chuckles left Sal. "Yes, Elek, a human. Now you'll get to try out the human languages you've studied so hard. He speaks English, so go with that one. And close the door before you alert everyone else. I don't want anyone to know he's here. I didn't want *you* to know, but I can't fart in the demon realm without you knowing."

Seeming to snap out of his shock with Sal's words, Elek whipped around and closed the door. He promptly dropped to his knees, bowing low to Sal. "Forgive me, my lord. I sensed you'd returned and I wanted to greet you."

"I know and I'm not upset." Sal waved his hand upward. "Now get your ass up and meet my human. Careful, though. Don't look into his eyes too long. He's a witch and will take control over your mind."

Having been staring at the pretty demon, Calvin shoved Sal on the chest. "That's not true!"

Sal laughed. "Hey, now you know how it feels."

"But it's true that demons can do that to humans."

"And you could compel him with the right spell." Sal leaned toward Elek as if speaking only to him. "You see, humans *are* dangerous."

Calvin rolled his eyes and moved by Sal, extending his hand to Elek. "I'm not dangerous."

Elek took a step back from Calvin's extended hand, staring at it with wide, crystal blue eyes.

Sal walked forward. He rested a hand on Calvin's shoulder. "Elek's never met a human before, so you might have to tread gently. I don't, though." He snatched Elek by the wrist and yanked him forward. "Be nice and shake the witch's hand. This is how humans say hello." He slapped Elek's hand in Calvin's and held them together, shaking them vigorously up and down. "Calvin, this is Elek, my head of household and my right hand demon. Elek, this is Witch Calvin, my lover."

Sal released their hands, but Elek kept his in Calvin's. The demon stared down at their joined hands, tipping his head to the side in a thoughtful and amazed look. He reached with his other hand, laying it overtop Calvin's so he held it in both.

Sal took Elek's hands and pulled them off Calvin's. "Okay, that's enough human warmth and energy for you." He flicked his hand toward the door in a shooing motion. "We're going to fuck, so you can run along now."

Elek jerked his head up with a startled look. "But I have to tell you, Count Amon will be arriving soon. He's come the past two evenings and said he would continue to do so until he speaks with you."

"What does that sniveling sack of rat balls want?"

Elek shrugged. "I offer each time to relay a message to you, but he refuses. He says it aggravates him enough having to continue speaking with a weak, lesser demon as myself."

Sal rested his hand on Elek's head. "Don't listen to him. As head of my house, you have full command over things when I'm gone. If he talks shit to you again, have him escorted out. You have my permission to do so and I'll be sure to instill that in him when I speak with him, which will be in a few moments since he just manifested outside the castle."

Calvin looked toward the window as Elek did. "You're not even looking at the window. How do you know that?"

Sal grinned at him. "Not much gets by me when I'm in my home territory." He glanced at Elek. "Let him in and bring him to the main hall…" He paused and turned his attention to Calvin. "Why do I have a feeling if I tell you to stay here, you won't?"

"Because you know me, and I've got a feeling this is bad business, so you might need some backup."

"I'm in my castle surrounded by legions of demons. I've got backup."

"But does any of that backup have the human power to compel or banish demons?"

Sal gazed at him for a long moment. He slowly put his attention back on Elek. "Bring him to my private chamber instead."

Elek bowed and darted toward the door.

Sal faced Calvin. "Now, you. I'm having Amon brought up here because I don't want you roaming the castle trying to find me, getting lost, and ending up the new toy for some of my demons, since without their true names, it kinda lessens your ability to control them. That door leads to my solar and it's the only way out of here." He pointed over his shoulder with his thumb. "And I'll be on the other side of it with Amon. Whatever you hear, do *not* come out. Agree?"

Calvin grumbled his displeasure, but nodded. "All right."

Sal cupped him under the chin. "It's for your own safety. If I had known Amon was being such a dick about wanting to talk to me, I wouldn't have brought you here. He's a shifty one and not a fan of humans."

Calvin laid his hand on Sal's chest and ran it lower, over the hard grooves of Sal's abdomen. "I'll stay out of sight."

Sal moaned, low and deep. "You keep touching me that way and I might end up sending him away."

Calvin glanced down to see the silken wrap around Sal's hips and how it was tented out. He brushed his fingers over the hard line. "Maybe you should."

"I—" Sal silenced, turning his head slightly, listening. "I have to take care of this." He spun around, storming toward the door.

Calvin could almost feel the anger rising off Sal. He took a few steps toward the door, pausing as Sal glanced back to him.

"Remember, stay out of sight," Sal said.

Calvin nodded. He remained in place as Sal closed the door, then rushed forward. Both hands braced on the door, he brought his ear close. Sal's voice boomed through the heavy door.

"Amon! Say one more belittling word to my demon and I'll rip your tongue out and shove it up your ass!"

A male voice, higher, a simpering tone to the words, replied, "Duke Sallos, your servant—"

"My servant runs my home and territory when I'm gone, and as such, acts with my authority and is to be given the same respect due to me. Is that clear?"

Silence followed, then Amon's bitter little voice spoke up again. "Most clear, Duke Sallos."

In a softer tone, Sal said, "Wait in my bedchamber for me."

Calvin assumed Sal was speaking to Elek, probably trying to give the other demon a chance to leave the room. And also, to send Elek in to make sure he didn't try to leave the bedchamber.

He stepped back and to the side of the doorway to not be seen.

The door opened, and he met Elek's gaze. Elek gave him the smallest of nods as he stepped in and closed the door over, but didn't latch it. The demon lifted his finger to his lips in a gesture for quiet, then motioned for Calvin to drop down. Calvin nodded and kneeled, knowing it would make him harder to spot being closer to the floor. He peeked out the crack of the door with Elek leaning over him doing the same.

The room was a half circle, the other half of the tower from the bedchamber. Black rugs of the same leather material as the one in the bedchamber laid over the stone floor, another fireplace burned with the green-tinted flames. There were two long sofas padded in deep red leather and two hardback chairs of black wood in the center of the room. A variety of weapons hung on the wall, but his attention was focused on the new demon standing in the center of the room.

Amon might be a noble demon, but he wasn't much larger than Elek. Two small, sharp horns jutted forward from Amon's broad, thick forehead. Where Sal's face remained human-like and beautiful when in his true form, Amon's features were hard and angular, thick cheekbones, deep sockets for his yellowish-green eyes, and a sallow complex. His long hair was a pale, sickly yellow. Wings extended out from Amon's back, but they weren't the grand wings like Sal had and were only slightly larger than Elek's.

Around Amon's neck rested a large constrictor snake, its scales matching Amon's hair in pale yellow hue. The snake opened its blood-red eyes to peer at Sal. Similar to his snake, Amon's tongue kept flicking out to wet his lips. Calvin wondered if the snake could grow in size as Beezle did and for some reason, found himself wishing for the crocodile entity.

"You're burning up my time, Count Amon," Sal said. "What do you want?"

Amon moved closer to Sal. "If the time of my visit is inconvenient, I could return."

"It's my understanding you've been returning. Every. Fucking.

Day."

Amon held up his hands in assent. "It's true. It seems your servant did as he said he would and told you I needed to speak with you. You're very hard to catch, Duke Sallos. I was beginning to think I'd have to cross into the human realm if I was ever to speak with you. You're spending much of your time in the United States, are you not? Georgia? Savannah?"

Calvin's heart beat faster. This demon knew a lot about Sal. Too much.

Sal tapped his own head with his index finger. "I'm mentally counting to a hundred right now. If you don't start getting to a point by the time I reach it, I'm going to hang you from my highest tower with your serpent as the rope."

Amon laughed. "You've always had a wonderful sense of humor, Duke Sallos."

"You know what's funnier? That you think I'm joking. I'm at twenty-five, by the way."

The humor dropped from Amon's expression. A flicker of insult moved over his face. "Once I begin to reveal my reason for being here, you'll be more than eager to listen."

"Forty-eight."

"I have a proposition for you."

"Forty-nine."

"One I think you'll be most eager to assist me with…"

"Fifty."

"Regarding Prince Sytri."

Silence.

Calvin swore his heart stumbled in its beats at hearing Sytri's name.

A smirk rose to Amon's lips. "Have you stopped counting now?"

Sal let out a snort. "No, but I'm counting slower."

"I'll take that as a good sign. I'm sure you're not aware, as you spend so much time in the human realm and even when you're here, you keep distance between you and most everyone else, but Sytri's authority is coming into question. When he gained his princehood, he was a fierce force to be reckoned with, as you personally know."

Amon paused, as if to let his final statement sink in with Sal. "However, many whispers followed his rise, that he was only able to take his position because of your strength. Had you asserted yourself, challenged him, fought him with your full strength, you would be a prince rather than only a duke."

Sal smiled in a show of his fangs. "Better to be only a duke, than barely a noble at all."

Calvin had to smile at Sal's shot back at Amon's rank.

Amon acquiesced to Sal's comment with a nod. "But if one who is unfitting to his position were to be…removed, then we both would move up in the hierarchy."

Sal nodded slowly. "This is a very dangerous proposition you're bringing to me."

"I don't feel it is. Not with your great strength. You're deserving of the rank of prince and also, of revenge. Sytri used you. Betrayed you. If anyone has the right to bring him down, it's you."

"And that's why you came to me, right?"

"Of course! To lend my support for you to gain the revenge due to you."

"How considerate. Here's the thing, what if I don't want revenge? What if I've let all that happened between me and Sytri flow under Bullshit Bridge? What if I find the very fact that you proposed this idea to me offensive and I've reached one hundred in my count and I'm about to hang you by your fucking snake?"

Amon narrowed his eyes. "Then I'd say you're making a grave mistake."

Sal stepped up to Amon, only inches separating them. "I'm

making a mistake? What you're talking about would bring war and chaos back to our realm and upset the hierarchy. Actually, no. Let me take that back. It probably wouldn't, because you'd never succeed. Sytri would have you spiked up your ass and out your mouth in front of his castle as a warning to any other dumbasses thinking about challenging his authority."

Amon's eyes widened with rage. "Your insults have gone too far."

The snake on his shoulders raised its head and hissed.

Calvin saw the strike coming, from both Amon and the snake. He flung open the door and surged through. "Demon Count Amon, I compel you to stand still!"

Amon's body jerked and tensed. Fear flashed through his eyes as his gaze landed on Calvin.

§ § § §

Sal whipped around. Damn it! He should've known Calvin wouldn't stay tucked away. His frustration faded as a smile threatened to break over his lips. Witchy Poo had balls. He had to give him that.

Calvin marched forward, pointing at Amon. "If you even think of striking him, I'll banish you from this castle so fast, you won't know what hit you."

Sal caught Calvin around the waist and pulled him to his side. The closer to him Calvin was, the safer he could keep him. He focused on Amon. "It's time for you to go. And now that you've spoken to me, I don't expect you to return." He glanced at Calvin. "He's free to move so he can go, yes?"

"Yes. He can leave."

A cold smile spread over Amon's lips. "You, Duke Sallos, have caught me off-guard. During the wars, it was said you always had a trick in waiting and this was a good one indeed. A human witch, of all things. While we may have our differences at the moment, your shrewdness has earned my respect." He slid back a step. "I do hope we can talk again in the future. Should you need anything, call on me."

"Probably best to not wait on me to do that." Sal lifted his hand, waving it for Elek to come out of the bedchamber. "Elek, see that the count finds his way out."

Elek rushed forward, passing Sal and Amon to lead the way toward double black doors. He opened one, allowing Amon to pass through, then followed and closed the door behind them.

Sal dropped his arm from around Calvin's waist and faced him. "I thought saying *stay out of sight* didn't leave a lot of wiggle room for interpretation."

"It didn't, but I couldn't stand there and let him and his hell snake hurt you."

Sal stared at Calvin. The witch's aura shone with protective energy…and emotions he didn't want to see. He shifted his sight to only see Calvin, not that it improved things with how damn sexy Calvin looked, hair still tousled from the earlier activities, his pretty face set with defiance.

Sal caught Calvin by the arm and with a sharp tug, yanked him forward so Calvin fell against him. "You're living up to the 'take no bullshit' part of your creed." He wrapped his arms around him and kissed Calvin on the head. "But we're not in your realm. Your magic may work here, but this is where all demons are strongest and you're more than a little outnumbered."

Calvin rested his head on Sal's chest. "I guess it wasn't the smartest thing to do."

"For the intention behind it, I wouldn't say that, but it wasn't the safest thing." Sal gently pushed Calvin back to look into his eyes. "I'm going to take you back to the human realm, then I'm going to have to come back here."

Confusion drew Calvin's slender eyebrows closer. "Why?"

"There's another demon I need to talk to."

"Sytri." The tone of Calvin's voice revealed so much in that single word—worry, concern, even jealousy.

Sal laid his hand on the side of Calvin's face. "I've got to warn him about Amon. I'm sure this was just Amon running his mouth, but Sy should know. Not so much to protect him, but to keep another war for power from breaking out."

"I want to stay."

"No."

"I want to be close to you. What if you need me?"

"I won't." Sal regretted the words as soon as he said them. The hurt they brought to Calvin's face made him feel pain. Damn it, how was he supposed to say no to him now? He was getting so witch-whipped. He let out a sigh of relent and laid both hands on Calvin's shoulders. "This time, I want your word you'll stay in my bedchamber. Promise me."

Calvin stared into Sal's eyes for a long moment. "I promise, unless—"

"No. No unless, no ifs, no buts. Amon is dangerous, but Sy is deadly. You either give me your promise you'll stay hidden or you're going home."

Calvin moved his head in a single, reluctant nod. "I promise."

Sal bent toward him, touching their lips together in a tender kiss. "Thank you."

A knock sounded on the other side of the door.

Sal turned toward it. "Enter, Elek."

The door opened, the fair demon sliding through and closing it. "I escorted Amon out with two sentinels and watched him vanish off the grounds."

"Good. Now I need you to send a messenger to Sytri's castle with a request for His Royal Pain In The Ass to come here. Not in those words, obviously."

Elek grinned. "Of course. Though, wouldn't it be nice to be able to use those words?"

"If he proves as much of a pain in the ass as he usually is, there's a chance I will. Before you send the messenger, sound the bells for everyone to stop with their fucking and go on alert.

Put sentinels at the doors and the bridge to escort Sytri inside, if he'll allow himself to be escorted. Once everyone is set and the messenger is off, come back up here. I'm going to have you hang out in my bedchamber with Calvin."

Calvin touched Sal's arm. "So he can make sure I keep my promise?"

Sal moved his attention to Calvin. "No. So if something happens to me, he can get you out of here safely." With his words, Sal saw the understanding and concern rise to Calvin's face. He didn't doubt Calvin now knew Sy was a demon not to be played with. He looked again at Elek. "If something does happen, take Calvin to Leraj and tell him I'm calling in the favor he owes me from when he decided to spread a damn pestilence and his human lover caught it and I cured him. He'll be able to take Calvin back to the human realm."

"I will, though, I know I won't have to. There's nothing Prince Sytri can do that you can't handle."

"Well, he's a little better at deceit than I am, and that's caught me off-guard and playing catch-up to him in the past. This should be a pretty straightforward meeting, but it's good to make sure we're all clear on things."

Elek nodded. "Shall I go issue the alert and send the messenger now?"

"Yes. I want to get this over with as soon as possible."

Elek bowed and spun toward the door.

Sal let out a heavy sigh and faced the opposite way, running his fingers through his hair as he walked toward the windows. "It's about to get a whole lot of awkward in here."

Calvin trailed behind him. "But Sy won't know I'm here, so it shouldn't be."

"*I'll* know you're here." Sal braced a hand on the stone molding of the window, placed his other on his hip. "No one enjoys having their ex and their current lover in the same space."

"You loved him," Calvin said, more than asked.

Sal stood silent for a long moment. "Stupidly, yes, I did."

"And he betrayed you for power and his position."

"In a nutshell." Sal faced Calvin and leaned back on the wall near the window. "You might as well know what happened, but first let me give you a quick rundown of our hierarchy, if you don't already know."

"I know the basics of the order, and that the titles are based on a demon's power."

"You got it. Where the vampires earn their titles from age and humans earn theirs by birthright, we demons gain ours through power. Other than the Emperor, the kings are the most powerful, and there are only a handful of them. You never want to summon a demon king. Ever. A demon king will always, without doubt or question, gain the upper hand on a human and once he does, he'll use your mind as his playground and fuck your soul.

"After the kings are the princes. The princes are slightly less ruthless, but not by much because most of them are aspiring to become kings. Following the princes are the dukes." Sal motioned to himself. "After us are the marquises, then the earls, then the counts. There are also knights and marshals, but those are more military titles. There're a lot of ranks, because we demons are an egotistical bunch. Throwing a cursory title at some shithead with a superiority complex is usually the easiest way to appease them. So, knowing that, you can see I'm pretty high up there in rank, but Sy is above me. And he pretty much stepped on me to get there."

Sal tipped his head back on the wall, looking up toward the ceiling. He didn't want to go much deeper into telling Calvin things between him and Sy, but at the same time, some odd sense told him it was the right thing to do. He cleared his throat and continued. "But to be fair to him, everyone was doing that to everyone else to gain power. We had wars for hierarchy before, but this was a particularly nasty one, launched when one of the kings had been destroyed."

"Destroyed?" Calvin asked. "You mean, he was killed? A

demon can be killed?"

Sal nodded. "But it's hard as hell to do. Totally decapitation will do it, but most mortal blades don't have the strength to do it. If you could immobilize the demon, there's a chance you could hack your way through their neck with a mortal blade, but you better hope to hell they don't break lose in the process. To really hurt or kill a demon, it takes a special weapon, one made from the bone of a demon. Like that." He pointed toward his bed, where mounted on the wall, a black-bladed longsword hung. "I used it to kill him." He directed his finger down to the leather skin on the floor.

Calvin's mouth dropped open. "That's…a demon's skin?"

"Part of it. The rest are the rugs in my solar. He was a big son of a bitch, brutish, beastlike, and he really pissed me off when he forced himself on one of my lesser demons. I was in an extreme rage and he underestimated my skill. After I killed him, I had his skin turned into rugs and his bones into weapons." At Calvin's silent stare, Sal cleared his throat. "So, now that I think of it, it's probably a little tacky to have the skin of my dead enemy as rugs in here. I'll have Elek move them out."

Calvin shook his head, seeming to come out of a shock. "No, it's fine. I'm just thinking maybe Sebastian should up your badass level a little higher on the scale."

Sal laughed softly. "He knows me as I am. I'm about as much of a pacifist as a demon can be. I far prefer being a lover rather than a fighter."

A grin curved a corner of Calvin's lips. "You won't hear any complaints from me about that."

A rush of desire moved through Sal at not only Calvin's words, but the attraction in his bright blue eyes. "And I give my word, I'll never give you a reason to complain about it."

Calvin walked toward him and rested his hands on Sal's hips. "I know you won't." Worry moved over his expression, and he nodded toward the skin on the floor. "But knowing what I do now, I'm glad you're here with me and didn't get killed in the war for hierarchy."

"Well, it wasn't my first war, just the nastiest." Sal lowered his voice and glanced to the side. "For a lot of reasons."

"Sy?"

"Yeah. The thing is, none of it was his fault. He was being who he is. I'm the idiot who thought there was something more. That he felt something for me. But all he saw was a stepping stone. We had combined our forces and together, we couldn't be stopped. We ran over any demon and their legions that crossed us. And after each battle, we celebrated. *Hard.* And it gave me all these grand delusions of us ruling over the demon realm with the pitter-patter of little lesser demons running through the halls of what would be our amazing castle.

"But, he had other plans. The war was coming to an end, the final hierarchy being established. It seemed he and I would both be granted the title of duke, and I really, I was fine with that. By then, I was tired of the fighting, and I still thought he and I could be happy together.

"He said we had one last foe to defeat, a demon already a prince named Tayish. We set the plan for my legions to attack from the south, Sy's from the north, and we would crush Tayish's forces between us. Only, I didn't know Sy had already made a deal with Tayish…to crush me. As I moved my legions in, Tayish turned his to meet me and Sy came in from behind. My demons and I were trapped between them. As soon as I realized what was happening, I rallied my legions to retreat. There was a break in Sy's lines, and my forces were able to push through.

"Sy's attack and deal with Tayish had won him the favor of the princes and the respect of the kings. When it was over, Sy was granted his princehood. And me, even though I'd retreated in the last battle, because of my earlier victories, I was given the title of duke. I really didn't give a fuck about a title at that point and once my castle and dukedom was established, I started going into the human realm more. It was around then that I met Valentin and Basil, when a witch summoned me and trapped me. I've seen Sy a handful of times since then, but never invited him here." Sal lowered his voice to a rumbling whisper. "Until now."

The deep tolling of bells reverberated through the castle and grounds. Sal glanced up. It was the call for everyone to go on alert. Elek had moved quickly in spreading the word.

Calvin took Sal's hand in his. "I know having him coming here isn't ideal, but you don't have anything to worry about from my end."

Sal gazed down at him. He caught him under the chin, brushing his thumb over Calvin's bottom lip, careful to keep his claw from scratching him. "I think you've enchanted me more as the man you are than you have as a witch."

"I like the sound of that."

"I don't. All this care and consideration, thinking of someone other than myself, is making my head hurt."

Calvin laughed and shoved him on the chest. "You'll get over it."

"I suppose it's a good kind of pain. Not my favorite type of pain, but it's growing on me."

"You have a favorite type of pain?"

Sal lowered his head closer to Calvin's. He shifted his voice to take on a rougher, huskier tone, filling it with sex and lust. "I love the feel of fingernails digging in and scratching at my back as I fuck someone." As he felt Calvin's warm breath wash against his lips, he also sensed the burst of desire through Calvin. He grinned. "Of course, I'm also a big fan of having my hair pulled and ass slapped."

Calvin's eyes widened a slight bit. "You bottom?"

"I've been known to. Who doesn't enjoy a good dick fucking them every once in a while?"

"I can think of a few that don't, but I know I do." Calvin brushed the backs of his fingers down Sal's cock pushing out the silken wrap. "And I also know who has the best dick I've ever had."

Gripping him by the waist, Sal hoisted him up, Calvin slinging his legs around him. Sal walked with him toward the bed. "There you go again, working your manly enchantment on me."

Calvin took hold of Sal's horns, smiling as he pressed their foreheads together. "I'm happy it's working."

"You're about to be real happy about it." Sal reached the bedside and laid Calvin back on the bed, bringing his body over him.

Angling his head, he laid a soft kiss on Calvin's neck and licked up the length of it. He pulled in the lingering scents of their earlier sex, all that delicious masculinity, and he wanted more of it, more of the energy that had radiated between them, of the heat, passion, and need. He wanted more of Calvin.

This sensation he was feeling for Calvin, the craving that was only satisfied when their bodies were pressed together, was so old a feeling it was unfamiliar to him now. It was nothing but a distant memory, yet it was becoming real again with each moment he spent in Calvin's presence. But the true test would be, would he feel the same when he stood face to face with the only other who'd made him feel the same way?

A chill shot through Sal, his body tensed. The door to the chamber beyond flew open, racing footsteps charging through his solar to the bedchamber.

Elek threw open the door. "He's here! He's already here!"

Sal eased up, sparing Elek a quick glance before looking down at Calvin. The worry had returned to Calvin's beautiful face. Sal cupped Calvin's cheek and gave him what he hoped was an encouraging smile. "It'll be all right. Just remember your promise."

"I will."

Sal kissed him, keeping it quick and chaste, then pushed off the bed and marched toward the door. He glanced back before stepping out, finding Calvin's gaze still fixed on him. His chest tightened with emotion that he didn't need to be burdened with… not at this moment. Emotion was a weakness when dealing with demons. He pushed it down and summoned his defenses. Looking away from Calvin, he moved through the doorway to face the one he'd avoided for so very long.

§ § § §

Calvin sprang off the bed, rushing to the door and dropping to his knees to peek out the crack as before.

Elek rested his hand on Calvin's back. His voice came in a whisper, "This might not be a good idea, since Sytri is sharper than Amon, but Lord Sallos didn't say we couldn't peek out. But don't move. Don't even breathe loudly."

Calvin moved his head in the smallest nod of acknowledgement, his gaze locked on Sal.

Rather than go toward the doors, Sal aimed for the windows. He hadn't yet reached them when a figure floated up and into view.

Calvin's jaw dropped. This could only be Sytri, and he was breathtaking.

His leathery black wings were moving in languid beats, Sy stretched a foot toward the windowsill. He touched down with his other foot and gripped the sides of the window, his wings fanned out behind him. The red sky framed him, and his long, straight ebony hair shone with the faint light. His skin was fair, ivory, and smooth. On top of his head near the front, two horns extended backward, long and spiraled. Dressed only in silken black pants, Sy had a torso of sharply defined muscle. His face held nobility, pride, and most certainly, sensuality. Sy's eyes were golden, the pupils slit like Sal's, and were framed by thick lashes.

Sy rested his gaze on Sal, a sensual smile on his lips. "Sallos. Dear, Sallos. It's such a pleasure to see you." His voice was deep and entrancing, and Calvin had to stop himself from being drawn into it.

"Yeah, right," Sal said. "I wasn't expecting you to show up so fast. It's not like you to rush over when you're called."

"Well, your messenger caught me at a good moment." Sy

hopped off the windowsill to land gracefully in the room. He sauntered toward Sal. "And I've been waiting for this for a long, long time."

Sal rested his hands on his hips, his stance casual and relaxed. "Yeah, sorry about that. I would've had you over sooner, but I've been busy. And also—and I can't express this enough—I haven't wanted to. Driving a barbed rod that's been sitting in fire up my dickhole would've been preferable to having you in my home."

Sy laughed, the sound rich and melodic. He stopped before Sal, their bodies close, nearly touching. He glanced down at the cloth of Sal's wrap pushed out by his hard cock. He reached toward Sal's cock and traced up the length of it over the cloth with his fingertips. "And yet despite your words, your body reveals the truth of how you feel about me being here."

Anger rushed through Calvin. He twitched forward, ready to burst through the door, but a strong hand grabbed his shoulder, sharp-tipped claws digging in. He glanced back and up to Elek. The pretty demon shook his head in warning. Calvin gave a grudging nod and looked back to Sal and Sy. He would give Sal time to handle Sy, but if Sy kept this shit up, he was going to have to break his word and banish the asshole back to his castle.

Sal let out a rough snort. "You probably shouldn't flatter yourself about that. You know me. I pop a boner over a candy bar."

Sy chuckled. "That's true." He looped his arms around Sal's neck. "But that doesn't mean we can't still make good use of it."

Sal glanced to the left, to the right, over at the fire. "Where the fuck is that barbed rod?"

The lust in Sy's eyes faded, along with the humor in his expression. "You can stop with your jokes."

"See, this where that human saying of, 'there's a lot truth in jest,' comes in."

Sy slid one hand forward to Sal's throat, stroking it with his clawed thumb. "I know you feel you have to put up resistance to retain your pride after what happened between us, but you can let it go. It's only us here."

Sal grinned at him. "That's an interesting version of the past you have, making it sound as though it was mutual with things going wrong between us. My memories have it that I wasn't the one who trapped you, attacked your forces, and tried to kill you."

"But you should have. To quote another human phrase, 'all's fair in love and war.' We had both, so all was fair game."

"Again, you're wrong. I had love. All you had was war."

Sy's voice dropped to a growling tone. "I had high expectations when I received your message and they're dwindling fast, as is my patience."

"I can tell, but then, you always did have a short fuse. Sorry if I'm not meeting your expectations. At least that's one thing that's unchanged between us. And by the way, that word I just said, 'sorry', it came out pretty easily. Granted, I didn't mean it, but still, I said it. You should try it sometime. Now would be a good start, such as saying you're sorry for betraying me and trying to kill me."

"You still can't let that go. Yes, I betrayed you, but for good cause, and I won't apologize for it. And if you really think I was going to kill you, that's the fault of your own stupidity. I had plans, goals, and you—"

"Speaking of plans and goals," Sal cut in, "Amon's plotting against you."

Shock flashed through Sy's golden eyes. "What?"

"You heard me." Sal lowered his voice to a threatening growl. "And if you want to hear more, take your hand off my throat before I rip it off at your fucking wrist."

Sy opened his hand and slowly drew it back. "How do you know that about Amon? Who told you?"

"A little demon named Amon. It came directly from him. He was just here and spilled it to me."

Turning, Sy paced a few steps away from Sal. "Why would he come to you?"

"Apparently, it's not much of a secret among our dear fellows how you screwed me over during the war."

Sy snapped his head around, shooting a glare at Sal.

Sal held up both hands. "Hey, I don't know why you're looking pissed off at me. I didn't tell you to try to kill me."

Sy spoke through clenched teeth. "I didn't try to kill you."

"Yeah, yeah, yeah. That song's already old. Anyhow, I wanted to let you know to watch your back. Amon and his snake are slithering about looking to bite you at the first chance they get."

"But why? I know he's desperate for more power and a higher position, but why is he targeting me?"

Sal moved to the couch that faced the bedchamber and dropped down in the center of it, his wings spread behind him. "Because you're an easy target, that's why."

Sy narrowed his gaze at him. "How so?"

"Think about it. You're one of the newer princes. More than a century may have passed since the war's end, but that's a drop in the bucket of time to our kind. And while I'm sure you've done great at building relationships among the princes and kings, most of them go way, *way* back. You might even still feel a bit like an outsider with them, don't you?"

Sy's expression softened. He turned away, walking toward one of the windows as if trying to hide how close to the truth Sal had gotten. "You have more thoughts on it. Continue."

"Since your ties aren't as strong, it means reinforcements might not jump as quickly to come to your aid. Or even, that there might be those among the nobility who feel you're undeserving of your title. On top of all that, you pissed off quite a few demons to get that title. I wasn't the only one you stepped on, and if you didn't wrong someone directly, you did so indirectly by killing an ally to them. Not that all the blame's on you for that. I was right there with you and everyone else was doing the same thing, but you know what assholes our kind can be.

"In Amon's beady eyes and small mind, you're the weakest of

the upper nobles. So he's going to hunt you, cut you out of the herd, and kill you. With help, of course, because he knows he's not strong enough to do it alone. I'm thinking since he came to me, he's going to everyone he thinks bears a grudge against you. He's trying to build a pack to hunt you down."

Sy rested a hand up on the stone molding of the window, tapping his claws against it. "What you're saying…it makes sense."

"Yeah, well, I'm not too bad at strategy, as you know."

Sy turned around to face him. "I do know. You're the first to come to me with this. So either you're the first he's approached, or others have agreed to join with him against me, or they simply don't give a shit if I'm attacked, except for maybe being happy for it. The loyalty you've shown to me is appreciated."

Sal burst out laughing. "Oh, sweetie, there you go again with flattering yourself. This is nothing more than me trying to stop another war. This world can't take another one. Amon killing you could be the spark needed to set things off again. Lower ranked demons will get all riled up over a count killing a prince, thinking they've got a shot to do the same. But if a prince destroys a count?" He shrugged his shoulders. "Who cares? Though, on that same line, I'd still try to avoid killing Amon, if you can. Maybe if you let him know that you know what he's plotting, it might be enough to stop him."

"If you're the first he's come to, then that might put you in danger."

Sal waved his hand in a disregarding motion. "He knows not to fuck with me. I already told him if he crosses me again, I'll hang him by his snake from one of my towers."

Sy laughed softly. "I believe that you did."

Sal stood and walked toward him. "So, now that you know Amon's up to his shithead ways, I hate to cut this short, but I'm getting ready to head back to the human realm."

A smile rested on Sy's lips. "You and your penchant for humans. Such an odd little quirk of yours and yet, charming in a way. Are you still in Savannah with your two vampires?"

Sal flung up both hands. "How the fuck does everyone know where I'm at?"

Sy caught a tendril of Sal's hair on his index finger, letting the silken red strands slide over it. "You intrigue many, with your ways of interacting with humans and vampires. And also, I didn't know where you were in the human realm until recently. Word spread of your battle with some vampires recently and it betrayed your location more than anything. So many vampires can't be killed without interest being raised about why and how."

Sal gave a nod. "That's makes sense."

"You must've come from there recently, too. I can smell the human cum on you." He touched Sal's chest. "There's even some lingering human warmth and essence on you. It's rather tantalizing, really."

"Why do you think I'm going back? Addicting little buggers, those humans."

Sy turned toward the window. "Yes, I know. That's why I stay here, where my mind is clear and not befuddled by human energy." He stepped up on the windowsill.

Sal shook his head at him. "I have doors, you know. You can walk right through them."

"But this is the more direct way, now isn't it?" Sy paused, then looked back at Sal. "Perhaps when you return again from the human realm, you'll invite me over again, or come to my castle to discuss…things."

"I wouldn't clear your schedule waiting for that to happen."

Sy contemplated him before facing forward again. "Right. Well, enjoy your humans."

"And you enjoy…whatever or whoever you do now."

A growl left Sy. He jumped from the window, snapping out his black wings.

Calvin sprang up and darted toward the window in Sal's

bedroom. He peeked out, watching Sy streak toward the ground, his wings open but not moving. He seemed about to crash and then, he was gone. He dematerialized in the air.

The door to the bedchamber burst open, Sal striding inside. "So, that was my ex. He's kind of a dick."

Calvin turned back around to him. "Yeah, he didn't exactly seem like a joy to be around."

Elek chuckled. "Dear Prince Sytri had no idea how close he came to getting banished back to his castle when he touched your cock, my lord."

"Maybe he didn't, but I did." Sal walked toward Calvin. "Thank you for practicing restraint. That would've gone a whole lot worse if you had busted out of here in all your witchy glory like you did with Amon."

"I gave him a pass because you asked me to stay hidden." Calvin held up an index finger in warning. "But I won't do it again."

"I wouldn't ask you to." Sal stopped in front of him and laid his hand gently on the side of Calvin's face. "It's time for us to go. Things have been too active around here for you to stay any longer." He turned to Elek. "I have one more duty for you to do while I'm gone. I need you to start assessing my demons and pick out six who you feel would be as close to trustworthy as possible to crossover into the human realm."

Elek's mouth dropped open, revealing the pointed tips of his small upper fangs. "My lord, why?"

"One of my vampire friends may be opening an establishment that needs some very special guards, ones who can take out a blood-crazed vampire if necessary. He asked if I could provide a few lesser demons to be of assistance, and I told him I'd look into it."

Elek walked quickly toward Sal. "If I may, my lord, I'd like to volunteer to be one of the demons."

Sal laid his hand on Elek's shoulder. "Sorry, but that's not going to happen. I need you here to manage things for me."

Elek lowered his head, his shoulders sagging. He peeked up again at Sal.

Sal huffed and spun half away from him. "Don't look at me like that."

Elek continued his mournful gaze at Sal.

Sal flung up a hand. "Goddamn it! Hanging out in the human realm is turning me into a weak ass. Fine! I'll take you over!"

Elek lifted his head, a bright smile shining over his face. "My lord, I'm so grateful. You won't regret it. And I'll get right to work on selecting more demons."

"Yeah, that's great. You do that. Actually, this might work out. I can make you captain over the demons so you can babysit them over there." Sal sighed. "This night has taken a fast decline. I'm ready to get out of here."

Calvin wrapped his arms around Sal's waist. "So am I. And I'm ready to take our night back to how good it started."

A rumbling moan of approval sounded low in Sal's throat. He glanced again to Elek. "Despite what I said to Sytri, I'll be back soon. I'll be checking in more frequently with the drama going on now."

"And I'll await your return, as always."

Sal patted Elek on the head. "Good demon." He glanced at Calvin. "Oh, before we go, there's something I want to give you." He walked across the bedchamber and stepped out to his solar, returning a moment later with a long, curved dagger in a scaly black sheath. He held it out to Calvin. "Here."

Calvin looked down at the dagger, then back up at Sal. He reached with a tentative hand and took it. The hilt was cast in dark metal, etched to be the body of a crocodile. He gripped it and the sheath, and pulled, revealing the ebony blade. Rather than reflecting light, the blade seemed to absorb it. "Is this what I think it is?"

"If you think it's a demon bone dagger, then yeah, it is. I don't like that Amon knows about you. I know you've got your magic to defend yourself, but I want you to be able to draw real blood if it comes down to that."

Calvin sheathed the dagger. "Thank you. I know you didn't come by this easily. It means a lot that you'd give it to me."

Elek leaned toward Calvin. "I think you mean a lot to him, for him to give you such a priceless gift."

Sal poked Elek on the chest with his index finger. "You. Don't bring that mushy shit into my castle. Now you've got work to do, and I'm getting him out of here."

Grinning to himself, Elek took a few steps toward the door. "Yes, my lord. Stay well and safe."

Sal caught Calvin by the arm and yanked him close. "It's really time to get out of here now."

Calvin wrapped his arms around Sal, holding him tight as Sal's wings folded forward and closed around him. "I'm ready."

He rested his head on Sal's chest, his mind racing with all that'd happened, all he'd seen and heard. But for all of those things, there was one that he hoped was true; Elek's words about him meaning a lot to Sal.

Chapter Eleven

Nathan stumbled hard, barely catching his balance before he fell. He glanced up, seeing that while his mind had been occupied as he walked, his legs had carried him to a church near his and Calvin's home. He spotted a bench off to the side of the sidewalk in front of the church and staggered toward it, feeling it was taking the last of his strength to reach it. He collapsed heavily on it, panting for his breath. After a moment, he shifted into a more comfortable position. Twenty-six years old and he felt like he was closer to one hundred and one. He'd only meant to go for a short walk to help sort through the thoughts that'd been haunting him, but he went further than he intended.

The first drops of rain pattered down on the bench, his head, his legs. He tipped his head back toward the sky. "When it rains, it really does pour."

He sighed and remained sitting. He didn't have it in him to make the walk back home right now. He could go into the church until the rain stopped, but for a reason he couldn't quite understand, a feeling of discomfort rose in him at the thought. Maybe he felt he didn't belong there anymore. He'd seen his brother summon a dark being, and all he did was earn a promise from Calvin to not do it again. Yes, he'd tried to fight the demon, but the beast was right; he didn't have the strength.

He couldn't protect Calvin any longer from anything. He certainly couldn't protect Calvin from himself. The things his brother did, he didn't understand them. The stones and crystals, the candles and incense, that journal Calvin called his Book of Shadows where he wrote down strange things…spells, he guessed. It had seemed harmless enough at first. He thought Calvin was only trying to find himself, exploring different things. He hadn't expected the witchcraft to last. But it had, and Calvin was clinging stubbornly to it.

He understood well there were forces in existence that many

people didn't know about, or didn't want to know about. Even the Church was quiet on the matters publicly, but that didn't stop them from having priests trained to handle exorcisms and banishments. He received cursory knowledge of it in seminary and had taken it upon himself to study it more. Had his body not begun to fail him, he would've pursued it to a greater extent.

Nathan closed his eyes. A few cold drops of rain landed on his face. When their father had passed, he might've only been sixteen, but he'd stepped up to be the man in the household, trying to do the duties his father had done and help their mother the best he could. He worked part-time after school, using what he earned to help pay for groceries and the home expenses. While he'd always tried to be a role model for Calvin, with their father's death, he doubled his efforts.

The day their mother passed on from her brave fight with cancer, he was struck with a sense of loss and hopelessness so deep, moving through every single day took more effort and energy than he had. He felt as though he was surviving on pure will alone, and that was fueled by his need to be there for Calvin. But he had needed something to be there for himself, too. That's when he entered seminary school.

His faith had always been strong, but finding a purpose, having a goal, those things brought him the comfort and strength he needed. Except he hardly had a chance to begin before that was taken away from him, also.

He was back to where he'd been, struggling through every day, but now with the addition of his body working against him. Once again, it was only willpower and his need take care of Calvin carrying him on. He feared it wouldn't be enough this time. Not with the things Calvin was doing.

That creature Calvin had summoned...he didn't know what to make of it. The demon was beautiful, he'd give it that, but he also knew demons could take on appealing forms to lure their victims in. The way it'd spoken was very human, though its actions were far from it, burning the phone number into the wall. He'd painted over it several times and the burned digits kept bleeding through.

And the demon's slit pupils, similar to a reptile or serpent, also betrayed the evil inside it. He wondered why it hadn't struck him with more force or attacked with greater ferocity. It certainly had the power. All he could think was that it had a plan to win Calvin, make him believe it was harmless, good, even kind.

The same sense of unease he'd felt several times since the incident moved through him. He'd known Calvin was gay since his brother was thirteen, when Calvin came to him to talk about the things he was feeling toward other boys. Despite what some teachings and beliefs held, he couldn't in good conscious repudiate his brother for his sexuality. He loved him. And, he wasn't a stranger to certain feelings himself.

He'd had intimate relationships when he was younger, had explored some of those feelings. He even thought that somehow Calvin's homosexuality was his fault. Had he, unknowingly, influenced Calvin? He'd never told his brother—or anyone—of the things he'd felt, the things he'd done, but somehow, someway, had it still come through? Perhaps unconsciously in his actions, things he'd said?

It was all things he didn't know, and probably never would. What he did know was the inner turmoil and heartache he'd suffered from those feelings. He couldn't find a way to justify them with what he'd been taught in his faith. But when he'd made the decision to enter seminary, to become a priest, he found peace in many ways. He could leave that part of himself behind, or at least, close it off, and focus his energy and time toward doing greater good through the Church.

But, he'd never really closed it off. Instead of trying to guide Calvin away from actions that were considered sinful, he instead offered him support and comfort. Maybe because he'd never had that himself. He couldn't blame anyone for that though, since he'd never sought it out. His fear of what others would feel toward him was too great. In that way, his brother was far braver than him.

He knew Calvin had partners, but nothing had ever moved into a steady and serious relationship. Until recently, with Calvin spending nights away from home with this mystery man. In the past week, Calvin hadn't spent a single night at home. He still returned every morning before work to check on him, take him to dialysis and pick him up, but once dusk began to fall, Calvin was walking toward the door with his backpack stuffed with clothes.

Two weeks had passed since Calvin had summoned the demon. Given that and the strange conversation they had where Calvin tried to convince him the demon could heal him, it seemed too much of a coincidence, too convenient, that Calvin had suddenly found a man to spend his evenings with. He hoped, so very much, that his suspicions were wrong, but deep down he could sense the truth in them. Somehow, he had to know for certain and once he did, he would call in every resource he could, use every last bit of his strength, to destroy that creature from ever coming near Calvin again.

"Why are you sitting in the rain, my son? Are you all right?"

Nathan startled at the gruff voice behind him. He twisted around, peering up at the priest standing behind him, an umbrella over his head. The man was older, grizzled, and not a priest he recognized. He'd attended this church, but that wasn't to say the man wasn't a visiting priest. The priest's black robes were faded and the white cleric's collar had an aged yellow tint to it. He couldn't blame the priest for his clothing being worn. The man could live humbly, more concerned with doing the good of his calling than anything material.

Nathan cleared his throat. "Yes, Father, I'm fine. I was only resting."

"You don't look well. Perhaps you should go inside, where it's warm and dry."

"I was actually getting ready to return home. And it's not raining too hard at the moment."

"If you would like, I can call a cab for you."

Nathan smiled at the old priest's thoughtfulness. "I'll be fine, but thank you."

The priest contemplated him for a moment. "You're troubled. I can see it. Tell me what bothers you."

Nathan gazed at him, then slowly lowered his gaze. "I'm not sure you'd believe me."

"I don't pass judgment, my son. That's the job of another." The priest glanced up and poked at the sky with his umbrella.

Nathan couldn't help but feel comforted by the priest's words. It'd been so long since he'd had anyone to talk to. He had a few friends, but none who he could tell about Calvin being a witch without fearing their judgment. Though, it was entirely possible that the priest, regardless of his words, would still judge him. It might be worth the risk. Here before him could be an ally if his suspicions were right. Someone who might have stronger connections with the Church than he did anymore, especially given the priest's age.

"It's my brother. I'm worried about him. He's doing things he shouldn't."

The priest stepped closer to the bench. "Such as?"

"He's a…" Nathan hesitated. The word, it was so hard to confess. He took a breath and forced his voice out. "He's a witch."

The priest's eyes widened slightly. "A witch?"

Nathan nodded. "I know it sounds crazy, but he is. And more so than simply practicing nature worship. He's worked on casting spells and most recently, he…he…"

The priest leaned closer to him. "Yes?"

Nathan pulled in another deep breath. "He summoned a demon. I saw it. The creature had purple eyes and slit pupils like a serpent's. And when I splashed holy water on it, the beast's skin burned."

"You have access to such things?"

Nathan smiled, though he felt only sadness. "I was in seminary school for a short time. It was my ambition to become a priest, until I became sick and couldn't continue my studies."

The priest gave a thoughtful nod. "I see. And were you able to banish the demon?"

"No. It left on its own." Nathan let out a disgusted snort. "But not before burning its phone number into a wall. Its phone number! The thing walks among us as if it's human!"

"As many of them do." The priest paced a couple of strides away. "The demon must be very powerful, and it sounds as though the dark one already has your brother in his clutches. I have matters I must attend to now, but I would like to see the marks this demon left in your home."

"Then, you believe me?"

The priest smiled. "I've been around for a very long time and I've seen things many others would never believe."

Relief rushed through Nathan. "I would be grateful for any help you can give. I live just a few blocks that way." He pointed up the sidewalk from where he'd come and gave the priest his address. "You're welcome to stop by at any time."

A smile spread over the priest's thin lips. "Thank you for the invitation. I will, very soon." He inclined his head to Nathan. "Until then, stay safe."

"Thank you. And thank you for listening and believing me."

The priest walked by him, reaching out, but stopping short of touching Nathan's shoulder. "It's my pleasure."

Nathan watched the old priest walk by the front of the church and turn, going around the side, probably to a private entrance. It hit him he hadn't gotten the priest's name, and he felt embarrassed by his poor manners of not introducing himself. He'd been so desperate to talk to someone, and who better than a fellow member of the church? Especially since the priest believed him. Given the priest's appeared age, he didn't doubt the elder had seen many amazing—and frightening—things.

"I'm not sure I'd trust that priest, if I were you."

Nathan whipped around at the sound of the male voice, a sweet tenor inflected with a refined English accent. He nearly gasped meeting the large brown eyes of the young man standing nearby under a dark green umbrella. Pale blond curls fell around the young man's face, and that face itself was strikingly beautiful, almost angelic.

Nathan pulled himself out of his shock. "I'm sorry?"

The young man walked toward him. "I said that priest, he doesn't seem the most trustworthy to me."

Nathan laughed softly. "He's a priest. Of course he's trustworthy."

The young man let out a snort. "Yes, because certainly no priest over the years, recent and distant, has ever proven themselves to be otherwise."

A sting at the accusation—and the undeniable truth in it—passed through Nathan.

"After all," the young man continued, strolling toward him. "Wouldn't a true man of compassion have offered his umbrella to another, who is obviously sick and cold?" He bowed forward, hovering his umbrella over Nathan and extending it to him.

Nathan gazed at him. The young man didn't seem he could be much more than twenty-two years old and yet carried himself with great maturity, and there was something in his eyes that made him seem far older than he appeared. Nathan slowly reached and took the umbrella from him. "But now you won't have an umbrella."

The young man sat on the bench beside him. "Oh, it'll take more than a little rain to do me in." He closed his eyes and tipped his face up toward the slate gray sky. "Actually, I'm very fond of the rain and days like this. Far better than how draining the sunlight can be. I can only handle it for a very limited time."

Nathan stared at him. For as lovely as this young man was, he seemed a bit…eccentric. "So, I'm guessing you heard some of my conversation with the priest. I didn't realize anyone was around."

"I wasn't so close, but I have exceptional hearing. Forgive my rudeness for eavesdropping. I too believe you about the demon and your brother being a witch, but I my opinion will vary greatly from the priest's."

"And what's your opinion?"

The young man turned to him with a sweet smile. "That goodness and kindness can be found in the most unexpected times and beings." He patted Nathan on the thigh and stood. "I wish I could stay and chat longer, but I really must dash. I'm absolutely famished and trying to hunt down some sustenance."

Nathan looked up at him, the feel of the other man's touch lingering on his thigh. "There's a good diner not far from here."

"I'm afraid my appetite is for something very specific, but thank you. And, good luck to you."

Nathan jumped forward, sliding on the bench as if it would bring him closer to the young man who was walking away. "I'm sorry, I didn't catch your name. I'm Nathan Blackwood."

The young man glanced back, wearing that same charming smile. "It's Malcolm. Malcolm Saint Clair." He faced forward and continued walking. "I'm sure our paths will cross again. I'm settling down here in Savannah for a while."

Nathan stared after him until Malcolm rounded a corner of the sidewalk and disappeared down another street. He sat back, his mind spinning with all the priest and Malcolm had said, along with conjuring his conversations with Calvin. It was too much to wrap his head around and now, the cold was beginning to seep through his skin and settle into his bones.

With a groan, he forced himself to stand and begin walking. He shuffled down to the corner and to the right, where Malcolm had disappeared, and couldn't deny the disappointment in not seeing him. Another thing that sent unease through him, but that was at least something he could control. He had another situation, more important, to take care of.

Chapter Twelve

"Only one more building to go," Basil said. "And I really think this is the one."

Sal leaned toward Calvin. "He said that two weeks and about fifty buildings ago."

Calvin snorted out a laugh.

Basil swung around on the sidewalk, pointing at Sal with the end of his mahogany cane, topped with a golden handle formed in the head and neck of an eagle. "Now who's the exaggerator?"

"I'm pretty sure it's still you," Sal said.

Calvin fully laughed, along with Valentin and Sebastian. In the three weeks since he had summoned Sal into his bedroom to ask for his help, he found himself welcomed into this small group. They made him laugh more than he had in ages, and he felt as though he had friends. Actual friends. It'd been longer than he could remember since he had anyone in his life who he thought of that way.

He'd never been one to make friends easily, and only had a handful of people he associated with when he was in school. It never bothered him, really. He was perfectly content and happy with his own company and that of Nathan's. But spending time with this little group brought him a sense of companionship he never knew he was missing.

Calvin grinned to himself. It would figure that after all this time, the ones he connected with and whose company he enjoyed turned out to be two vampires, a former blood slave, and a demon. And the latter made him the happiest of all.

He looked up at Sal walking beside him in his human form. His demon had proven over the past weeks that he was insatiable when it came to sex, but he felt the same way when it came to Sal. He constantly wanted and craved him, whether in his human form or demon. Really, though, for all the things he adored about

Sal, the sex was a bonus.

Whether it was having dinner together or lying in bed after sharing their bodies, he felt happy and safe. Sal made him laugh, told him the most amazing stories from demon and human history. But, it was also bringing to form a problem for him. The way he felt toward Sal was growing stronger, and he wouldn't be able to deny it to himself or to Sal much longer.

He was falling in love with him.

Or had fallen. That was probably more true, but he was still trying to push it back for a little longer. There were many times that Sal seemed to care about him, but love? Broaching that might be enough to scare even a demon duke.

Sal draped his arm around Calvin's shoulders. "What's on your mind, witchy poo?"

Calvin slipped his arm around Sal's waist. He reached up with his other hand, taking Sal's hand that hung over his shoulder. "Nothing you want to know about, I'm sure."

Sebastian spoke up from behind them. "I'd go with that too, seeing how you were looking at him."

Valentin added his elegant voice. "Yes, I'd have to agree. I'm certain his thoughts were a tad too mushy for our dear demon."

Calvin chuckled and glanced back at Sebastian and Valentin walking hand in hand. "That's why I'm keeping them to myself."

Sal let out a huff. "I'll have you all know, I've built up quite the resistance to mush."

"Yeah, we could tell last night when you were making gagging noises at me and Valentin," Sebastian said.

Sal stopped and spun around, swinging Calvin with him. "Oh, come on! You guys take it to a whole other level!" He shifted his voice to mimic Sebastian's tenor. "I love you, Valentin." He changed his voice to sound that same as Valentin's English accented baritone. "I love you too, 'Bastian." He changed back to Sebastian's voice. "Eternity won't be long enough for me to be with you." He bent forward, his mouth open, and pointed inside with his index finger. His voice returned to his own. "Gag! Puke!"

Calvin could barely keep his laughter under control.

Basil moved to Sal's side, nodding at Sebastian and Valentin. "You two do lay it on a bit thick."

A smirk curved Valentin's lips. "You're only saying that because you don't have anyone to lie on at all."

Basil spun around, marching up the sidewalk. He raised his cane, pointing skyward. "I'm a man of business, my dear cousin. I haven't time for such trivial affairs."

Sal snorted. "Sounds like the battle-cry of a man who needs to get laid. You know, when I bring my demons over, I'm sure any of them would be up for a fuck."

"That's lovely," Basil said, the tone dry and revealing he felt the opposite.

"I'm just saying maybe you should drop the high and mighty attitude and take what you can get. If that means fucking some demon ass, you should jump on it."

"I believe Sal may be onto something," Valentin chimed in.

"Perhaps you all should be less concerned with what I'm doing with my cock and more interested in that matter at hand." Basil stopped and turned toward a red brick building rising three stories high. He held his arms open. "We're here!"

Calvin gazed at the building, tipping his head back to take it in. He wasn't sure it was up to Basil's grand gesture of introduction. Even with only the moonlight and streetlamps to light it, the brick appeared dingy with years of city dirt having collected on it. Some of the stone molding had chipped and cracked, but he could see it had once been beautiful with intricate carvings and stone faces spaced every few feet, some smiling, some glaring or frowning, others appearing to be weeping. The guardians of the building, he thought. The windows had wooden shutters closed over them, or plywood for the ones missing shutters.

They were in one of the oldest areas of Savannah, and the

building had a nice location with the Savannah River directly across the street. It seemed, though, while many of the neighboring buildings had continued to be cared for and updated, this one had been forgotten.

Valentin moved closer to the wooden door. "Are you sure this is the right one?"

"Yes!" Basil said. "I was here yesterday evening with the agent. You need to see the inside. It has tons of character." He reached for the blackened steel door handle, but the door didn't budge. "Damn. It's locked. I didn't think it would be."

Sal snickered. "Why would you? Look at it. Who'd want to break into it? It's a wreck."

Basil shot him a glare. "It's not a wreck. There's endless potential here."

Sal folded his arms across his chest. "Yeah, for a money pit."

Basil tapped the door with the head of his cane. "Just get over here and open the lock for me. I don't want to break the door in."

"Probably better off if you did. You'll want to replace that rickety ass thing, anyway."

Basil continued to glare at Sal.

Calvin looked at him, grinning. "You should probably help him. I'd like to see the inside, too."

Sal rolled his eyes and walked toward the door. "This is a waste of my mighty demon power."

Sebastian stepped forward to stand at Calvin's side. "Right, because they're put to far better use toasting marshmallows with your fingertip."

"It was easier than hunching over that puny fire you guys had going the other night." Sal laid his hand flat on the door near the handle. A click announced the lock had opened. "There. You're welcome."

Basil gave him a nod of gratitude. "Thank you." He gripped the door handle and opened the door. "Gentlemen, welcome to

Ambrosia."

Valentin arched a slender eyebrow. "*Ambrosia*?"

Basil turned to him. "That's what I thought I'd call the club, since blood is our ambrosia."

Valentin stared at Basil, silent.

Sebastian leaned toward Calvin, speaking in a loud whisper. "I think Valentin is trying to decide if he wants to express or not how he feels that's a bit exaggerated."

"That's exactly what I was thinking," Valentin said. "Thank you for expressing it for me. And Basil, it sounds as though you've already made your decision on this building. Having us here is nothing more than a formality in gaining our approval."

Basil held up a finger in rebuttal. "Not true. If you see something you don't like with the building, I want you to speak up."

Sal leaned a shoulder against the stone molding around the door. "I don't think there's enough hours left in the night for that."

"Then if you say nothing, I'll take your silence as agreement." Basil swung around to walk inside.

Sal motioned to Valentin. "See what you've gotten yourself into? He's going to make you a silent partner."

Valentin extended a hand to take Sebastian's and walked with him to enter the building. "I'm not entirely opposed to that, since I'm still trying to get comfortable with this idea. Baz does have more of a business mind than I do, though, and he's done exceptionally well by us. But I'm not going alone in this. You said you'd be in charge of security."

"Not exactly. I said I'd bring some demons over and babysit them when I have time." Sal gave a nonchalant flip of his hand. "I'm putting the managing duties on my most trusted demon."

Sebastian clapped Sal on the shoulder as he walked by. "Pawning the responsibility off on someone else. Wouldn't expect anything more. Less, certainly. But not more."

Sal swatted at Sebastian's hand. He looked at Calvin. "Aren't you going to defend me against these guys?"

Calvin walked toward the door, offering an apologetic smile at Sal. "I would, but it's just so damn hard to defend against the truth."

Laughter and snickers came from inside the building.

Sal caught Calvin by the arm, yanking him close and giving him a rough kiss. "We already have one smartass human hanging out with us. Why don't you try being the nice one in the group?"

"Hey!" Sebastian shouted. "I'm nice! Most of the time."

Calvin put his arm around Sal's waist and walked inside with him. "I have a feeling you'd get bored with anyone who was too nice."

"He absolutely would," Valentin said. "He can't be around anyone who's wholly nice and selfless. It makes him nauseous." He held a hand toward Calvin. "Not that you're not wonderfully nice and selfless, of course."

"It's all right, I know what you mean." Calvin patted Sal on the chest. "As it is, I probably toe the line to of being too nice for him."

"Uh, no," Sal said. "Anyone who gets in a demon's face and threatens to banish him so fast his head will spin off his body has enough of a mean-streak to hold my interest."

Sebastian snapped his fingers and pointed at Calvin. "So that's how you keep him in line. Nice work, man!"

Sal flung up a hand. "It wasn't directed toward me!" He gestured around the space. "Anyhow, back to this whole mess. Baz, are you going to turn on some lights? We might be able to see fine, but our dear humans might need some light to see what a glorious wreck this place is."

Basil's voice carried from the other side of the room. "I was trying to remember where they were. I think I've got them. And it's not that bad!"

Lights flicked on, sluggishly and with a low hum. The

overhead lamps burned with a soft yellow glow, growing brighter as they warmed with the electric current.

Valentin looked up at the lights. "So, the electricity needs to be rewired."

Basil walked around the room, giving a twirl of his hand. "Details, details." He stopped in the center of the room, leaning to the side on his cane. "What do you all think?"

Calvin gazed around the large room. It appeared to have been a pub back in its glory days, with the long wooden bar to the left. A few chairs, some of them broken, were stacked against the wall on the right. There was a broad open doorway to the right leading into a spacious sitting room, where a flight of stairs on the far wall traveled upward. Only the bottom half of the stairs were visible, as part of the wall enclosed them.

There was another doorway on the opposite side of the barroom directly across from the entrance, darkness beyond, but Calvin guessed it led to another room. Behind the bar, he spotted one more door. Cobwebs hung thick in the corners, on the old black steel chandeliers, the candle sconces. The floor was solid hardwood and bore the scratches, nicks, and wear of its many years.

The building definitely needed work, but he could sense the age in it, saw the character in the old building's scars, and how with some cleaning and polishing, those scars would make it all the more beautiful.

Valentin turned in a circle, taking it in. "Basil, when was the last time you fed?"

"Last evening. Why?"

"That doesn't explain it, then. I'd thought perhaps you'd gone too long without blood and you were starting to go mad."

"The building's not that bad. It can be ready to open in a month."

Valentin spun around, facing him. "A month?! Now you *are* exaggerating."

Basil held up a hand and bowed his head as he acquiesced. "Perhaps a month is a bit optimistic. But definitely no more than three."

"There's a month's worth of work in this room alone. I haven't even seen the room behind you or behind the bar. Or the other two floors."

"And cellar," Basil added. "There's a grand old cellar with stone arches, solid wood shelves, even some old wine and mead barrels."

Valentin shook his head at him and turned away, resting his elbows on the bar.

"This is why you never could come up with business ventures on your own. Because you can never look beyond the immediate to see the big picture down the road." Basil held his arms out to the sides. "This room would be where guests would enter. Picture it cleaned with Victorian décor creating the ambiance. The bar would be fully stocked, of course. There, one the end, we'll have the absinthe fountain."

Valentin lifted his head, glancing back at Basil. "Absinthe?"

"Oh, look who's suddenly giving his attention. Yes! Of course we'll have absinthe. I know you were heartbroken when our fountain was broken during our move here."

Valentin turned around, reclining on the bar. "You have more of my interest now."

Basil pointed back to the doorway on the right side of the room. "Through there is a sitting room, where our guests can chat with donors. Behind me, there are three smaller rooms that could be offices. I think we'll have that area closed off for only us, or when we're speaking with a particular client in private. Over there," he aimed his finger at the door behind the bar, "is a kitchen and that's where the cellar can be accessed."

He walked across the room, into the sitting room, directing with his cane up the stairs. "The top two floors have rooms, since this used to be a pub and inn. I'm thinking the second floor is where we could set up the rooms for servicing our clients. The next floor could be private rooms for any donors who want to live here.

"I'll have cameras installed in the blood boudoirs with a live feed going down to one of the offices, where one or two of Sal's demons can monitor them at all times while a donor is with a vampire. The front for the club will be as though we're a high-end, member only bar to the public and authorities. Really, so long as the right people are getting their money and the records are in order, I don't foresee any issues, and I've already looked into the requirements."

Valentin tapped his fingers on the bar, his face concentrated. "It seems you've got it all planned out."

"The building itself practically planned it out. It's set up perfectly for this kind of operation. The real estate agent says it's one of the oldest buildings left in Savannah and it's said back in its day, this place was a favored spot by pirates on their way to the Caribbean."

Valentin rolled his eyes. "Nothing like tales of glory gone by to make it shine through the grime. Of all the buildings you've dragged us to, this one is in by far the worst shape."

"I'll agree to that." Basil laid a hand on the thick wooden banister. "But through the years and all that's been thrown at her, she's survived and remains standing. Not unlike us."

Valentin sighed, seeming to relent further. "Damn you and your sentimentality." He looked at Sebastian. "What do you think of it? Your opinion weighs heavy here since you'll be managing the donors."

Sebastian strolled around the room, his gaze roaming and taking it in. "I like it. A lot. I know it looks like mess, but I'd take it any day over that shithole I was kept in. This place has the potential of having class. I can see it how Baz is talking about, plush couches and chairs, ornate rugs over the floor, leather stools at the bars, paintings and mirrors on the walls. It could become a comfortable place for vamps and donors to get to know each other before going upstairs."

"Exactly!" Basil said. "You're seeing my vision for it perfectly. I do want this to be an area where vampires and donors can mingle. And while yes, this will be a blood house, I want it to be as organic of an experience for our clients as possible. We vampires—and by *we* I mean vampires of sophistication, such as you and I, Valentin—know that part of the pleasure of the hunt is in the wooing of our prey. I want our clients to woo our donors."

"I really like the sound of that." Sebastian walked toward Valentin, a sensual smile on his lips. "I still remember how odd of a vampire I thought you were, with the way you took the time to seduce this lowly blood slave."

Valentin extended a hand toward Sebastian. "I still think you're right on me being odd, but you were never lowly."

Sebastian placed his hand in Valentin's, and Valentin lifted it to his lips. Closing the distance between them, Sebastian turned and leaned back into Valentin. "And since you keep on wooing me even knowing I'll give you blood whenever you want it, I'll agree with Baz's statement."

Valentin dipped his head down, brushing his lips up Sebastian's neck in a trail of soft kisses. "Because my pleasure comes in pleasuring you."

Sebastian closed his eyes, happiness and bliss shining over his beautiful features as his vampire prince wrapped him in his arms.

Sal let out a loud huff. "All right, now that I'm about ass deep in the syrupy goop those two are spewing out, I think it's time to blow this place." He grabbed Calvin's hand and looked at Basil. "You got anything else for us, Baz?"

"Well, I did want to ask Calvin his opinion on the building, if you think you can control your nausea long enough."

Sal rested a hand on his stomach, as if trying to calm it. "I'll try to keep it down, but if those two keep it up, don't hold it against me for puking all over the floor of your lovely establishment."

Calvin chuckled and rubbed Sal on the back. "Try to be strong for a couple more minutes." He put his attention on Basil.

"I'm with Sebastian. There's something about this building, the feel to it, that I love. I think it deserves to be restored and given new life."

"Right you are. Now here's a question for you." Basil strolled forward, motioning to the walls, the ceiling, with his cane. "This building has seen a lot of lives pass through. Do you sense any spirits residing in it?"

"Excuse me!" Sal blurted out. "Demon, here! I'm a little bit aware of otherworldly beings, you know."

Basil gave him an exasperated glance. "Well then, do *you* sense any spirits?"

Sal shifted his weight from one foot to the other. "Uh, not at the moment."

"Not at the moment," Basil repeated. "Then, at another moment, you might?"

Sal flipped his hand in a nonchalant motion. "You know how spirits are. Always coming and going."

"So what you're saying is, you don't know."

"I don't believe that's what I said at all. I said, there's nothing here right now."

Basil rolled his honey-brown eyes and turned to Calvin again. "As I was saying, do you feel there could be spirits here?"

Calvin tried not to laugh at another huff from Sal beside him. "Honestly, I'm sensitive to spirits, but I can't tell if there's anything here. The building does feel comfortable and welcoming to me, if that means anything. I'm not getting any negative vibes. If you want, I can get together some things and do a cleansing when you're getting ready to make your move on this place."

"That would be most helpful and appreciated. Thank you." Basil contemplated him for a moment. "Besides witchcraft and demon taming, what other skills do you have? I know you said before you had started in community college, but hadn't continued because your mother became ill and the loans were already getting out of control. If you could go to school, money as no object, what would you study?"

Calvin lowered his gaze, thinking for a moment. "When I had started college, I was going into accounting, because I'm good at math and I thought it could get me a decent job. But what I really wanted to study was history, specifically the Middle Ages and Early Renaissance." He brought his gaze to Basil again. "That would be my choice, to learn about the past and maybe teach at the college level."

Basil laid his hand over his heart. "So you'd want to be a scholar?" He looked at Valentin. "You hear that, dear cousin? He's a man after our own hearts."

Sal laid an arm around Calvin's shoulder. "Hey, go get your own witch."

Basil smirked at Sal. "Was that a hint of jealousy in your tone?"

Sal snorted and lifted his chin with a defiant tilt. "Of course not. I'm a demon and above such petty emotions."

Valentin spoke up. "But perhaps not so above others, judging how you were looking a Calvin a moment ago when he was speaking about his passion for history."

Calvin looked up at Sal, hoping to still catch a glimpse of the look Valentin had seen, but Sal turned his head away toward the door.

"I don't know what you're talking about, my fangly friend, but I do know it's time for Witchy Poo and me to get out of this joint and go have some real fun."

Basil walked toward them. "Fine, fine. We all know that's code for you saying you want to fuck, but I have one more question for Calvin." He rested a hand on Calvin's shoulder. "I know being a witch takes a lot of skill in being organized with your spells and items of your craft, not to mention study in knowing how to cast spells and when. That along with your proclivity toward math and scholarly pursuits, how would you like to help out in this venture? I'm thinking you could be our administrator, do the books and keep the member records. And obviously, we'd pay you far more than that grocery store you're at now."

Calvin's mouth dropped open, a stutter of shock slipping out. "Are you serious?"

"Of course I am. Though, I must warn you, who've I've chosen as head of security is a real pain to deal with."

Calvin turned a grin on Sal. "He does have his moments, but I think I can handle him."

Sal pointed to his own chest with his thumb. "Are you kidding? I'm the main reason to take the job."

Basil nodded. "I agree. So he can keep you in line." Before Sal could reply, he put his attention on Calvin again. "So, what do you say?"

Unable to contain his excitement, Calvin threw his arms around Basil. "I say I'm honored and flattered and absolutely yes, I'll do it! Thank you!"

Basil laughed and hugged Calvin back. "You're welcome, dear. You'll do brilliant, I know it." He released Calvin from the embrace and rested his arm around Calvin's shoulders. "And there we have it. We're all in agreement on the building?" His gaze went to Valentin.

His arms around Sebastian, Valentin bowed his head in a single nod. "Yes, we're all in agreement."

Sal brought his hands together in a loud clap. "Great! It's decided and we can stop talking about it now. Go straight to the action. When you need me, let me know. Until then…" he snatched Calvin by the arm and yanked him away from Basil. "Give me back my witch."

Sebastian glanced back at Valentin. "Did that seem possessive to you? It looked possessive to me."

"Yes, most definitely. It goes along quite well with the way he was gazing at Calvin a moment ago."

Taking Calvin by the hand, Sal walked toward the door. "I'm done with all of you tonight."

Basil called out. "Have a good night, then. Thank you again, Calvin."

Calvin glanced back. "And thank you!" He managed to get the last word out before Sal pulled him outside. He quickened his pace to match Sal's. "Well, somebody doesn't like it when the teasing's turned on him." A smirk rose to his lips. "Was it getting a little too close to the truth?"

Sal gave a grunt for his answer. "You're hungry, I'm guessing. What do you want to eat?"

Calvin caught how Sal blatantly ignored his question, but decided to let it go. Not answering gave him a good idea of the answer, and he was overjoyed that it could be true. He shifted toward Sal, their pace slowing together, walking with their arms touching. "In a few more blocks, we'll be hitting the commercial area, with all the shops and restaurants. We can walk by there and when something looks good, we'll stop."

"Sounds like a plan." Sal walked in silence for a moment. "It's a good thing Baz is doing, bringing you and Sebastian on to help with his blood house. I know he'll be generous in what he pays you. You could probably even go back to college. Work for him at night, take classes in the afternoon. That's was Sebastian's going to do. Hell, you might even be able to go to the same school.

"And you know, if you had any questions about what really went down during those time periods, the Middle Ages and Early Renaissance, you've kinda got a good source here." He gestured to himself. "Then if you wanted to stretch your studies out to a later period, Valentin and Baz could cover anything from the late 1600's on. It's something to think about. Between the three of us, we could help you become one of the greatest human historical scholars ever."

Calvin gazed up at him. "I'm in shock. You *do* pay attention when I talk."

Sal leaned toward him, his lips close to Calvin's ear. "It's more than your body that interests me, you know."

"I think that's the most romantic thing you've ever said to

me."

"Some of Valentin's and Sebastian's mush must've splattered onto me."

"I'd be okay if you didn't wipe it off right away." Calvin listened to Sal laugh, and pulled his hand from Sal's to wrap his arm around him. The Savannah River flowed with waters as dark as the night sky to their left. Old style lampposts lit the area with a soft golden glow. The walkway along with river was park-like, but being on the outside of the main historical district, it was quiet, no tourists or any other people strolling about. He spotted a small public restroom building and nodded toward it. "I need to hit that real quick."

"You want me to go in with you?"

Calvin aimed a smirk at him. "I don't know. Are you interested in watching me pee?"

Sal shrugged. "Golden showers have never really been my thing, but if you think you're into that, I'm game for trying it again."

Calvin laughed and shoved Sal away. "No, I'm not!" He paused. "Wait. What do you mean, *again*?"

His lavender eyes gleaming with wickedness, Sal shifted close to him once more. "I've been around for a long time. There's not much I haven't done."

Staring at him, Calvin nodded slowly at the revelation. "Then I can't believe you're not bored with me yet. Going by all the things that can be done and what you've probably done, I'm pretty damn vanilla."

Sal shook his head. "You'll never bore me. It's not the actions of it that make it good. It's the emo—" He stopped the word short before completing it.

"It's the…what?"

"Nothing. Lost my thought." Sal flipped his hand toward the restroom. "You gonna hit the head, or what?"

"Yeah, I'm going." Calvin walked toward the restroom door

and threw a grin back at him. "And by the way, that was the most romantic thing you *almost* said to me."

A snort of defiance left Sal, and he crossed his arms over his chest.

Snickering to himself, Calvin traveled along the narrow opening around a corner to the restroom itself holding three urinals and stalls and as many sinks. Two men stood in front of sinks and the dingy mirror. On the steel shelf below the mirror were small packets of white powder, dried green leaves in a plastic bag, cigarette wrappers, a syringe with an uncapped needle.

He quickly looked away, but not before catching the eye of one of the men and noticing the other looking at him, as well. He ducked into a stall and locked the door behind him, hurrying to take care of his immediate need.

Shit, shit, shit. He didn't know if the guys were in the middle of a deal or if they were buddies laying out what they had for the night, but either way, it would be his damn luck to walk into the middle of it. He zipped up and turned toward the stall door. Taking a deep breath, he unlocked it and walked toward the sinks as though nothing was out of the ordinary. He noted the paraphernalia was gone, but the guys were still there…between him and the door.

"How's it goin'?" one of the guys asked.

Calvin glanced toward them from washing his hands and gave a smile. "Good. How about you guys?"

One in a faded, tattered jean jacket shrugged. "All right. Been kind of a boring night. We've been looking for some fun."

Calvin turned off the water and pulled some of the brown paper towels from the dented and scratched white holder. "I hear you on that."

The second, wearing a black leather jacket, took a step closer to him. "You're looking for some fun, too?"

Calvin moved to step around the guy. "On my way to it now. You guys have a good night."

The man grabbed him by the arm. "Hold on, now. What's your hurry? Pretty young guy like you, two handsome guys like us. Here. Alone. You don't have to go anywhere else for fun. We've got all the fun you need right here." The guy grabbed his own crotch.

Calvin jerked his arm out of the man's grasp. "I don't want any trouble. Let me go."

The man in the jean jacket stepped forward. "No trouble here, baby. Like we said, only fun." The last word left the man in a snarl, and he lunged for Calvin.

Calvin twisted away, avoiding the man's grab, but stumbled back into the other guy. The second man snatched Calvin's arms, yanking them behind his back.

The first grabbed Calvin by the hair while his companion held him. "We tried to be nice about this. You should've just gone along with it." He swung with his right fist toward Calvin's face.

Locked in the other man's hold, Calvin couldn't dodge, couldn't defend himself. The man's fist slammed into Calvin's left cheek and corner of his mouth, snapping his head to the left. Pain blinded him and shocked his body. He was flung hard to the side toward the sinks, the edge of one catching him in the stomach and driving the wind out of him. His glasses, already knocked loose from the hit, fell off and into the sink basin. Rough hands grabbed him again from behind.

The lights above burst, raining glass over Calvin and the men. Only one of the lights remained, flickering on the edge of erupting. It took Calvin milliseconds to realize what was happening.

His demon had arrived.

Calvin wrenched his head toward the open doorway. Sal rounded the corner, a fury in pure rage. He launched toward the man holding Calvin and flung him back. The man hurled through the air, crashing into one of the stalls. The second man dove at Sal, his fist raised. Sal caught it in his hand, his demon claws out, gouging the man's hand. He twisted the other's hand, hard and fast. Screams from the man followed the snapping of bones.

Calvin snatched his glasses out of the sink and put them on. He gathered some strength, leaning back on the sink, stunned. Sal was losing control. His pupils had become slits, his horns were emerging, his body expanding in muscle and height to stretch his clothes to their limits.

The man stared up at Sal and screamed again, but not in pain. His pain seemed to have been forgotten in the face of fear. The other attacker shot out of the stall, running for the door.

Sal lashed out, catching the man's arm. "I don't think so, asshole." He jerked the man's arm up and wrenched it. The sharp point of a bone tore through the leather jacket. The man opened his mouth, but only a gurgle came out, the pain having stolen his voice.

Sal grabbed him by the throat, then reached down and took the other by the hair. He dragged them both toward the far wall. Hauling them up, Sal slammed them into the wall, pinning them there by their throats. His voice left him in a deep rumble. "A moment ago, two against one wasn't a fair fight. But now with me being the one, it's a little more than fair, isn't it?"

Calvin looked at the men, their eyes wide and wild with fear. He shouldn't feel the touch of vindictiveness rushing through him, but he also felt certain if these men had attempted what they had with him, they'd done it with others…and may have been successful. Still, he didn't know how far Sal would go and he didn't want him to kill them. He pushed off the sink, walking toward him. "Sal."

Sal's focus remained on the men. His canine teeth had shifted to his demon fangs. "How does it feel to be helpless?" He squeezed each of their throats, blood welling around his claws. "How does it feel to be reminded how weak you are? How pathetic?"

Calvin stopped at Sal's side. He glanced at the men, gasping to pull in the slightest bit of air. He laid a hand on Sal's shoulder. "Sal, I'm okay. Let them go and let's get out of here."

"They hurt you." Sal slowly looked away from the men to him. Fresh rage lit his lavender eyes. "They drew your blood."

Calvin touched his fingers to the corners of his mouth and looked down at the blood staining them. He realized then he tasted the coppery tang of it in his mouth.

Sal pulled the men off the wall and smashed them back onto it again. "I enjoy humans and this realm, I truly do, but some humans make it a better place by leaving it."

His hand on Sal's shoulder, Calvin placed his other hand on Sal's arm. "I can't argue that, but I don't want you to be the one to make that happen. And something tells me these guys are going to change their ways after tonight." He touched Sal's cheek with the backs of his fingers and caressed down it. "Please, I don't want you do to this. Let them go."

Sal closed his eyes in a long blink. He opened them again and while his eyes were still in their true form, the rage in them had faded. He took a deep breath and as he exhaled, he released the men. They crumpled to the floor at his and Calvin's feet.

Calvin took Sal's face in both hands and turned his head toward him. He placed a soft kiss on Sal's lips. "Let's go."

Sal nodded. His horns retracted, as did his fangs and claws. He returned fully to his human form. He took a step back from the men, started to turn away, then spun back. He kicked out, nailing the one in the jean jacket in the head. He kicked again into the other's stomach. "Fucking douchebags." He took Calvin's hand and walked from the restroom with him.

Calvin breathed deep the night air, cooling his heated skin. He realized he was trembling, his adrenaline draining away and taking his strength with it. His legs were weak, and he wanted to lean on Sal's strength, but summoned what little he had left to steady himself. He needed to seem strong for Sal, even if he knew Sal could sense the exact opposite from him.

Sal guided him around the building where it faced the river and blocked the view of the street, though no one was in sight. He touched Calvin's cheek, brushed his thumb over the corner of his mouth, sending his power through him to heal the injuries. He pulled Calvin to him, wrapping his arms tight around him. "I'm taking you home."

Calvin embraced him, gripping the back of Sal's shirt in two fists. "When you say 'home,' do you mean my place, your place here, or the demon realm?" He lifted his head, forcing a smile for Sal. "There are a few options."

Sal gazed down at him, his expression gentle, but had no humor in it. "I mean my place here."

Calvin stared at him for a moment. Sal's mood was different. He was always joking, sarcastic, but at that moment, Sal was only serious. He rested his head on Sal's shoulder. "Good. That's where I want to go."

Sal continued to hold him. Calvin waited for the icy touch of demon magic to chill him, the weightlessness of dematerializing, but it didn't come.

Sal squeezed him tighter. He bowed his head, his voice left him in a rough whisper. "I'm sorry I didn't get in there sooner."

Calvin shook his head slightly. "You came in more than enough time."

Sal moved his head in a small nod. "Ready?"

"Yeah."

Sal's power and magic flowed through Calvin, the coolness refreshing him. The world slipped away and a sense of safety came with it disappearing. In an instant, the atmosphere was weighted again, and when Calvin opened his eyes, he was in the familiar surroundings of Sal's bedroom in the mansion.

Sal slowly released him, only to take Calvin's face in both hands. He brought their lips together, the kiss tender, but restrained. "You should rest—"

Calvin gripped a fistful of Sal's hair and pressed their mouths together, pouring his emotion into the kiss. He didn't need to use words to tell Sal what he wanted. His emotions would speak clearer for him.

Sal's hold on him tightened. He slid his tongue over Calvin's, taking control of the kiss with his hunger. He pressed against Calvin, making him step backward toward the bed. Reaching the bed, he broke the kiss. He lifted Calvin's glasses off, setting them on the nightstand, then helped Calvin out of his shirt and tore his own over his head. Calvin stepped out of his shoes and barely had the last one off before taking hold of Sal's jeans and opening them. Sal reached for Calvin's jeans, each of their movements quick, desperate to get each other unclothed.

Calvin shoved Sal's jeans and briefs off his hips. Sal grabbed him by the waist, lifted him, and set him back on the bed. He pulled Calvin's jeans off the rest of the way and climbed onto bed with him. Calvin met him in a fervent kiss and slid back toward the center of the bed, Sal moving with him.

Calvin eased to his back, one hand buried in Sal's long red hair. Kneeling between Calvin's legs, Sal braced himself on one hand and reached down with his other. At the warm and slick feel of Sal's lubed fingers on his hole, Calvin passed a low moan into Sal's mouth. Sal rubbed the outside of Calvin's hole, then pushed two fingers into him. Calvin arched up toward him.

He rolled his ass, rocking it to get Sal's fingers deeper inside him and let Sal know how much he wanted him. He opened his eyes and found Sal's gaze on him. There was an intensity in Sal's eyes that Calvin had never seen before, but it made his heart pound faster, sent his emotions soaring higher.

Calvin rested his hand on Sal's cheek. "I need you."

Sal pulled his fingers out. His palm filled with lube, he stroked his dick and brought it to Calvin's hole. He guided the head in and placed both hands on the bed, gazing down at Calvin as he sank his cock deeper into him. "You have me."

Sal kissed him hard and began thrusting, driving his cock deep into him, the head of it stroking Calvin's gland. Calvin held onto him, digging his short fingernails into Sal's back. His needful moans filled the room, and he had no control over stopping them. Not with how Sal was sending jolt after jolt of pleasure through him and pushing him closer to coming.

Sal's thrusts were quick and strong. He captured Calvin's lips in a heated kiss. In the kiss, in Sal's body and the energy emanating from him, Calvin sensed a possessiveness and strength of emotion so powerful, it was overwhelming.

Sal pushed one arm under Calvin's head and gripped his opposite shoulder, holding him, pressing their bodies tighter, driving his cock into him with more urgency. He kissed Calvin on the temple and whispered, "Come for me. Let me feel all your emotion and energy."

Sal's words, his voice deep with lust, were like a trigger for Calvin. The last threads of his control began unraveling. Every thrust, his cock grinding between his and Sal's body, pushed him closer to the edge. He clung to Sal, electric heat rushing through him as his climax took hold of him. The pleasure filled him and as Sal had wanted, he let his emotions go, pushed out his energy and what he felt for Sal into the release. He hadn't finished when Sal's loud moans joined his shouts of ecstasy as his demon came with him.

Sal slowed to a stop and brought their lips together again, the kiss calmer than before. Calvin combed his fingers through Sal's hair, his body relaxing into the satisfaction Sal had given him. The kiss eased to an end, and Sal drew back, caressing Calvin's cheek as he slid his cock out of him.

Calvin watched him walk toward the bathroom, then pushed himself up toward the head of the bed. Sal returned, offering a towel to him.

Calvin took it and began wiping himself clean. Glancing up, he caught Sal watching him and gave him a grin. "You've been staring at me a lot since we got back."

Sal leaned down to him and took the towel back, his lips nearly touching Calvin's. "That's what you get for being hot."

Calvin laughed. "I'm not so sure I buy into that demon flattery of yours."

Sal tossed the towel to the floor and climbed into bed with him. He pulled Calvin to him. "You should. It's the truth."

Calvin smiled and laid his head on Sal's chest. His emotions were still running strong, and he wondered, should he say it? Tell Sal how he felt? Or would it be too much? No, he didn't think it would be. There was no way Sal couldn't know how he felt about him, so saying it would only be putting his voice to those emotions. But he wanted to say it, to make sure Sal didn't have any doubts.

Calvin took a deep breath. "Sal, I…I want you to know—"

"I know." Sal kissed him on the top of the head. His voice softened, filled with warmth. "I already know."

Calvin closed his eyes and exhaled a contented sigh. "I thought you did. I just wanted to make sure."

Sleep pulled at Calvin and wrapped safely in the arms of his demon duke, satisfied in body and spirit, he let it claim his consciousness.

Chapter Thirteen

Sal stared at the horizon. The golden light of the rising sun was beginning to banish the last darkness of night. Reclined in a lounge chair by the pool, he stroked Beezle on the head and back. The little black croc dozed on Sal's bare chest, an occasional gurgle, almost purr-like, came from him.

Though Sal petted Beezle, his was barely aware of his actions. His attention and thoughts were focused on what he had to do. He'd existed for eons and despite what he said about never forgetting anything, his earliest years of when he came into being were shadowed memories now. But through the eons of his life, he'd made a special point to lock away what he knew where the most important things.

Last night was one of them.

Whispers of emotion had tried to speak louder to him recently and he'd always managed to shut them up. He didn't want to hear what they had to say. He didn't want to acknowledge the truth of his growing feelings for Calvin. Last night, though, he couldn't keep his emotions down. They *screamed* inside him, and he'd reveled in it. And he'd lost control, in more ways than one.

It began with the douchebags attacking Calvin. He had almost fully shifted, in front of strange humans, and if Calvin hadn't stopped him, he didn't want to think what he might have done. But that rage, it was so powerful, so consuming. What those assholes had done and tried to do to Calvin lit a spark that roared into an inferno inside him. All he'd wanted to do was hurt those pieces of shit. *Bad.*

Yet, for all the power of that rage, there was something stronger. When Calvin spoke to him, touched him, that one emotion he'd tried to stomp down rose inside him. It conquered the rage and turned it into compassion for Calvin, making it so he wanted was take care of him and make him feel safe.

He'd known for a while how Calvin felt about him, but when

he took him last night, asked Calvin to let go and let him feel it, he'd been overwhelmed. Calvin's aura radiated with love for him. The worst of it was, it felt as if it were a reflection of what he'd been trying to keep down inside himself.

And that's why he needed to stop this.

Sal didn't need to look behind him to know Calvin had stepped out of the mansion. Though Calvin's bare feet made only the softest brush over the ground, he heard him. More than that, he'd felt him. Another reason this needed to stop. It was too much, too deep, too close.

Calvin sat in the lounge chair beside Sal's. He smiled at him and reached to pet Beezle's head. "I wondered where you were when I woke up. Watching the sunrise?"

Sal kept his gaze on the horizon. "Or night fade. However you want to look at it."

Calvin fell silent. Sal sensed the tension growing. His witch… *the* witch, knew something was up.

"What's wrong?" Calvin asked.

Sal took a deep breath. Fuck, he didn't want to do this. But not doing it now would only draw it out. It was inevitable that this had to happen. He turned his head, meeting Calvin's bright blue gaze. "You know, when we went into this, for me it was more or less needing to scratch an itch that'd been bothering me for a while. I'd been thinking about you, wanting you, ever since the bullshit at the blood house. And sure, there was that warm fuzziness of maybe getting to save your brother's life, but really, it was all about getting a chance to fuck you."

Calvin let out a humorless snort. "That's sweet. I don't like where you're going."

"No, I don't think you will, either." Sal lifted Beezle off his chest and sat up, swinging his legs over the side of the lounge chair and facing Calvin. He held Beezle, but kept his attention on Calvin. "It's probably time for us to cool it for a while."

Calvin held Sal's gaze. He nodded slowly. "So, I start to let you know how I feel about you, and now you want to bolt, right?"

Sal held up one hand, as if to ward off the idea. "No, because to be fair to both of us, I knew how you were feeling about me before last night. The only difference is, last night you really put it out there."

"Which is what you wanted me to do. You said it, to let you feel my emotions and energy. I did, and look at where we are now."

Sal closed his eyes, trying to collect himself. This was going bad fast. Not that he'd expected it to go well, but Calvin was sharp, astute, and logical, even when it came to emotions. Getting by him was no easy task.

His voice softer, Calvin said, "You know, you're not the only one here who's sensitive to emotions. I might not be able to see auras, but I've picked up things from you about how you feel toward me. At least, I thought I did."

The last sentence hung like a question, and Sal knew Calvin was looking for affirmation. Should he give it or not? Sal opened his eyes to Calvin's gaze. Hurt was shining in Calvin's eyes. He was already bringing so much pain on him, he couldn't deny him this. "What you've sensed from me is right and true, but it doesn't change the situation."

"I'm not sure I even fully understand the situation, or what's brought this on all of a sudden."

Sal placed Beezle on the ground and sat forward, his elbows on his knees. "The situation is, I'm a demon, you're a mortal. And what brought this on is that shit you've been picking up from me."

Calvin pushed his glasses up and rubbed his eyes. "Okay, we're a little closer to me getting it, but not quite there. Is this about you having another allergic reaction to the mushies?"

"No, this is more. This is me trying to stop us from going further and getting hurt worse in the long run. You don't know how much it means to me that you accept me for what and who I am." Sal lowered his gaze, his voice hushed, became rougher.

"Really, you don't. I've shown you the real me and seeing that, you lov—" He cut the word short and cleared his throat. "Your feelings have kept growing." He lifted his gaze to Calvin's again. "But it'll never work out."

"Why?"

Sal couldn't help but smile, even though he knew it held only sadness. That sweet mortal innocence, Calvin really didn't understand. He reached across the distance between them and took Calvin's hand. "Because someday, you'll die. You're going to grow old and while I can deal with that, I'm not sure I can take standing by and watching you leave me to go where I can't follow."

He watched the emotion rising in Calvin's face, unshed tears making his blue eyes shine.

His voice a rough whisper, Calvin said, "There has to be a way."

Sal shook his head. "There's not." He paused for a moment. "Well, there are two ways. You could become a vampire, but you'll be trading your witch's power for vampiric ones. A vampire may hold onto some of their humanness, but they're not human, so calling on human magic doesn't work real well for them."

Calvin squeezed Sal's hand. "I'd give it up if it meant I could be with you."

Sal laid his other hand over Calvin's. "I wouldn't let you do that, change who you are for me. It wouldn't make you happy, losing that part of yourself, and in the end, you'd grow to resent me."

"I wouldn't."

"You say that now, but you need to think long and hard about how you'd feel not being a witch anymore."

"Being a witch isn't about casting spells and working magic. It's following a spiritual path of harmony with the world."

Sal opened his mouth to counter, but realized his had nothing to combat the truth of Calvin's words.

"What's the second way?" Calvin asked.

"It's so ridiculous, there's not much point in talking about it."

"I want to know. If there's any way, I want to know what it is."

Sal let out a sigh of relent. "I've never even known this to happen. If it has, no demon's ever talked about it. But if a mortal saves a demon's life, the demon is bound to them by the Powers, what we call our sources of our power, to give the mortal one thing that they desire."

"You mean, like a wish?"

"Kind of. But seriously, since most mortals are more interested in banishing demons and most demons would rather be destroyed than saved by a human, the chances of that ever happening is pretty much zero."

"But I did save your life."

Sal gave him a confused look. "No, I'm sure I'd remember if you had."

Calvin pushed on Sal's shoulder. "At the blood house! If I wouldn't have freed you from the salt binding, you would've been trapped there for who knows how long."

Sal lifted a hand, teetering it back and forth. "That's kind of a gray area. Technically, my life wasn't in danger. I was just trapped. And since you put me there to begin with, it was your fault I was there. Besides, it's said when it happens, the demon is supposed to feel something like a snap inside them, a tie to the human, putting you even more under their control until you finish the deal and give the human what they want. I think we both know I didn't get that."

Calvin lowered his gaze. Sal knew Calvin's mind was racing and he hadn't accepted they couldn't be together yet, which also meant, Calvin was thinking of the only available option.

As if to confirm it, Calvin asked, "Can a vampire feed from a demon?"

"If any demon's ever let a vampire do it, they've never told me or any other demon I know. Our blood is different, same as our life essence. We're living, but not in the same sense as a human. I know Baz and Valentin have never even hinted at wanting a taste of me." He paused at the thought. "And now that I think about it, that's a little insulting."

A single laugh escaped Calvin, but it held little humor. "But, even if I couldn't feed from you, Basil's opening the blood house. I know a lot of vampires use feeding as a way for sex to, but it doesn't have to be that way. It can be just getting your food and moving on, like Baz does. It wouldn't be cheating."

Sal took Calvin's other hand so he held both. "No, it wouldn't be. But there's a lot more you need to consider than how you'd get your food. You'd need to come to terms with losing a big part of yourself. And that's why we need to cool it for a while."

"When you say 'a while,' what do you mean? A week, a month, my mortal lifespan?"

Sal opened his mouth, but couldn't get the answer out. To say it would cement it, make it permanent. And yeah, he knew saying "a while" left it open, but now that he was here in this moment, looking into Calvin's eyes, his ebony hair still tousled from bed, his soft and sweet features, he couldn't bring it to a close.

Calvin sat back, his hands slowly sliding out of Sal's hold. "So that's it."

Sal stared down at the ground. He couldn't reply. It was a rare thing for him to not have words, but none were coming to him. Probably because he'd said what he didn't want to, and what he really wanted to tell Calvin, he wouldn't let come out.

Calvin stood, his head turned away from Sal toward the sunrise. "You might think of it as the night growing weaker, but I think of it as light growing stronger."

Sal forced his head up, looking at Calvin. The warm, early morning light washed over him. It seemed as if the sun itself was illuminating Calvin's inner and outer beauty.

Calvin looked down at him. "I know our definitions of *a while* aren't the same. If you feel that we need to take a step back from each other, fine. But…" He bent toward Sal and took his face in both hands. He brought their lips together in a tender kiss. He eased back, looking into Sal's eyes. "I'm not giving up that we can be together." He stepped back, caressing Sal's cheek until the distance between them grew too great. He walked toward the mansion. Reaching the door, he stopped and looked back. "And I know you didn't want to hear it last night, but I'm saying it now. I love you, Sallos."

Calvin's words shot through Sal, bringing both joy and pain. And the reply screamed in his mind, but he kept his lips closed and swallowed it down.

Calvin walked into the mansion and disappeared.

Sal crumpled forward, his hands buried in his hair. This wasn't supposed to happen to him. Sure, it'd happened before, but that was one-sided on him. The other side of his supposed love had betrayed him and tried to kill him with a horde of demons. But this…this was real.

And he was letting it go.

Light scrapping along the cobbles made Sal open his eyes. Beezle had shuffled close to his feet and the little croc's yellow gaze was locked on him.

Sal pointed down at him. "Stop judging me."

A rumble came from Beezle. He spun with amazing speed, whacking his hard, scaled tail into Sal's leg.

"Ow! You little…" Sal let the words fade unsaid, watching Beezle doing an annoyed waddle toward the pool. In the distance, the engine of Calvin's Honda Civic grudgingly started.

Sal collapsed back on the chair, closing his eyes tight against the sun…and his emotions. He did the right thing. If they would've kept on the way they were, eventually Calvin would get hurt, much worse than what he was feeling right now. As he aged, Calvin would eventually grow to resent him. And while he might be able to heal any illnesses that would hit Calvin, eventually Calvin's body would fail him. Nothing could stop time from taking Calvin away from him. Better to let it end now, while Calvin was young and could find love with another human…

An ache spread through Sal's chest. He was a fucking demon. This shouldn't be happening to him. He shouldn't feel this way. Too much time in the human realm and around humans that was it. Nothing else. He needed to go back to the demon realm, stay there for a long time, and get his strength back, in more ways than one.

Now if only he could work up the motivation and energy to go there.

Sal opened his eyes again. The sky was already bluer than moments ago, but it was empty. No clouds, no birds, nothing. All around him felt the same way, as though there was a void, something missing. More than once in his existence he'd felt alone, but few times had it struck him stronger than in that moment.

Chapter Fourteen

Calvin walked out of his bedroom, head down, showered and dressed for work. It was the last place he wanted to be, but he'd called off the day before after Sal had dropped it on him about needing to take some time apart. He still didn't know if he fully accepted it, but it was slowly sinking in that what he had with Sal might be gone.

The night before was the first in weeks that he'd spent at home. Nathan was surprised, but he'd also been able to tell his brother was happy. When Nathan asked why he wasn't going out, he'd replied with was a shrug and "I'm just not." He saw in Nathan's eyes that his brother wanted to press more and was glad when he didn't. The thing was, it made him realize that in so short a time, how close he'd gotten to Sal, Sebastian, Valentin, and Basil. They'd become part of his life.

And they still would be. Regardless of his and Sal's intimate relationship, he was going to help Basil with the blood house and take that job. He had to. He needed the opportunity and the money. And most of all, it would keep him close to Sal.

Calvin stopped walking down the hall before turning into the family room. He closed his eyes, fighting back his rising emotions. After he'd left Sal, he only made it a little way down the road before he broke down in tears. He pulled off to the side, unable to see the road, and let his hurt pour out of him. He tried to keep a strong façade in front of Sal, but same as with knowing he loved him, he was sure Sal saw through it. Throughout the rest of the day, it would hit him in waves and he'd hardly slept. He couldn't sleep without Sal's cool, strong body beside him.

Damn it, this couldn't be the end for them. He wasn't going to let it. He loved Sal and if it took giving up being a witch and becoming a vampire to be with him, then that's what he would do. He would let some time pass, but only to prove to Sal even more that he was firm in his decision.

"Are you okay?"

Calvin startled at Nathan's voice. He snapped his head up and opened his eyes. His brother stood in the family room, holding Buster and looking at him in concern. Calvin took a deep breath and walked forward. "Yeah, I'm fine. Have a headache, that's all."

"You don't look good. Maybe you're coming down with something."

Calvin shook his head and walked toward the rack where their coats and jackets hung by the front door. "I think I'm just tired."

"Or suffering from a broken heart?"

Calvin paused, his hand on his jacket. He glanced back at Nathan. "What?"

A gentle smile rested on Nathan's lips. "Last night, there were times during dinner and when we were watching TV, you looked like you were lost in your thoughts and whatever you were thinking had you close to tears. The man you've been seeing, did something happen?"

Calvin looked away from him, tried to force his voice to be steady, but it left him rough with hurt. "We're…taking a break for a while. Things were getting a little intense for him. Emotionally. So, we're backing off seeing each other for a while."

Nathan walked across the room to him. He rested his hand on Calvin's shoulder. "I'm sorry."

Calvin forced a smile and patted Nathan's hand. "I gotta get to work."

Nathan nodded and stepped back from the door. "If you want to talk—"

Calvin opened the door. "I do, but not about him." He poked Nathan on the chest. "I want to talk about you and what I can do to help you."

Nathan's expression hardened. "We've already talked about it. There's nothing you can do that I would accept."

"If you would open your mind, hear me out and understand—"

"I listened to you before. Twice."

"No, you didn't. Certainly not the first time and even though you didn't shoot me down the second time, you didn't fully open your mind, either."

"And I never will. Not as long as your way of healing involves witchcraft and evil."

Hurt, frustration, anger, surged up inside Calvin, and even though his brother hadn't caused all of it, he'd played a part. "Stop being so fucking stubborn and goddamn ignorant!"

Nathan startled back. "Calvin!"

Calvin looked away from him. He reached for his jacket again and pulled it off the hook. "I'm sorry. I'm not feeling like…me right now."

Nathan sighed and stepped closer to him again. "It's all right. I know you're hurt, and I'm the only target around."

Calvin tugged his jacket on and mumbled, "Yeah."

"And I know you don't want to hear this, but since you've gotten deeper into your…craft, you've changed. That thing you summoned a few weeks ago, I have a feeling that wasn't the first time you've summoned it, and I know you've seen it since. This anger inside you, I'm afraid that monster's the cause."

Calvin clenched his teeth. It took every bit of his willpower to keep from snapping at Nathan again. He yanked open the door, shooting Nathan a quick glance. "You're right. I didn't want to hear that. I'm going to work. I'll be home this afternoon."

Nathan took the door to close it. "Be careful and have a good day."

"I will. You too."

Calvin walked down to the sidewalk, turning in the direction of his work He would never be able to get Nathan to open his mind to Sal healing him. He had thought he could do it, but his brother would never accept that Sal wasn't evil, or that his craft wasn't putting him on the direct path to Hell. If only his brother knew that it was because of him, he'd entered into a deal with a demon, but what he'd gotten out of it was more than he ever bargained for; he'd fallen in love.

Chapter Fifteen

Seated on the leather sofa, slouched low, Sal stared at the TV, petting Beezle lying on the cushion beside him. Usually, he found the blood and gore of a zombie apocalypse hilarious. Now, it was nothing but images flashing before his eyes, hypnotizing him, entertaining him just enough where he could block thoughts of Calvin…for a few minutes at a time, at least. He hadn't made it back to the demon realm, which now seemed for the better. There were only two distractions there, fucking and fighting, and he wasn't in the mood for either of them.

Not in the mood to fuck. Sal let out a rough snort. This was only the second time he could think of when that wasn't an option to make him feel better. He'd broken things off with Calvin yesterday morning. He should be over him by now. Sure, it might take humans a long time to get over an ended relationship, but he was a demon. He was above such things. Really, he was.

And if he kept repeating that, it might become true.

He looked down at the pint of chocolate ice cream in his hand. It was nearly melted and since he'd squeezed a half bottle of chocolate syrup in the container, it was now a swirl of lighter and darker chocolate, more liquid than solid. He lifted the cardboard carton to his lips and started drinking. There wasn't ice cream and chocolate in his homeland, either. More reasons to stay here.

Along with being close in case Calvin should need him…

"You jerk!"

Sal peeked over the ice cream carton at Sebastian, his face focused in anger, blue eyes locked on him. He lowered the container. "What'd I do now? Use the last of the toilet paper again?"

Sebastian stopped in front of him, pointing down at him with his cell phone. "You know damn well what you've done!"

Opting to try and divert Sebastian's attention, Sal smiled up at him. "Has anyone ever told you that you're hot as hell when you're pissed off?"

"Yes, I have."

Sal leaned to the side, peering around Sebastian to Valentin. The vampire stood in the doorway, leaning one shoulder on the frame, his arms folded across his chest, one foot crossed over the other. He looked the picture of sophisticated annoyance. Basil stood beside Valentin, resting his forearm up on Valentin's shoulder. While Basil was more casual in his jeans and button-down shirt compared to Valentin's dress pants and thin cashmere sweater, Baz didn't look any less annoyed.

Sal lifted the carton to take another drink of melted ice cream. "Wow. I've managed to piss off all three of you and don't even know how I've done it. Can you guys enlighten me in case I need to do it again someday?"

"If you get second chance, you better not fuck it up again!" Sebastian turned his phone toward himself, tapping at the screen with his index finger. He turned the screen toward Sal and shoved it in his face. "This is what you've done to piss us all off."

Sal read the text messages on the screen starting with one from Sebastian to Calvin.

Hey, man! I was planning on heading into town this afternoon. When do you get off work? We can meet up and do some shopping before you come over tonight.

Calvin's reply followed. *I get off at 4:30, but I don't think I'll be coming over. I guess Sal didn't tell you, we're not together anymore.*

What?! What happened?

He said we need to cool it for a while.

Sal touched the phone screen and flicked up to read the next messages. *Okay, this is too much to get into in text messages. I'll meet you after work and we'll talk. In the meantime, I've got a demon's ass to kick.*

Don't be mad at him. He's just doing what he thinks he needs to.

He's wrong, and he doesn't know what the fuck he's doing! I'll see you later.

Deciding he didn't need to see more, Sal looked up at Sebastian. "I'm glad you guys are still going to hang out. He needs that, people he can call friends. He doesn't have anyone except for his brother and that dude probably isn't long for this world if he doesn't let me help him."

Sebastian's mouth dropped open, a shocked cough escaping him. "You can't be serious." He spun around to Valentin and Basil. "Please tell me he's not serious."

"No, he's not," Valentin said. "He is, however, desperately trying to cover how he really feels."

Sal snorted. "I'm a demon, boys. I don't have *feels*."

Basil strolled forward. He tipped his head back, inhaling deep. "Smell that, lads? That's the smell of bullshit in the air."

Sal shook his head, focusing on his ice cream again. "There you go with your exaggerations, Baz."

Valentin followed Basil. "No, I think he's spot on with this one. You like to pretend you're above such things as emotions and needing anyone, but you're not. Far from it. Your needs are exactly why you spend more time in this realm than your homeland."

Speaking into the ice cream container as he lifted it to his lips, Sal said, "I have no idea what you're talking about."

"Then allow me to enlighten you," Valentin continued. "You were betrayed in your homeland. You'd wanted love and trust, and you were stabbed in the back. And you know amongst your kind, you can never have the kind of relationships you desire, ones where friends are true, where you can feel safe giving your love and trust to a partner. And while Baz and I have never been intimate with you in our bodies, we are in every other way, and sometimes, those ways are more important, more special. You spurn mushy emotions, but they're exactly what you crave. You get that from us and you were getting it from Calvin, on the grandest scale."

Sal lowered the ice cream container and stretched for the bottle of chocolate syrup on the end table beside him. "Well, thank you for that, Doctor Wyndham. Where'd you get your PHD in demon psychology, anyway? Paranormal U?"

Basil glanced at Valentin. "The demon doth protest too much, methinks."

Valentin made a monosyllabic noise of agreement. He flipped his hand toward Sal. "You're the very proof. Look at yourself. You're a mess. You have ice cream spilled on your shirt, dried chocolate around the corners of your mouth, your hair looks like rats were fighting in it. You've made the mistake of breaking up with him, you know it, but my guess is, you don't know how to fix it."

Sal popped the cap on the chocolate syrup and tipped his head back, squeezing a thick stream directly into his mouth. He swallowed and brought his head forward, pointing at Valentin with the bottle. "Wrong. It was the right thing to do, so there's nothing to fix."

Basil rested his hands on his hips. "Then it's your turn to enlighten us as to why you think such ridiculousness is true."

Sal shot Basil what he knew was a frustrated and exasperated glare. "Now you're the ones who can't be serious. You and Valentin know damn well why Calvin and I couldn't keep things going with us. Two little things called immortality and mortality." He flicked a hand at Valentin. "You're almost in the same situation with Sebastian, except he knows without a doubt that he wants to become a vampire someday.

"Calvin thinks he wants that, but I don't think he's fully comprehended that if he does, he'll lose most, if not all, of his abilities as a witch. And honestly, I don't even think that's something he can comprehend until those powers are gone. He says being a witch isn't only about casting spells and working with other powers. It's a spiritual path he can still follow as a vampire, but come on. How well do you think he'd cope when he feels that connection and energy gone from him?"

His voice calmer than before, Sebastian said, "I don't know. And honestly, you don't either. Only he can tell you that and it's his choice to make, if he wants to. Maybe to him, being with you is more important than anything else."

Sal stared up at Sebastian, partly impressed, partly annoyed that a young mortal was schooling him on life. He set the ice cream carton and chocolate syrup on the table and sat forward. He looked up at Valentin and Basil. "If he really wanted it, would one of you do it?"

Valentin and Basil shared a look. Valentin cleared his throat to speak. "If there were no doubts in his mind or yours, yes. But we'd need to hear you give a true declaration of your feelings for him. I'd want to hear you say it, that you love him."

Sal flung up both hands. "What the fuck difference does it make if I say it or not?"

"Because if you say it, then you've accepted it."

Sal rolled his eyes. "I don't think you're taking enough blood from Sebastian. You're running short on being able to supply your brain and your dick, and your dick's winning out if that's the kind of logic you're coming up with."

Valentin shrugged. "Believe that if you want, but to me, it seems you're still living in denial."

Sal gazed at him for a moment longer, then slowly lowered his gaze. He glanced at Beezle, another unanswered question moving through his mind, but with a possible answer standing in front of him. He reached toward the little croc. "I need to borrow a tooth for a second, Beezy." He opened Beezle's mouth and ran his index finger over one of Beezle's sharp teeth. He pulled his finger out before blood spilled in Beezle's mouth. The black croc yawned and nearly closed his eyes, peering at him through slits, as if bored and mildly curious at the same time.

Sal stood up, looking at the blackish blood, a faint red tint to it when the light hit it just right. It welled out of the wound, thick and rolling down his finger, but the gash was already sealing. He extended his finger toward Valentin and Basil. "I need one of you to taste my blood."

Basil pulled his head back and turned away from Sal's finger.

"I'll pass, thank you."

Sal looked at him. "Why? What makes it so bad compared to a human's?"

"Well, first off, look at it. It's not very appetizing looking, now is it? And the scent…"

"What?"

Valentin sighed. "It's hard to explain. Human blood has the most alluring scent. Every vampire would describe it differently and every human has a taste unique to them. To me, I think of it as roses and wine. Alluring and delicious. Your blood, it's like turpentine."

Sal let out an offended cough.

Basil stepped forward. "Maybe not quite that bad. Perhaps more like a very potent alcohol." He gestured to Valentin. "And there you have it. Two vampires who have two different opinions on the vileness of your blood."

"Vile?!" Sal blurted out. "Damn, Baz, that's pretty harsh coming from one of you blood connoisseurs." He looked down at his finger, the wound closed and the blood still wet on his skin. "I guess it answers the question I had, though."

"You want to know if he could feed from you," Sebastian said.

Sal nodded. "Yeah."

Silence fell over them for a brief moment, broken by a loud exhale from Valentin.

"Fine, I'll do it. I'll taste your blood."

Sal snapped his head up. "Seriously?"

Valentin took the last few steps to stand directly in front of him. "Yes. It's just that little bit and it's been out of your veins for a while, so I'm sure it's lost a lot of its potency, as human blood does."

Basil shifted forward, pushing Valentin out of the way. "No, I'll do it. We don't know what could happen, so it's better if it's me."

Valentin gave him a confused look. "What do you think could happen?"

"What if demon blood is toxic to us? Even a small bit like that? You have someone who needs you." Basil's gaze went to Sebastian. "I don't."

Sebastian took Valentin's hand and laid his other on Basil's shoulder. "I'm not sure this is a good idea."

Basil flashed a bright smile. "Oh, I'm sure it'll be fine. I'm probably thinking the worst and blowing it out of proportion." He turned to Sal and took him by the wrist. "But, you never know." He stared at Sal's finger.

Sal waited a few seconds before his impatience gave out. "Are you going to do it?"

"Yes! I'm working up to it. Don't pressure me." Basil continued to gaze at the blood, then looked into Sal's eyes. "This is a bit awkward, you know. Me about to take your blood."

"It's a few drops on my finger. It's not like I'm asking you to bite me on the ass cheek."

Basil made a grumbling noise in his throat. "When was the last time you washed your hands?"

"Just lick the damn blood!"

With resigned sigh, Basil opened his mouth and pushed Sal's finger in. He scrunched his face, as if tasting something strong, and pulled Sal's finger out of his mouth again, cleaned of blood. "Well, that has a bit of a bite to it."

Valentin moved closer to him. "How do you feel?"

"Other than having that taste in my mouth, I'm fine. It's very potent with energy and life essence, and it doesn't go down smooth, that's for sure."

Sal laid his hand on Basil's shoulder. "Normally, I'd be offended, but I'm too damn grateful right now for your help. So do you think a vampire could feed from a noble demon?"

"I couldn't say for certain from that little bit, but I would definitely advise taking it in small doses. To compare your blood and human blood to liquor, where a human's blood can be relished and enjoyed like a full glass of fine wine, your blood is like taking a shot of hard liquor. Throw it back fast and get it down. It even has a distinct burn to it. But as for the after effects or prolonged issues from drinking it over an extended period of time, obviously we don't know the answer on that."

"But it might be possible," Sal said. "This gives hope that it could work."

Valentin laid his arm over Sebastian's shoulders. "Yes, it does, but you also shouldn't be opposed to him feeding from a donor if he needs to. While that little taste of your blood hasn't killed Basil…yet…who knows if a demon's blood can sustain a vampire in the same way a human's blood, or even one of our own, can. We vampires can feed from each other and survive because we were once human. You aren't and never were."

Sal frowned at him. "Thanks for the downer. Next time I need some cheering up, remind me to avoid you."

"I'm taking your side on that," Basil grumbled. "Hasn't killed me *yet*. I feel like I should be waiting to see if I survive the next few hours." He spun toward Sal, swinging and landing a punch into Sal's shoulder. "If your demon blood starts to kill me, I'm warning you now, I'm clamping onto your neck and taking you with me."

Sal grinned at him. "So, what you're saying is, despite all your bitching, you liked it."

"I suppose one could acquire a taste for it."

Sal rested his hand on Basil's shoulder and softened his voice. "Thanks, Baz."

Basil laid his hand over Sal's. "You're welcome." He gave a little shake of his shoulders to rid himself of Sal's hand. "And that's about enough of that. Your gratitude is making me uncomfortable."

Sal chuckled and stepped back, sitting on the sofa again. "I was starting to get an icky feeling with it, too."

Sebastian sat beside him. "So are you going to call Calvin and talk things out?"

Sal sagged back on the couch. "Not yet. He needs some time to think about what he wants. Me being around would do nothing but weigh his thoughts in one direction. I mean, who wouldn't be swayed knowing they could have all this?" He gestured down at himself.

"Right," Sebastian said, drawing the word out. "Maybe you should brush your hair, wash your face, and put on a clean shirt before you start flaunting."

Sal brushed his hand over his hair, the tangles smoothing away, and scrubbed at the corners of his mouth with the back of his hand. "Better?"

"Slightly. And I think you should call him sooner. You're putting him through hell."

"I—" Sal stopped as his phone chimed on the end table beside Sebastian. He dove over Sebastian's lap and snatched it, turning it over to look at the screen. "Interesting."

"What is it?" Valentin asked.

Sal slowly sat up, his gaze still on the screen. "Looks like someone pretending to be Calvin is texting me."

Basil stepped forward, concern filling his handsome face. "What? How do you know?"

"Well, the number isn't Calvin's and it says, 'Hey babe, it's me. What are you doing right now?' Calvin's never called me *babe* and he never will. It's not his style."

Sebastian looked down at the phone. "Then something must be wrong. Someone's trying to lure you out."

Sal's fingers moved with flashing speed in replying back. "I'm going to try to get some information and when I find out who this is, I'm going to rip their fucking head off and piss in the stump of their neck." He typed back, deciding to play the game. *I'm just hanging out, baby. What's this new number you got?*

A reply came a moment later. *New phone. You need to come over. I'm so fucking horny for your big dick.*

Sal snorted. "If I wasn't so pissed right now, I'd find this amusing." He typed, *Oh yeah? Are you at your place?*

Yes. Come and get me.

Sounds like you want it bad, so that means I'm going to make you work for it. How's starting off with a golden shower sound?

Sebastian looked up from peering down at Sal's phone and watching him reply. "Eww."

"That's what Calvin would say too, so that's why I wrote it."

The reply came through. *Sounds like you know what I want. Give me all you got, just get over here fast.*

"Yep. Definitely not Calvin, which means I'm talking to someone who's about to die." He typed back, *On my way. Be ready for me.*

Oh, I will be.

Sal stood and stuffed his phone in the back pocket of his jeans and turned toward the sofa, holding out one arm. "Beezle."

The crocodile entity vanished in a puff of black smoke and reappeared draped over Sal's shoulders.

Basil took a quick step forward. "We'll go with you. You might need help."

Sal glanced at him. "I appreciate the offer, but what good are vampires against a demon?"

Sebastian laid his hand on Sal's arm. "You think a demon has Calvin?"

"From how the bastard was talking, yes, I do. The question is, which one? I know a couple who might like to get their claws on him to get at me and they know I've been hanging around in this area. I've manifested a lot around his place, so between that and his energy, it's like shooting up signal flares to where we are. It wouldn't take much for either of them to track him down." Sal shook his head. "Damn it! I should've known to be more careful."

Valentin moved to Sebastian's side. "All the more reason for you to let us help you."

"Sorry, kids, can't let you do that, and I don't have time. I'm leaving. Now." Sal summoned his power on his final word and as he dematerialized, the last thing he heard were his friends calling his name.

Chapter Sixteen

Sal manifested in Calvin's bedroom. If he wasn't feeling so murderous, he would've been amused by the smell of paint and his number still burned and clear on the wall, where recent coats of paint had tried to cover it.

From under Calvin's bed, Buster peeked his nose out, then the rest of him emerged. He rushed toward Sal, tail flashing back and forth in happy wags.

Sal bent down, petting him on the head. "Smart poochy, hiding in here. I think it'd be best if you stay." He added some compulsion to his final word, ensuring the dog would remain in the room. He slipped Beezle off his shoulders to the floor. "And you stay here too until I call for you."

He stood up straight, extending his senses. Calvin wasn't here. He didn't know if he should be relieved by that or not. On one hand, it could mean Calvin was safe. On the other, it could mean he was being held somewhere.

But there were two others in the house and one of them, he knew well.

Sal walked to the bedroom door and out to the hall. Voices drifted toward him, hushed in tone, but his sharp hearing picked up every word.

"What did you say to it when you texted it?"

The second voice, gruff and low, as if it belonged to an aged human, replied, "Things that would have sparked his interest."

"Where is it? Why hasn't it shown up yet?"

"He's here."

"What?! Where?"

"He'll show himself soon." The aged voice spoke up. "Won't you, *demon*?"

Rage surged through Sal. His true form began to emerge,

claws replacing nails, fangs lowering, horns manifesting. He stalked down the hallway and stopped at the threshold to the family room. Nathan had his back to him, but the other "man" faced him.

A sickening smile spread over the old priest's face. "And there you are. My, but you do look angry, half in your true form."

His voice rumbling, Sal said, "And you look as disgusting as always, Amon, but this tops it. A priest? Really? Let me guess. You got a look at Nathan there, saw he was touched by that power, so you thought by appearing as one of his brothers, it'd win his trust. That's low even for you. But I don't give a fuck about what new lows you've sunken to. Where's Calvin?"

The priest looked at Nathan. "You see, as I said, the demon will try to confuse us, turn us against each other. We must be brave and not be swayed by anything he says." He shook his head and glanced at Sal, then back to Nathan. "I'm afraid he's attached to your brother even more than you thought."

Sal stepped into the room, his gaze locked on Amon. "This is the last time I'll ask. After this, I'll start ripping off body parts until you tell me. Where is Calvin?"

"Now. Do it now." The priest reached toward Nathan, but didn't touch him. "We must exorcise him. Destroy his very being if we're to free your brother of the hold he has over him."

Sal turned his gaze to Nathan. The man's pretty green eyes were wide with fear. He hadn't shaved in a few days and the black stubble hid some of his paleness, made his face appear not quite so gaunt with illness, but he could sense Nathan was weaker than the last time he'd seen him. Calvin's brother was fading from this world and the man had no clue how much losing him was going to hurt Calvin.

Sal noticed in the crucifix in Nathan's hand, the vial of clear water in the other. Both items shone with sacred energy, but with how weak Nathan was, he didn't think the man would have the strength to throw around the power needed to do much damage to him.

Sal pointed at Nathan. "You need to put that shit down and listen to me. I know that asshole beside you looks like one of your brothers, but he's not. He's one of mine. And he's going to hurt your *real* brother if you don't let me take care of him."

"Don't listen to him," the priest said. "He's doing exactly as I said he would. You see that now."

Sal walked further into the room, his gaze on Nathan. "Where's Calvin? Do you know where he is? That he's safe?"

Nathan opened his mouth, no words leaving him at first. "I—"

The priest rushed a step closer to Nathan. "Don't answer him! Don't converse with him!"

Sal jabbed his index finger toward Amon, his voice boomed through the house. "Shut the fuck up!"

The priest swung his hand toward Sal. "You have to do it! Now!"

The last control Sal had over his anger snapped. He lunged, clearing the distance between him and Amon in an instant. He slammed into Amon, driving him back into the wall. "Pay attention, Nathan. If he was a real priest, I wouldn't be able to do this."

Sal snatched the dingy white cleric's collar. His claws scratched Amon's throat, and he ripped off the collar, throwing it to the floor. He spun around, swinging Amon, and flung him to the floor, also. "Show your true self to him!"

Searing pain lashed across Sal's back. He whipped around, facing Nathan who held the vial of water high, ready to slash it down at Sal again. "What'd I tell you about that shit? It fucking stings!"

His voice trembling as much as his hands and body, Nathan brandished the crucifix before him. "Demon Sallos, you are not welcomed here."

Slight dizziness rushed through Sal's head. His body felt the barest hint weaker. He reached toward Nathan. "Found out my true name, huh? And who told you? Him? How do you think he knew it? Because we come from the same place!"

Nathan held the vial aloft. "Stop spinning lies."

"You really don't want to do this. That guy back there," Sal pointed over his shoulder with his thumb, "isn't who or what you think he is. I'm serious. If you don't like me because I'm a demon, trust me, you'll fucking hate him."

With a burst of courage and strength, Nathan marched a step toward Sal. "Be silent, demon! I know nothing but lies come out of the mouths of your kind."

Sal snorted. "Tell me about it." He glanced back to Amon. "You really worked him over good, didn't you?"

Ignoring Sal, the priest focused on Nathan. "You can do this. Gather your strength. Destroy the demon before he claims your brother as his own."

"Little late for that. I've already made him mine." Shit. Him and his damn mouth. Sal spun toward Nathan, holding up both hands. "I don't mean that in a bad way. If he doesn't want me, he can walk at any time. I don't…for lack of a better word…possess him."

Nathan's expression hardened. He marched forward, the crucifix before him. "Enough! I command you to leave my brother alone!"

Sal backed up for the steps Nathan advanced. "Listen, if we could talk this through—"

"Silence! I command you to be silent!"

Sal's jaw locked shut…not of his own will. The heated energy of the power Nathan called upon moved through him, but it was rough and barely controlled. While Nathan had a gift for summoning it and the blessed tools, as in any fight, the one with the most skill would be victorious.

Sal focused his energy, called upon his power, and the icy wave of it washed the heat away. "You need to stop this!"

Nathan swung the vial of water in a downward slash. The

spray of it splattered across Sal's chest.

Sal winced. Steam rose from the marks, and the hiss of his skin burning beneath the T-shirt filled his ears. "We've been over this before. You're a baby priest. You don't have what it takes to banish me."

Nathan slashed again with the holy water, advancing on Sal. "You're not welcomed in this house."

Sal flinched when the water splashed over his arm, leaving a red welt. "Stop it!"

"You're not welcomed in this world." Nathan flung more water, the drops hitting Sal in the abdomen.

Sal doubled forward. Fuck, the one stung like hell. His head spun, and he could feel the strength draining from his body. Words Calvin had said to him floated through his mind…

Three things are needed to cast a spell. The need. The knowledge. The emotion.

Nathan might be physically weak, his skills and talents not honed, but he definitely had those three things going for him. If this man ever gained more knowledge and sharpened it, and his health was returned to him, he would be a powerful force.

"He's weakening," the priest said. "Keep going. Finish him!"

Nathan raised the vial over Sal's bent over form. "Go back to your world."

Sal cried out, the water slashing across one cheek. He dropped to one knee. He didn't want to strike out at Calvin's brother, but if the guy didn't knock this shit off soon, he wasn't going to have a choice. He put his hand over his cheek and looked up at Nathan. "Why can't you get it? Calvin is so desperate for you to live, he summoned me to save you."

Nathan's gaze was locked on him. "Being saved by a creature like yourself is worse than death."

"Ignorant bastard! He loves you! He'll do anything for you!" Sal held Nathan's gaze. "And I'll do anything for him. That's why I'm here, because that fucking asshole behind you used Calvin as bait to call me out. You think I'm stupid? Do you think I didn't know it was a trap? Of course I did! But I didn't care, because all I wanted was to know Calvin was safe. We're on the same side! We both want to protect him!"

He saw it then, the slightest break in Nathan's hard expression.

"Don't listen to him!" the priest shouted. "He's using your emotions, your weakness, to get to you."

Sal slowly started to stand. "You and I have the same weakness — Calvin. We both want to protect him, watch over him, do what's best by him. I can tell you, getting rid of me isn't it. But getting rid of him," he flicked his head toward Amon, "will keep Calvin safe."

The priest pushed himself up off the floor, rushing closer to Nathan. "Lies! Silence him!"

Sal saw exactly what he needed in Nathan's gaze; doubt. "If you have any doubts, turn that shit on him. You know what it does to me. If he's human like he claims, it won't do a damn thing to him."

Nathan's gaze hardened again, resolve set in his face. He twisted around, a stream of water flew from the bottle…and landed across the priest's face.

Amon screamed, reeling backward, hands covering his face. Steam seeped through his spread fingers.

Sal stood up, a breath of relief escaping him. "Since I'm always one to say I told you so…I fucking told you so!" He looked back at Amon. "That shit stings like a bitch, doesn't it, Amon?"

Nathan didn't acknowledge Sal. His eyes were wide with horror. He stumbled back a step. "I didn't think it would do anything. He's…he's a…"

Amon spread his fingers, peeking between them with yellowish-green eyes. "Worthless human." He rose to his feet, dropping his hands from his face, revealing it in full demon form, a red slash running from his left eye, across his nose, to his right cheek. His horns began to emerge from his forehead. In a puff of yellow smoke, the snake entity manifested around his shoulders. He walked slowly toward them. "But it doesn't matter. You may have been too weak to banish him, but you weakened him enough. And that's all I needed."

Amon shifted, and Sal saw the attack coming. He braced himself, prepared for the strike…and the door flew open. He snapped his head toward it, his gaze locking with Calvin's.

"Sal!" Calvin rushed a step forward.

"Calvin, no!" Sal shouted. "Get out of here!"

"Perfect timing," Amon hissed. He lunged for forward, but rather than Sal, he aimed for Nathan.

Sal jumped for Nathan, shoving him out of the way. Nathan flew to the side, crashing hard to the ground. Amon's claws ripped across Sal's chest, but the pain yielded before excruciating tearing in Sal's abdomen. Cold and hard, the black blade of a demon bone dagger sank into Sal's stomach. He looked down at it, his blood welling around the blade.

Amon leaned close to him and whispered, "When you turned me down, keeping your loyalty to Sytri, I changed my plans. You, with your witch, showed yourself to be the greatest threat, but with a very clear weakness— humans. And you bared it again now, leaving yourself vulnerable when you saw a threat to that man. But I want you to know, you won't be the last. Sytri *is* next. I'm nothing if not patient. Rank by rank, I will become a king."

"Sal!" Calvin ran toward him.

"No!" Sal grabbed Amon by both arms, throwing him back. Amon's hand remained clenching the dagger, and the blade jerked out of Sal's abdomen.

Pain blackened Sal's vision. He dropped to his knees, but summoned all the power he could. He looked up at Calvin and lifted his hand. "Stay back!" He forced out his will, slamming it into Calvin. As if fighting against a powerful wind, Calvin's progress stopped. He stumbled backward, unable to stop himself from being pushed by the force of Sal's power back out the door. With a last effort, Sal willed the door to slam closed and sealed it, as he did for all the outer doors and windows.

He sagged back against the wall, one hand over his abdomen, and whispered, “I’m so sorry, witchy poo.” On his next thought, he called for Beezle.

Black smoke erupted in front of him, Beezle taking solid form and growing between him and Amon. His long tail whipped back and forth, his yellow gaze already focused on Amon and the snake.

Sal glanced at Nathan on the floor, and their gazes met. He knew in that moment, Nathan realized he’d been wrong. Sal brought his gaze back to Amon, locking him in a glare. “Looks like it’s down to us. Let’s finish this.”

Chapter Seventeen

Calvin pulled and pounded on the door. He shoved his hand into the front pocket of his jeans, tearing out his keys and jamming one into the lock, but it would turn. He gripped it with both hands, trying to turn it was so much force, the key bent. The door stayed closed and locked solid, sealed with Sal's magic. He raced away from the front door, running toward the side of the house and around back to try that door, but he knew it would be the same.

He was at work when the text from Sebastian came, telling him Sal was in trouble and might be at his house. He ran out of the grocery store, not a word to anyone, and since he only lived a couple of blocks away from the store and didn't drive to it, he didn't stop running until he burst through the door.

How had this happened? Amon, was that piece of shit using his brother to get to him? Or to Sal? Or both of them? It was too much to think about and understand without being able to talk to Sal or Nathan. He needed to put his mind to getting inside the house. Amon had stabbed Sal with a demon bone dagger. He was hurt…he might even be…

No. He couldn't, wouldn't think of that. He wasn't going to lose Sal.

Calvin reached the back door, falling into it with his momentum too great to stop. He yanked at the door. It wouldn't budge. Sebastian, Valentin, and Basil were coming, but breaking through Sal's power would be too much even for the vampire princes, especially with the sun draining them. They had a limited amount of time they could be out before the sun's poison would make them sick, and pushing beyond that could mean death.

He hit the door with the side of his fist and braced both hands on it. His head bowed between his arms, spells and incantations flashed through his mind. None of them would work. He may know how to summon a demon, how to compel one, how to banish, but he had no idea how to break demon magic that was already in place. He had so much more to learn in his craft. He needed to figure out some way to use what he already knew.

His mind grasped hold of an idea. It could very well be one of his worst ideas ever, it might make an already dangerous situation deadly, but it was all he had.

Calvin spun away from the door and dropped to the ground, frantically smoothing the dirt away. In his mind, he conjured the symbols he needed and etched them into dirt with his finger, hoping he remembered them correctly. He didn't bother with drawing a circle for containment. He didn't want to contain this demon.

He slammed his hand down on the ground, pouring his will, energy, and emotion into the symbols. He took a breath and called upon the only one who might be able to break through Sal's spell. "Demon Prince Sytri, I call upon thee. Hear me, Prince Sytri. Hear me and come into this world. Come to me!"

A rumble of power chilled the air around him. A light wind lifted, charged with energy that made the hairs on his arms stand on end. Sytri was manifesting. He slowly lifted his gaze and looked upon the demon prince.

Sy was in human form, but no less beautiful, as like Sal, his facial features were the same in his demon form. His skin was fair, flawless, his features delicate but also, striking in their beauty. His smooth, long black hair hung nearly to his waist. He was tall, slender, and at that moment, he had his golden eyes focused on Calvin.

At his side stood a wolf, as tall as Sy's hip, broad in body. Its black coat was thick and long. With its head lowered, eyes of electric blue locked on him, a tendril of unease moved through Calvin. This must be Sy's entity companion. Calvin wondered how big the wolf could get, because it looked fearsome enough as it was.

A smirk curved a corner of Sy's lips. "I know you. Or I should say, I know your scent. It was all over Sallos when I saw him last."

A single amused laugh left him. He looked away from Calvin, gazing around the area. "A witch. Only Sallos would make a witch his lover. For a long term, at least."

Calvin pushed himself up, standing and facing Sy. "Sorry, there's no time for the current boyfriend to bicker with the ex. Sal needs our help."

Sy arched a slender eyebrow. "He told you about me? Now that's even more amusing."

His patience at an end, Calvin pointed back at the door. "Forget about that! He's in there with Amon and he's dying! He needs help!"

"Yes, I'm aware. I can sense their energy, and his is fading."

When Sy made no move toward the door, Calvin thought he was going to erupt with frustration and anger. "So help him!"

Sy turned his gaze away from Calvin, looking at the sky, the trees, everything around. "It's been so long since I've come to the human realm. The energy here gives quite the rush. I think I might be starting to understand why Sallos spends so much time here." He slowly brought his gaze back to Calvin. "Interesting that you should summon me, yet not make an attempt to contain me."

"I don't want to keep you trapped in a circle! I want you to break Sal's spell, go inside, kick Amon's ass, and heal Sal! I know you've got the power to do all of those things!"

Sy laid a hand over his chest, as if flattered. "Indeed, I do. But whatever made you think that I would?"

Calvin locked his gaze with Sy and stepped up to him. "Because he loved you. Because he was probably the only one in your eternal existence who ever has and you betrayed him. Because even despite that, when he thought you could be in danger, he warned you. Because you owe him. And most of all," he stabbed his finger into Sy's chest, "because I fucking said so!"

Sy's smirk returned, broader than before. "I like you. And I see a little more clearly why Sallos does, too. Your facts are a bit skewed, but since Sallos doesn't know the full truth, I won't hold it against either of you." He placed his index and middle fingers on Calvin's chest, pushing him aside with what seemed no effort.

Calvin stumbled back, but caught himself quickly.

"Since you amuse me, for a human, and I do despise Amon, I'll help." Sy sauntered past him to the door. He gestured back to the wolf. "Stand by the witch, Lucien. He won't harm you."

Moving with long strides, Lucien trotted toward Calvin.

Sy laid his hand on the door and glanced back at Calvin. "You'll want to stand back. This is going to be rather impressive."

Golden energy erupted from Sy's hand. Blue light flashed around the door, Sal's spell resisting Sy's power. A growl of frustration and effort left Sy. His golden power flashed with greater brilliance, slowly overcoming Sal's, but still, the power of Sal's spell held strong. Sy placed his other hand on the door, and Calvin felt the burst of energy rush out of the demon prince. In a blast of blue and gold, the spell broke…along with the door. The cracking and splintering was deafening, wooden shards flew through the air.

Calvin covered his face with his arm and when he peeked over it, he stared at the gaping, smoking opening where the door had been, blackened around the edges.

"That took a bit more force than I expected," Sy said. "Even dying, Sallos's power is formidable." He glanced back to Calvin. "Shall we?"

Calvin jumped into a run, racing past Sy. "Come on!"

He ran through the kitchen, stopping at the entrance to the family room. Sal lay on the floor on his side, a pool of blackish blood under him, and Nathan behind him. From the trail of blood across the floor, Calvin deduced Sal had put himself between Nathan and Amon. Nathan was conscious, staring at Amon, but he could see the helplessness and fear on his brother's face.

Beezle, huge in size but much smaller than he could be, guarded both Sal and Nathan from Amon and the yellow snake, which was coiled on the floor in front of Amon, far thicker and bigger than Calvin had seen it before. The small room wouldn't allow for Beezle to grow much larger and still be able to maneuver.

The room itself was trashed. The legs of the coffee table were nothing but sticks beneath it. A lamp was broken, the recliner was overturned. The sofa had been thrown against the far wall and the TV lay on the floor with spider web cracks across the screen.

Sal lifted his head, looking at him. His voice came weak and rough. "Calvin, get out of here."

"No, I'm not leaving you!" Calvin ran for Sal.

"Perfect timing," Amon said.

Nearly to Sal, Calvin looked to the side and fear washed through him. The snake launched half of its coiled body into the air, its blood-red gaze on him. Its mouth opened, revealing hooked, sharp teeth.

Too fast. It was coming too fast, and he couldn't dodge it.

Beezle spun, the black croc's body a blur with his speed. He surged up, great jaws opened wide and snapped closed on the snake, whipping it back with a powerful shake of his head. The snake's head smacked into Calvin's arm, close to latching onto him. Beezle shook his head back and forth, his teeth tearing through the snake's yellow skin to the molten flesh beneath. An ear-piercing and chilling scream came from the snake.

"Nyal!" Amon shouted.

On his word, the snake vanished, leaving only yellow smoke in Beezle's jaws.

Calvin slid to his knees at Sal's side, laying one hand on Sal's shoulder, the other on his cheek. He looked down at Sal's abdomen, the shirt soaked with blood. "What do I need to do? How can I stop it?"

Sal placed his hand over Calvin's. "I don't think this is one your magic can fix, witchy poo."

Nathan reached toward him. "Calvin, I'm so sorry."

Calvin took Nathan's hand, holding Sal's in his other. "It's okay. We're going to get through this. All of us."

High pitched giggles filled the room. Calvin glanced back at Amon.

"Ah, human hope. It's such a cute thing, how it continues to strive when there's no point. And there's absolutely none here. Your lover is bleeding out and your brother was marked for death long before I came here. There's nothing, *nothing*, you can do for either of them. Except stepping aside and allowing me finish Sallos before he suffers more."

"Oh, I don't know if things are quite that dire."

Calvin looked toward the kitchen, where Sy leaned against the doorway between the two rooms, Lucien at his side.

With a graceful flick of his hand, Sy motioned toward Calvin. "He's a witch, you know. All he needed was a chance at you. I've given him that, now the rest is up to him." He glanced at Sal and shook his head. "Really, Sallos. You should've let your witch fight this battle for you."

Sal looked up at Calvin. "I can't believe you summoned my ex for help. If I live through this, I'm going to be so pissed, I probably won't fuck you for at least a day."

Calvin grinned at him. "I'd like to see you try to do that, because I sure as hell won't make it easy on you not to."

A smile broke through the pain on Sal's face, and he squeezed Calvin's hand.

Amon faced Sy. "This is no fight of yours, Prince Sytri. You've only been forced here by that witch. Leave while you have the chance."

Sy laughed. "Oh, Amon. If you truly think I'm so stupid, you deserve to be killed because every breath you take is air wasted. Regardless, at this point, I'm only spectator. I'll deal with you in our realm, after the witch banishes you back there."

The front door flew open, Basil running through, Sebastian and Valentin behind him. They each surveyed the room, their gazes resting on Calvin and Sal. Calvin watched the rage rise in their faces, but it shone the clearest on the vampires, a red tint highlighting the icy blue of Valentin's eyes and the honey-brown of Basil's.

Basil marched across the room, Valentin and Sebastian following. He gripped the mahogany shaft of his cane and pulled, freeing the hidden sword. Valentin did the same with his ebony shafted cane. Both vampires took up spots in front of Calvin and Sal, Beezle in front of them with low, rumbling growls leaving him.

Sebastian knelt beside Nathan and behind Sal, placing his hands on Sal's arms. "You're bleeding! Why aren't you healing?"

"He was stabbed with a demon bone dagger," Calvin said for Sal. "It acts similar on a demon as any knife would on us."

Basil focused on Amon. "I don't know who you are, but you've fucked with the wrong demon."

Amon laughed. "Vampires? There's nothing you can do to me!"

"Maybe they can't, but I can." Calvin stood and stepped between Basil and Valentin. He moved ahead of Beezle to stand against Amon.

Sal tried to sit up. "Calvin, get behind Beezle."

Without turning around, Calvin said, "Sebastian, try to keep him still, please. I really don't want him to die before I finish banishing this bastard."

Amon crouched low. "You're like all humans, thinking you have the strength and right to control a demon. But I thank you for your arrogance in stepping closer." He jumped for Calvin.

Calvin closed his fingers around his silver pentacle and shouted. "Demon Amon, stop!"

Amon stumbled, his body stiffened, seeming to not want to obey him. Rage filled Amon's face, and he continued to push forward.

Calvin called upon his need and desire again, pushing it into his words. "I compel you, Count Amon, by speaking your true name, stop!"

Amon froze, completely rigid, but he trembled as though he was fighting against Calvin's spell.

Calvin marched closer to him. "You don't have the strength to fight me. You don't belong in this world. You're not welcome here, and I command you to go back to your realm."

Amon's form wavered, fluctuating between transparent and being solid. His strained voice left him with halting words. "I… will not…obey you."

Calvin stopped in front of him, a half arm's length away from the enemy demon. "You don't have a choice. You have no power here. You're forbidden in this home." He thought of Sal behind him, what this piece of shit had done to him, and channeled his emotions into his words. "Your strength and power are nothing. I banish you from this world! On my will, so mote it be!"

Amon was flung backward, Calvin's words carrying the force of a physical blow. The demon screamed, smoke rose from his flesh, and he vanished with a burst of energy.

A wave of lightheadedness washed through Calvin. The pentacle felt hot in his hand, and he slowly opened his fingers to release it. He swayed slightly, but caught himself. There was weakness in his muscles, as though he'd expelled a great deal of energy. Near him, Beezle shrunk in size. The crocodile gave him an affectionate bump on the foot with his nose, then wandered toward Sal. Lucien trotted after Beezle. Sniffing the croc and Sal, the wolf wagged his tail in obvious recognition.

Sy's voice filled the silence. "Now that was the most entertaining thing I've seen in ages. I never praise humans, but given the situation, I have to say well done, witch."

Calvin spared him a quick glance. He spun around and rushed back to Sal, taking Sal's face in both hands. "How are you?"

Sal smiled up at him, but his voice was weaker and softer as he spoke. "I'm not sure, now that I know who the real badass in this relationship is."

Calvin choked out a laugh and brushed Sal's hair away from his forehead. He looked at Sy. "Now you. Heal him. And my brother."

Sy strolled further into the room, stepping gracefully around the debris. "And what will I receive in return?"

"What will you…" Calvin stammered, his anger rising fresh. "I summoned you here to help!"

Sy stopped at Sal's feet, looking down at him and Calvin. "And I did that. I broke Sallos's spell and admitted you into the house. If you want me to heal your brother or Sallos, you're pushing your luck in requesting two favors without restitution, dear witch."

"Fine. What do you want?"

Sal clasped Calvin's arm, though his grip had no strength. "Calvin, no. Don't make a deal with him."

Calvin rested his hand over Sal's. "I have to." He focused on Sy again. "So? What do you want?"

Sy sighed and looked up toward the ceiling, his lovely face thoughtful, his hand moving in long strokes over Lucien. "So many possibilities. But let's agree on this." He lowered his gaze, meeting Calvin's. "Should I ever require your services as a witch, you'll assist me."

Calvin shook his head. "Too open-ended. I'll assist you once, with one spell, no more than that. And it can't be in an action against Sallos, any human, Valentin, Basil, or anyone else I call my friend or family."

Sy extended his hand down to Calvin. "Agreed."

Calvin took Sy's hand. "Done. Now heal them."

Sy tipped his head to the side. "Which one?"

"What the hell do you mean, which one?!"

"Oh, I see now." Sy tsked and shook his head. "Silly mortal, you didn't listen closely enough to my words. I said I could heal one *or* the other of them, and that you were pushing your luck in requesting two favors. As in, healing both of them would be two favors, not counting me breaking Sallos's spell to allow you inside, which I did of my own goodwill."

A low growl escaped Sal. "Fucking sneaky ass bastard."

Sy laughed. "Not really. Were half your blood not spilled on the floor, I'm sure you would have caught it. I have to take my advantages where I can. However, witch, if you'd like to make another deal—"

"Goddamn, shut the fuck up for three seconds, Sytri," Sal snapped. "You still talk as damn much as ever." He gave Calvin's arm a small squeeze. "You don't have to cut another deal with him. He's trying to confuse you. Heal me and I'll heal your brother."

Sy huffed and rolled his eyes. "Forever the do-gooder and still so adept at spoiling my fun."

Calvin laid his hand on Sal's cheek and bent down to him, placing a tender kiss on Sal's lips. "Thank you." He looked toward his brother. "Nathan, you agree?"

Nathan gazed at Calvin for a moment, then glanced at Sal. He nodded once. "Yes, I do."

Calvin twisted around to Sy. "No more games. No more deals. No more dragging your ass. Heal Sallos."

Sy moved toward Sal. "Fine. Step aside, witch."

Calvin shifted around to Sal's head and guided him gently down to rest it on his lap.

Sy swung a leg over Sal, standing with one foot on either side of Sal's hips and eased down until he was sitting astride him. He grinned at Sal. "One of many familiar positions for us, isn't it, dear Sallos?"

Sal managed a fierce glare. "If I wasn't dying right now, I'd kick your ass."

"He might still get his ass kicked as soon as he finishes healing you," Calvin growled. "Or banished so hard, he'll wish he had his ass kicked."

Sy laughed. "You two are quite the couple, I must say." He held up his index finger. The nail lengthened and changed into a sharp claw. He hooked the claw over the neck of Sal's shirt. "I have to see what I'm working with."

A grumble of annoyance sounded in Sal's throat, but he seemed too exhausted to waste many more words on Sy. Calvin fought to keep control over his anger. Trading words with Sy would only give him more excuse to delay in healing Sal.

With a downward jerk of his hand, Sy cut through the shirt's collar. He continued to draw it down, slicing through the material. He flipped the cloth to each side, revealing Sal's torso and wounded abdomen.

Horror shot through Calvin, a sick and sinking feeling roiled through his stomach. Sal's abdomen was slick with blood, so much so that it was difficult at first glance to make out the wound, but Calvin refused to look away. The dagger had been driven into the center of Sal's stomach and ripped toward the right. Staring at the wound, he didn't know how Sy could heal it, but if the demon prince could, there would be few favors that Sy could ask of him that would equal the gratitude he'd have.

Sy shook his head. "Amon certainly wasn't playing around. Gut wounds are always the worst and so tricky to heal."

"But you can do it, right?" Calvin asked.

Sy let out a single laugh. "Can I do it? Dear witch, do you have any idea who you're talking to? I'm a prince of demons. There's very little I can't do."

A growl proceeding his words, Sal said, "Except shut up. That's always been a challenge for you. You think you can stop talking long enough to help me out here before I die?"

Sy let out a nostalgic sigh. "How things have changed. You always used to be the patient one. Now look at you, all rush, rush, rush. But I suppose I can see your point in this situation." He hovered his hands over Sal's wound. "I'll save you. Again."

"What do you mean, *again*?" Sal asked.

"Shhh, you don't want to hear that story right now."

Soft green energy emanated from the palms of Sy's hands. It grew stronger by the second, illuminating Sal's stomach. A hushed groan came from Sal. He closed his eyes, rolling his head on Calvin's lap toward him.

Calvin stroked Sal's hair. "Are you all right?"

"Yeah. He's blocked the pain."

"Believe it or not," Sy said, "I do have a few shreds of compassion in me."

Calvin focused on the wound. It didn't appear to the closing or healing. He glanced at Sy. A frown curved the demon's lips and his expression turned more concentrated. The light from his hands strengthened, and Calvin could feel Sy's energy flowing out of him.

Sy closed his eyes. The light between his hands and Sal's abdomen became too intense for Calvin to continue looking at it. He lowered his gaze to Sal's face. The lines of pain around Sal's eyes had smoothed. He looked peaceful, almost relaxed. Calvin continued to stroke Sal's hair, his face, and Sal reached back with one hand, taking Calvin's other hand in his. Despite the blood covering Sal's hand, Calvin gripped it and held on tight.

The room was silent. It seemed everyone was holding still, not even wanting to breathe for fear it could break Sy's concentration. Though fearing he would see Sy wasn't making progress with healing Sal, Calvin forced his gaze to Sal's abdomen. He nearly gasped aloud in shock. The light had dimmed slightly and the wound was almost closed.

After a few more moments, the green light softened, then faded out completely. Through the blood covering Sal's abdomen, Calvin could see once again the hard lines of Sal's muscles and smooth skin.

Sy shook out his hands. He stretched his arms over his head, arching his back. "Now that was a test of my skills. But, as you can see, I passed brilliantly." He swung his arms down and patted Sal on the stomach. "You may be a bit tender for a little while, but you'll live to fight and fuck another day."

Sal made no effort to get up, but he did open his eyes, looking at Sy. "Thank you. I owe you one."

Sy stood, grinning down at him. "No. Your witch does."

Sal braced a hand on the floor and pushed himself up, turning to Calvin. "I don't know if I should say I'm sorry, or thank you. Both, I think."

Calvin wrapped his arms around him. "Owing him a favor is a small price to have you alive and healed."

Sal tightened his hold on Calvin. His voice dropped to a rough whisper. "You saved my life."

Calvin froze, the words and the meaning behind them striking him hard. He eased back, keeping both hands on Sal's shoulders. "Are you serious?"

Sal nodded it. "I felt it when Sy began to heal me, like a click inside, a tie to you." He smiled and touched Calvin's cheek with the backs of his fingers. "So it looks like I owe you *real* big."

Sy waved both hands in front of himself. "Hold on. I'm the one who healed you, ergo, I'm the one who's saved you."

Sal fixed Sy with a stern look. "Wrong. You wouldn't be here if he hadn't summoned you. He banished Amon. And he made the deal to get you to heal me. All of his actions have been toward saving me."

Sy snorted and folded his arms across his chest. "That's seems rather skewed, if you ask me."

"Not according to the Powers, because I can feel the bond and subtle pressure that I owe him a favor."

Sebastian added his voice to the conversation. "But what does that mean?"

Sal glanced up at him. "It means since he saved me, the Powers, what we demons call the sources of our power and magic, have gifted me with the ability to give him any one thing that he wants."

"Anything?" Valentin asked. "As in, immortality as a human?"

Sal turned a smile on Calvin. "See that? Even he's got a good guess on what you'd want."

"Well, we were having that conversation about one of us making him a vampire and you having Basil taste your blood right before this happened, so it didn't seem a far off assumption."

Calvin snapped his head toward Sal. "You did all that for me?"

"You know, I'm sitting in a puddle of my own blood right now, so my memory's a little sketchy at the moment."

Basil stepped forward. "Yes, he did, and my memory of what his blood tasted like is quite clear."

Calvin shook his head in confusion. "I think I need the whole story from the beginning. How did all of…" he glanced around the destroyed room and flipped his hand toward, "this, happen?"

"It's my fault."

Calvin looked toward his brother.

Nathan sat up, leaning back on the wall, his gaze focused down. "All of it's my fault. From bringing that *thing* into the house to…Sal being hurt. That creature never would've hurt him if I hadn't weakened Sal trying to banish him, and if Sal hadn't been trying to protect me and make me understand that he wasn't the enemy."

Calvin and the others listened while Nathan explained how he'd met Amon, believing the demon was an old priest who seemed supportive in his need to break Sal's hold over Calvin. He'd met with Amon twice to discuss banishing Sal, told how he'd feared he wouldn't be strong enough to exorcise him, but Amon offered him endless encouragement. Pain filled Nathan's voice, but also Calvin heard how his brother was sickened that the one he'd put his trust in had been the true enemy and that he could err in judgment so badly. Sal took over the story from his end about rushing to find him, with Sebastian filling in the gap of how he texted Calvin, then him, Valentin, and Basil coming to help.

Stunned, Calvin worked to sort it all out. Above everything he was told, one thing rang the strongest; Sal had wanted to protect him.

"I'm sorry," Nathan said. "For everything. An apology is small for the damage I've done, but I hope I can make it up to you, Calvin." He lifted his gaze to Sal. "And you."

Sal reached over to Nathan and patted him on the head. "It's okay, little priesty. No hard feelings. Normally I'm good at holding a grudge, but I'm going to let this one go since we're practically family." He draped his arm around Calvin.

Calvin grinned at Sal. "I think you've really scared him now."

Sy's golden gaze moved over them. "This is fascinating. A human having saved a demon's life. A vampire tasting a demon's blood. The whole part about a demon deceiving a priest is an old story, that's happened countless times, but still interesting hearing it from the priest's point of view. Sal, you have a very interesting life here."

"That's me. The life of the party, wherever I go."

Sy made a noise in his throat that said more than words how he disagreed. He looked toward Sebastian, Valentin, and Basil. "Two vampires. It's been a very long time since I've been around any of your kind. You two must me the infamous vampire companions of Sal."

"We tend to look at it as the other way around," Valentin said.

Basil nodded. "He's similar to a stray cat. We fed him once and he continued to show up."

Sy's gaze settled on Basil. A sensual smile curved his lips, and he walked toward him. He stopped before Basil, so close to him their chests nearly touched, and Basil leaned back to put more space between them. He glanced down to Basil's right hand and the ring with a thick gold band and a large, brilliant ruby set in it. He took Basil's hand. "Your rank among vampires is that of a prince?"

Caution in his tone, Basil said, "Yes, it is."

"Well then, from one prince to another..." Sy lifted Basil's hand, placing a kiss on his knuckles. "It's a pleasure to meet you."

Basil slid his hand back and out of Sy's grip. "I'm not entirely sure if I should say likewise or not."

An amused smile rested on Sy's lips. "And you've tasted demon blood? I've heard the bite of a vampire is quite pleasurable."

"It can be. We're also able to rip out half a throat if we're inclined to do so."

Sy tipped his head to the side, contemplating Basil. "Your energy, it's much cooler than a human's. It's rather refreshing."

"That's nice. Listen...Sytri, is it?"

"Sy, in this realm. No need to share my true name too much."

"Right. Well, *Sy*, I'm gathering that you haven't spent a great deal of time in the human realm, but here, we have a concept of personal space and quite frankly, you're invading mine." Basil placed the eagle head handle of his cane in the center of Sy's chest and pushed, driving Sy back a couple of steps. "That's better."

Sy chuckled and turned away, walking toward the front door, the black wolf padding after him. "I like your friends, Sal. They're amusing."

"Hey!" Sal snapped. "You still need to tell me what you meant by saying you were saving me *again*."

Sy opened the door and glanced back. "Do you really want to get into that now?"

"At least the condensed version, yeah."

Stretching a hand up on the doorframe, Sy leaned his forearm against it and drummed his fingers on it, looking to be contemplating on whether he wanted to reveal what he'd meant. After a long moment, he let out a sigh. "Fine. Toward the end of the wars, the princes determined you were more of a threat to their power than I was. With us having our forces joined together, they basically believed you were bolstering my strength. A couple of my spies both reported that there were plans to assassinate you, and that by doing so, it would eliminate two threats at once, since it was thought I wouldn't be a problem without you.

"With that knowledge, I approached Prince Tayish to form an allegiance to defeat you. I knew if you lost in battle, you wouldn't be granted the title of prince, you would be a duke, and hence, no longer a threat to them. Also, I was certain my betrayal would crush your spirit to where you would no longer continue fighting, further eliminating you as a threat. And along with those two things, it would also prove my strength wasn't dependent on you. Since we both still live, I'd say my plan was a glowing success."

Sal stared at him, his mouth hanging open for a brief moment. "You betrayed me to save me?"

"How do you think it happened that my lines of demons received a mixed signal during that final battle, which created an opening allowing the majority of your legions and you to retreat? Had you ever known my demons or me to make such a mistake before?"

Slowly, Sal lowered his gaze, mumbling, "No."

"Of course there was the added bonus that with your defeat, I gained the title of prince. As Tayish said, the princes were willing to accept me, because me alone was far better than the both of us together. So, as the humans say, two birds, one stone."

Sal lifted his gaze in a glare. "At least you got something." His hardened expression softened. "Then, that explains when I sent a message that I wanted to see you, why you came so quickly. You were hoping we—"

"I wouldn't travel too far down that road. All I was hoping for was a good fuck for old time's sake. So, there you go. Now you know." Sy turned to walk out the door.

"Where the hell are you going?" Sal asked.

Sy looked over his shoulder. "Since I'm here now, I thought I'd spend a little time sightseeing. Perhaps I'll become like you and begin spending more time in this realm."

"That's just great." Sal looked at Calvin. "Shouldn't you

banish him or something?"

"That'd be kind of rude since he healed you."

Sy nodded to Calvin. "Well said, witch. And now, I'll take my leave. Don't worry, I can find my way back home when I feel the need to return."

"Sytri…Sy," Sal called. "Seriously, thank you for working with Calvin."

Sy glanced back, a smile on his lips, and bowed his head in acknowledgement of Sal's gratitude. "Gentlemen…" his gaze went to Basil, and he winked at him, "Vampire, until we meet again." He stepped out with Lucien, closing the front door behind him and the wolf.

Basil let out a loud exhale. "He's exhausting."

"Tell me about it," Sal said. He glanced around the room, petting Beezle beside him. "We really trashed this place."

Calvin glanced back to Nathan. "It's a good thing I'll be starting a new job soon. We've got a lot of stuff to buy and a whole backdoor and part of the wall to replace."

Nathan's eyes widened. "Was that the explosion right before you came in?"

"Yeah, Sy kind of blew it up."

Nathan stared at him, then sighed, as if he simply accepted it. "You didn't tell me you'd gotten a new job. I hope it'll pay well."

Basil stepped forward, wearing a bright smile. "Oh, it will. He'll be working for me, Basil Warrick. Behind me is my cousin, Valentin Wyndham, and his partner, Sebastian Beaumont. We're friends of your brother and we've known Sal for, quite literally, centuries. No doubt he can be obnoxious at times, but he truly is one of the good ones, and while he jokes that he has a black heart, it's really golden."

"Aww, Baz, that's the sweetest thing you've ever said about me," Sal said.

"Yes, I know. And taking a lesson from you, I feel some bile at the back of my throat over speaking such mushiness."

Sal laughed and rested a hand over his abdomen. "Shit, don't make me laugh. I'm still sore."

Basil rested an affectionate hand on Sal's shoulder and offered his other to Nathan. "But as I was saying, it's lovely to meet you."

Nathan reached with a hesitant hand to take Basil's. "You're really a…vampire?"

"Yes, Valentin and I are both vampires, but I'm sure we could probably correct a few false ideas you're thinking now, if you're basing what we are off certain movies or books. Yes, we drink blood. Yes, we're immortal. And we're certainly faster and stronger than humans, and we have numerous other abilities, but a lot of the weaknesses are false. For example, I rather enjoy churches, and blessed artifacts don't bother us. The sun is troublesome, but we don't incinerate the instant it touches us. Really, you can think of us as human, but with several upgrades."

Calvin watched Nathan slowly nod and stare at Basil. His brother looked like he needed to lie in bed, curled into a ball for a few hours to figure out everything that'd happened.

Nathan let out a heavy breath and ran his hand through his hair. "I don't think my life is ever going to be the same."

Sebastian moved closer to Nathan. "No, it won't. My introduction to vampires was pretty rough, having been a blood slave, and just like you thought all demons were bad, I thought I vampires were horrible. And then I met Valentin and my world changed again, for the better. I know you're going through a hell of a shock right now, but I promise you, you're surrounded by the good guys now."

Nathan gave him a smile. "I appreciate hearing that."

Calvin slid across the floor and wrapped Nathan in a hug. "I'm glad you're okay."

"So am I. Thanks to your demon."

"Hey now," Sal said, waving a hand. "Let's take it easy on the possessives here."

Calvin looked at him. "You're saying you're not?"

"No, no, I'm not saying that. It's just different when I say it and someone else does."

Calvin rolled his eyes, but his smile remained.

"Well, since we're going to be here until the sun sets, we'll help with picking up," Basil said. He pointed at Sal. "But not you. You need to rest. I'm sure Sebastian would be willing to drive you home so you can get cleaned up and be in your own bed, then he could come back for us."

Sebastian nodded. "Absolutely."

Calvin turned to Sal. "You should go and rest. I need to figure out a way to secure the huge hole your ex blew in my house, then once that and everything else is settled, I'll come back with everyone."

Sal gazed at him, silent, and Calvin could sense his hesitation to leave. He rested his hand on Sal's cheek. "I think I've proven I'm not half bad at taking care of myself and others, even a badass demon like you."

Sal took Calvin's hand and brought it to his lips, placing a kiss on the back of Calvin's fingers. "You've proved more than that."

In Sal's gaze and voice, Calvin heard what Sal really meant behind the words. He gripped Sal lightly by the horns, pulling him in for a kiss. He meant to keep it chaste, but his emotions soared at feeling Sal's lips on his and as Sal started opening his mouth, he did the same.

The kiss eased to an end, but he didn't want it to. He wanted to press his body against Sal's, to give himself to him, be joined with him. He knew Sal needed more rest, though, and he certainly couldn't start stripping in front of everyone and having his way with his demon duke.

Calvin sat back from the kiss and stood, holding both hands down to Sal. "Do you think you can stand and walk if I help you into the car?"

"Yeah, I'll be all right." Sal got to his feet with a pull from

Calvin. He stumbled and swayed, as if a wave of dizziness hit him. He gripped onto Calvin to steady himself, and Calvin held onto him. Sal shrugged out of the ruined remains of his shirt, letting it fall to the floor. His horns, claws, and fangs retreated, leaving him back in his human form.

"Before you head out there," Basil said, "Calvin, do you have anything to wrap him in? He's a mess, and I really don't want to try to explain to a detailer what's all over my car."

Sal huffed. "Just when you started to be sweet to me, Baz, you go and say something like that."

Basil held up his index finger. "It's not that, and I think the fact alone that I'm letting you in my Range Rover covered in blood proves that I am tremendously sweet and compassionate, but why make more of a mess than there needs to be?"

Nathan started to push himself up. "I'll get a blanket for him."

Basil turned back to him, helping Nathan to stand. "That's most gracious. Thank you." He left the family room with Nathan and they walked down the hallway.

Valentin went to Beezle and picked him up. He stroked the little croc on the head, then handed him to Sebastian. "I'm sure he'd like a lift home, also."

Sebastian cradled him in one arm. "And I think he's earned a long rest, too."

Basil and Nathan returned, Buster trotting behind them. Basil tossed a green blanket around Sal's shoulders and helped him to wrap it around his body. "There we go. Now let's get you out to the car."

Calvin guided Sal forward and out of the house to the Range Rover parked in the drive. He opened the passenger door for him, keeping a hand on Sal's arm to steady him as Sal sat inside. He turned to Sebastian and took Beezle, placing the little croc on Sal's lap. As Sebastian walked around the front of the SUV to the driver's side, Calvin leaned in, kissing Sal one more time.

"I'll see you soon," he said.

Sal squeezed Calvin's hand. "Try to make it as soon as you can."

"I will." Calvin glanced up, seeing Valentin braving the sunlight for a few moments to kiss Sebastian. When Valentin backed away from the SUV and closed the driver's side door, Calvin gave Sal's hand another squeeze, then slowly released it and closed the passenger door.

He walked back to the porch, Valentin standing behind him inside the shade of the doorway. The SUV's windows were tinted too dark for him to see Sal, but he knew Sal's gaze was on him and he lifted his hand in a wave. He watched the SUV pull away, mixed with wanting to follow, but also relieved that Sal was safe. He turned to go back inside.

He didn't know if he fully comprehended all that'd happened, all he'd done. Sal said he'd saved him. He didn't know much about the Powers that demons believed in, but he did know that a stronger connection had been forged between Sal and himself, one that went far beyond any deals or owed favors.

Chapter Eighteen

Sal snapped awake, bolting up and ready to deliver a deathblow to his enemy. Only, there was no enemy, no Amon. He was in his bedroom in the mansion…alone.

He took a deep breath, mentally telling himself the fight with Amon was long over, he was alive and most importantly, Calvin was safe. But Calvin also wasn't there. He didn't sense him, Basil, Valentin, or Sebastian in the home. He looked toward the windows, pale moonlight streaming through. The hour was late. Everyone should've been back by now.

Sal stretched toward the nightstand and picked up his phone, seeing a missed call and two texts. He unlocked his phone and went to his messages.

Hey, I tried to call, but you must be sleeping. Just wanted to let you know things are taking a little longer than we thought trying to secure the backdoor, but it shouldn't be too much longer before we're done.

The second text read, *We're on our way back. I hope you're doing okay. I'm worrying since I haven't heard from you. Can't wait to see you.*

The last text was sent only ten minutes ago, so Sal typed back, *Just woke up. Still feeling a little out of it, but doing better.* He paused for a moment, trying to decide whether or not to type the last part on his mind. Fuck it. Calvin had saved his life. *I can't wait to see you, too.*

He set the phone back on the nightstand and eased to his back with a wince. Since he was shirtless, wearing only black athletic pants for comfort, he looked down at his abdomen and ran a hand over where the wound had been. There wasn't a mark to be seen. Sy had done a hell of a job healing him. Despite being tender internally and in his muscles, he was feeling better, his body recovering from the blood loss with far greater speed than a mortal or even a vampire, but the fight and damage from the dagger had taken a lot out of him. He should go back to the demon realm. He would regain his strength faster there and in his true form, but he didn't want to leave Calvin alone here. Even though Calvin had thoroughly kicked Amon's ass, he wanted to be close.

Sal closed his eyes, his thoughts drifting through what'd happened…and the emotions he couldn't deny any longer. They haunted him more than getting knifed and nearly killed. Ever since Sebastian brought him home and left him to return to help the others, he'd had no option than to face those emotions. Throughout his shower and into sleep, he felt it deep and strong, and now that he'd acknowledged it, there would be no going back from it.

He was in love with Calvin.

He knew it before, but he'd been able to squash that shit down, bury it, hide it. Or so he thought. It'd been a fight within himself, love wanting to come out, give all those warm, fuzzy feelings, and him stomping the hell out of it and telling himself to knock it off. He was a demon. Calvin was a human. He was immortal. Calvin…wasn't. Love needed to stay away because all it'd bring in the long run was pain.

That's all it had done in the past. Even with learning the truth of why Sy had betrayed him, it didn't change the hurt that betrayal brought. Instead of making the deal with Tayish, Sy could've come to him and together, they could've beat the hell out of any demon wanting to assassinate him. But that's not what Sy did. Sy could sugarcoat it anyway he wanted about wanting to save him, but in the end, what he'd done had ultimately been good for Sy in winning him his princehood. The most learning about the reasons for Sy's betrayal of him did was lessen the animosity between them where they could recover their friendship. Maybe.

So, he knew well the crap love brought with it, including fear. He'd felt the latter potently today, fearing Calvin getting hurt. Fear of not being able to protect him. Fear of losing him. Why the fuck couldn't love come on its own? Why did it have to bring so much baggage with it?

But, there was also one other emotion that love had brought to him. He was happier than he'd been in ages. Maybe he could deal with everything else because of that. Really, he didn't have a choice. He was in love with his witch. He couldn't change that and if he was going to be honest about it—like he was with everything else right now—he didn't want to.

The big question was, what would Calvin ask of him? He had a strong feeling what it would be and he hoped he was right.

The creak and whine of the garage door opening below came to him. Sal pushed himself up with a burst of energy and out of bed. He reached the stairs, jogging down them as everyone walked into the entrance hall. He paused a few steps from the floor, surprised to see Nathan was with them, but didn't give it much thought as he looked at Calvin. Relief and a sense of peace moved through him, as if he hadn't fully felt at ease or didn't quite trust that Calvin was safe until that moment. Calvin looked up at him, and as he met Calvin's blue eyes, he knew without a doubt, he was fucked. Or as some would call it, in love.

Calvin smiled up at him. "Hey. You already look a lot better."

Sal cleared his throat and finished walking down the steps to greet him. "Yeah, Sy healed me well enough where my body's taking over now. I'll be fine by tomorrow." He opened his arms, and Calvin stepped into his embrace. He held him tight and bowed his head, whispering, "I'm glad you're here."

A loud, exaggerated sigh interrupted before Calvin could respond.

"Such sweetness, my poor old heart can't take it," Basil said, a hand over his heart. "It's too adorable." He smacked Valentin on the arm with the back of his hand. "Look at our demon, Valentin. Just look at him."

Valentin nodded in agreement. "I know. This must be how parents feel when their child finally finds the one they want to spend the rest of their life with."

His arm around Valentin's waist, Sebastian wiped away a nonexistent tear. "I think I'm going to cry."

Sal shot them a playful glare. "Laugh it up, smartasses." He looked at Calvin, who was snickering softly, and gave him a light shove. "And I don't know why you're laughing!"

"So many reasons," Calvin said. He flicked his head toward Nathan, who stood back watching them while holding Buster and looking generally uncomfortable. "Nathan's going to stay the night here. Baz and Valentin were nice enough to invite him, since the house isn't the most secure right now. Sebastian and I went down to the home store and bought big sheets of plywood to cover the hole where the backdoor was, but it wouldn't take much to kick them in."

His voice soft, Nathan said, "And I appreciate you all letting me stay here."

Basil patted him on the shoulder. "It's nothing. As we told you, you're among the good guys now."

Nathan smiled at him and seemed to relax a slight bit.

Basil turned his attention back to Sal. "By the way, we've asked Calvin to move in here. We know you want him to, but we thought we'd save you the struggle of asking yourself. He said he wanted to talk to you about it first. I told him to do what he wants and you'll go along with it."

Sal's mouth dropped open, only a cough coming out.

Laughing softly, Calvin shifted his backpack on his shoulder and looped his arm through Sal's. "I think with that getting dropped on you, I better get you back in bed." He looked at Basil. "Which guest room do you want Nathan in?"

Basil waved him off. "We'll get him settled. You take care of your demon."

Letting Calvin lead him back up the stairs, Sal pointed back at Basil. "Quit talking about me like I'm his new puppy!"

"More like his old dog," Basil said. "Good luck teaching that one any new tricks, Calvin."

Everyone laughed, even Nathan, and Sal couldn't help but smile. He faced forward, walking with Calvin up the stairs. "See what you've done? They think I'm some kind of lovesick puppy."

Calvin turned a smirk on him. "You mean you're not?"

At the top of the stairs, Sal turned left with Calvin. He pointed to his own chest with his thumb. "Hey, I've got control over my emotions. Everyone can tease me all they want. I'm demon enough to take it."

Calvin veered into Sal's bedroom. "We know. That's why we're teasing you. That, and I think we're all pretty damn happy to be able to tease you."

Sal stopped at his bedside and turned to him, watching Calvin slide his bag off his shoulder and set it in a chair. The humor had vanished from Calvin's face with his last words, and Sal understood then how much everything had affected him. Calvin had shown his bravery in more ways than banishing a demon. He'd also shown it in keeping himself together to get Sy to heal him and take care of his brother and the house. Calvin had done nothing but put on a brave face, and now that they were alone, he could see Calvin's façade beginning to crack.

Sal stretched a hand out to him. "Hey, come here."

A few quick steps brought Calvin to him. Calvin threw his arms around him, holding him tight, burying his face against Sal's neck. "When I got Sebastian's message, I was so scared for you and Nathan. Then when I came in and I saw you laying there…all that blood around you…" Seeming not able to finish his words, he squeezed Sal tighter, pressed into him more.

Sal rested one hand on the back of Calvin's head, holding him with his other arm. "I know. It looked bad, but you were amazing." He touched his lips to Calvin's cheek, giving him a kiss and also letting him feel his smile. "Sy was right. I should've let you fight for me from the start."

Calvin let out a laugh and lifted his head. His fear, relief, and love had overcome him to the point where tears shone in his witch's beautiful blue eyes. Calvin blinked, two tears escaping. Sal gently lifted off Calvin's glasses and set them on the nightstand, then wiped the tears away with his thumbs. "I'm proud of you, witchy poo. You're a hell of a man and an incredible witch."

"So does that mean you're done pushing me away now?"

"What it means is…" Sal brought his lips close to Calvin's,

"I'm going to drive you insane by wanting to be with you all of the time."

Calvin's breath left him in a rush. He closed his and Sal's mouths together in a heated kiss. Sal slid his tongue along Calvin's, a moan passing from Calvin's mouth into his. He drifted his hands under Calvin's shirt, caressing the smooth skin of Calvin's back as he edged the shirt up. Calvin eased back from the kiss, letting him lift the shirt off. He dropped it to the floor and reached for Calvin's jeans. Putting his lips to Calvin's neck, Sal kissed, licked, gently nipped, and breathed in Calvin's clean scent, knowing Calvin must have showered before coming over.

He finished drawing the zipper down on Calvin's jeans and hooked his thumbs over them and Calvin's briefs, lowering them together. He went to his knees and locked his gaze on Calvin's dick, so hard it strained out from Calvin's body. Sal leaned close to Calvin's body, breathing in his masculine scent, and let out a groan. "You haven't come since we stopped seeing each other, have you?"

"No."

Sal heard the need in Calvin's voice. "Neither have I." He touched the tip of his tongue to Calvin's balls and licked up, leaving a wet line from Calvin's sac and along the underside of his shaft. "We're going to have to change that for both of us." He drew the tip of his tongue over Calvin's slit, cleaning it of pre-cum. He opened his mouth wider and took the cockhead in.

He moved down Calvin's shaft. The head hit the back of his throat, and he kept going, swallowing it and taking Calvin's full cock into his mouth. Calvin gasped and gripped a fistful of Sal's long, red hair. Sal slid back up the shaft, swirled around the head with his tongue, and dove back down it. He rubbed both hands up Calvin's thighs, felt the tension in the muscles, and knew Calvin was already fighting against his rising pleasure. Sal moved one hand to Calvin's sac, gently fondling his balls.

Calvin tossed his head back. "Fuck, Sal. It feels…so…good."

Sal slowly sat back, Calvin's cock slipping out of his mouth.

"That's good, but I don't want you to come yet. I want you to come with me, when my dick is deep inside you."

Calvin reached down, taking Sal's hands and guiding him up, then claimed his lips in a passionate kiss. He pushed against Sal, pressing him back toward the bed. He broke the kiss as Sal bumped into the edge. "Maybe you should slip into your true form. You know, not take unnecessary energy away from your body to heal by keeping up your human form."

A knowing grin slid over Sal's lips. "That's so thoughtful of you."

Brushing his smiling lips over Sal's, Calvin said, "That's just the kind of guy I am."

Sal pushed his pants off and began to slowly loosen his hold over his human form. "You most definitely are."

As his height grew, frame and muscles thickened, Calvin kept his hands on him, caressing, stroking, admiring him as he took on his true form, and that alone was nearly enough to make him climax. His horns grew out, thick and spiraled, and his wings emerged. He stretched them out with a groan. He knew Calvin's other motive in suggesting he go into his true form, but his dear witch was right in how it would save his energy and be more comfortable.

Calvin leaned his body into Sal's, going up on his tiptoes to get closer to his lips, though, Sal still had to bow his head for Calvin to reach them. "Beautiful," Calvin whispered before touching their lips together in a gentle kiss. He eased back and nodded toward the bed. "You lay back. Let me do the work tonight."

Sal sat on the bed and slid up toward the headboard. "I like the sound of that." He propped the pillows against the headboard and leaned back on them. His wings spread over the bed and hanging over the edges. He gripped his cock in a fist, grinning at Calvin. "I'm ready."

"You always are." Calvin opened the nightstand drawer and retrieved the bottle of lube. He climbed onto the bed, straddled Sal's thighs and sat with his cock resting against Sal's.

Sal took them both in a loose grip. He cupped the back of Calvin's neck with his other hand and a gentle pull brought Calvin to his lips. Their tongues brushed along each other. Calvin rocked his hips, his cock sliding along Sal's.

Sal moaned low in his throat. He tightened his grip, increasing the friction of their hard cocks rubbing together. His need to have Calvin strengthened, as his control against coming weakened. Sal ended the kiss, Calvin's warm breath washing against his lips. "I need inside you."

Calvin reached for the lube and popped it open. "I need that, too." He filled his palm full with the clear liquid and took hold of Sal's cock.

Sal closed his eyes, a long groan leaving him as Calvin smoothed the silky fluid over his dick from base to tip, pleasuring him as much as preparing him. He slowly opened his eyes and picked up the lube, slicking his fingers. Retracting his claws, he reached behind Calvin and rubbed the outside of the tight hole. He pushed two fingers into him. Calvin's breath hitched in his throat. He dipped his back, pushing his ass back toward Sal's hand.

Sal thrust his fingers deeper into him. "That's perfect, beautiful, how you want it from me."

Calvin straightened and placed a hand on Sal's shoulder for balance. He brought his ass over Sal's cock, guiding the head to his hole. He looked into Sal's eyes as he began easing down on it. "I don't want it from anyone else. And I never will."

Sal held onto Calvin's hips, pure bliss surging through him as Calvin took in his dick. Calvin settled all the way down the hard rod. He closed his eyes, moaning as he rolled his hips.

Sal ran his hands up Calvin's chest, gazing at his witch's beautiful face and the pleasure filling it. "What else do you want from me?"

Calvin opened his eyes. He took Sal's hands, locking their fingers together, palm to palm. He braced against them and Sal's strength as he began moving up and down Sal's cock. "I want to hear you say that you love me."

Sal knew he probably should've been surprised at the request, but in an odd way, it made him happy. He allowed a smirk to curve his lips. "Is that what you're going to use your demon wish on?"

"If I have to."

Sal held Calvin's gaze, took in the seriousness. He didn't doubt Calvin knew how he felt, but it was clear Calvin needed to hear him say it. He drew one hand out of Calvin's and laid it on Calvin's cheek, caressing along his cheekbone. "You don't have to." He brushed his thumb over Calvin's lips. "I love you, Calvin."

Sal felt the surge of emotion from Calvin. He switched his sight to see Calvin's aura and it radiated with golden energy… with love.

Calvin fell forward, wrapping his arms around Sal's neck. "I love you, too."

Sal brought their lips together, pushing his emotion into the kiss for Calvin to feel the truth of it. He caressed down Calvin's back to take him by the hips again, thrusting up to meet each downward push of Calvin's ass. Their kiss came to an end, but Calvin stayed leaning close to him, their lips nearly touching.

"What else do you want from me?" Sal whispered.

Calvin exhaled a few fast breaths before he seemed to be able to find his voice again. "I want…I want you to give me immortal life. To not grow old or become sick. To live eternally as a human and still be a witch, so I can be with you…forever."

From deep inside, a stirring of power rose within Sal unlike any he'd ever cast before. He'd wondered when Calvin made his request, how he would make it happen, and it seemed the Powers and instinct were going to guide him. With each second, the strength of power increased. He could feel it spreading through his body. Before it overpowered him, he had to ask Calvin again. "You're sure that's what you want?"

Calvin nodded. "Yes. Without a doubt."

As if Calvin's confirmation was the last thing needed for the spell to be cast, the power surged through Sal in a dizzying and pleasure-filled rush. He dropped his head back, moaning loud, thrusting up into Calvin with more urgency. Calvin's voice blended with his in ecstasy, and he held onto Sal tighter. Opening his eyes, Sal saw they were both wrapped in the soft blue light of the spell's power, but around Calvin, it was a halo of radiance.

Calvin rode Sal's cock, breathing fast, moaning his pleasure on each exhale. "It feels…so…incredible. And I'm close. So… close."

The energy, power, and pleasure radiating around them and through them, Sal knew he couldn't hold back much longer either. He gripped Calvin's cock, pumping it in quick, strong strokes. "Come with me."

Breathing hard, fast, desperate, Calvin thrust back on Sal's cock, grinding his ass on Sal's hips. He clenched Sal's shoulders, shouting his pleasure as he came. The first shot of cum landed on Sal's chest and he let go of his control, following Calvin into climax. The pleasure and power blazed between him and Calvin, overwhelming him. When it slowly began to fade, his mind felt as if it were floating, his body extra sensitive to every touch from Calvin.

Calvin slumped forward, resting against him, his head on Sal's shoulder. Sal brushed his fingertips up and down Calvin's back, savoring the warmth of his body against him and the lingering ecstasy. He turned his head toward Calvin, nuzzling into his hair and grinning. "I really hope your brother is still downstairs, otherwise there's no doubt he heard us fucking and that's going to be really awkward over breakfast."

A laugh broke from Calvin. He sat up, giving Sal a light push on the chest. "We need to work on your romantic-after-sex-talk."

Sal caught him behind the neck and pulled him down for a kiss. The kiss drew to a gentle end, and he brought his hand forward on Calvin's cheek. "Seriously, though, how do you feel?

Any different?"

"I feel amazing, but…" Calvin smirked at him, "I can't tell if your magic or your dick has me feeling this way."

"Well, if I had to take a guess…" Sal motioned toward his crotch in answer.

Calvin laughed and glanced to the side, toward the tall windows and the night beyond. "But I think it worked."

"How do you know?"

"I can see clearly, perfectly, without my glasses."

Sal gazed at him for a moment, then flicked his gaze to Calvin's glasses on the nightstand. "That must've been a side effect. The spell must've healed or corrected anything with your body."

Still looking toward the windows, Calvin's voice was soft as he spoke. "I'm going to miss wearing them."

"We can always get you some with plain glass lenses."

Calvin nodded slowly.

Sal gripped him lightly under the chin and turned Calvin's head toward him. "You doing okay with this?"

A smile rose to Calvin's lips. "I'm so happy, I don't even know where to begin with expressing it or even understanding it. I've never felt anything like this before." He laid his hand over Sal's. "On a lot of levels. All I know is I wouldn't change any of it."

Sal sat up, bringing his lips close to Calvin's. "I wouldn't either. And I'll say, I'm fucking ecstatic over what you wanted from me."

Calvin wrapped his arms around Sal's neck, closing their mouths together.

In the kiss, emotion flowed between him and Calvin, pure elation, and strongest of all, love. He made a silent vow with his kiss to Calvin, never again would he try to deny or push away the love he had for his witch.

Chapter Nineteen

The back of the mansion shone with soft yellow ground lights, keeping the night and shadows at bay, and giving a warm feel to the area. The scent grilling steaks wafted through the air, along with wood smoke from the fire crackling in the stone and brick lined fire pit. Calvin reclined in a lounge chair, smiling as he watched Sal play with Buster.

A week had passed since Sal had given him the greatest of gifts, his love. And immortality, too. He'd adjusted and fully accepted his decision with the latter. He was overjoyed with the first.

Since Sal had given him immortality, he'd made a point of testing small spells and all had been successful. The day before, he went to Basil's building that was to become Ambrosia and performed a cleansing of the space to ensure no negative energies or entities were there. After he'd finished, Basil, Valentin, Sebastian, and Sal noted how the place seemed brighter, despite the cleaning and remodeling having not yet begun.

He couldn't express his relief at still being able to cast. He'd been ready to give up being human and any power he had if it meant he could be with Sal, having both was something he hadn't given hope to. Now that he did have Sal and was still able to use his power, he fully understood what it was to feel blessed. It made him determined to use the long life ahead of him to continue studying his craft and to use it for the good of others.

The door opened behind him, and Calvin glanced back to see Basil and Nathan walking out with drinks and going toward the round, glass-topped patio table. He smiled as he looked at his brother. Three days after the fight with Amon, when Sal regained his strength, Nathan consented to Sal healing him.

It was still so clear in his mind. The house was a mess from the fight. All that could be cleaned up was, but the carpet and padding had to be ripped out of the family room, since demon blood wasn't exactly easy to clean. Standing in that disheveled family room, Sal had approached a nervous looking Nathan and said, "You know, usually when I heal someone, I do it with a kiss."

Nathan's mouth had dropped open, he'd stumbled a step back. "What?!"

Sal burst out laughing. "I'm just fucking with you, little priesty. Your brother would kick my ass if I kissed you. I do prefer to at least touch someone when I'm healing them, because the contact helps the energy to pass from me to them, with none getting dissipated into the air, but in your case, I'll hold my hands close to you."

Sal then did as he said, letting his power flow out to Nathan. The effect on Nathan was almost instant. He stood straighter, light began to come back into his eyes, and the pain that had become ever present, vanished.

But something else changed with his brother, too. Also in Nathan's eyes, he saw gratitude and acceptance toward Sal. Maybe even more so than his own, Nathan's entire life would be different from then on. His brother's mind had been forced open, and now he was positive Nathan understood that whether someone was human, vampire, or demon, each was an individual not to be judged, but to be accepted for who they were.

Of course, coming face to face with demons and discovering vampires were real was pretty much enough to blow anyone's mind open, he supposed.

Calvin looked back to Sal, who was squatted down in front of Buster, a red ball in one hand, petting the little terrier mix with his other.

Sal stood and tossed the ball. "Catch!"

Buster sprang into the air, snatching the soaring ball. The dog clamped onto it with small teeth and pranced with his head high, his prize in his mouth, back toward Sal.

"What a good poochy!" Sal patted and roughed up Buster's fur, then glanced at Beezle laying at the edge of the pool. "You see that, Beezy? That's how it's done."

A low grumble came from Beezle. He turned and slipped into the water.

"And there he goes into the pool," Basil said with a sigh. "Why won't your demon reptile go down to the lake if he wants to swim?"

Sal swung around to face Basil, hands on his hips. "Because the pool water's warmer and he likes it. Quit your bitching. Having that cute pool guy come more often to clean it wouldn't be a bad thing for you."

Basil lifted his glass of wine to his lips, taking a sip before setting it down on the table. "Except for the fact that he appears to most definitely be a sun worshipper given his tan, and I'm always asleep when he's here during the day, save for the one time you pushed me out of bed to gawk at him."

Sal rolled his eyes. "You're exaggerating. I didn't push you out of bed."

"No, I think you did," Valentin said, standing at the grill. "I heard the thump of him hitting the floor."

"I nudged him. He fell out of bed on his own."

"Because you startled me!"

"You shouldn't scare so easily! You're a damn vampire!"

Laughter echoed through the area from everyone.

Sebastian, sitting in the chair beside Calvin, gave him a light push on the arm. "Any regrets about moving into this crazy joint?"

Calvin looked toward him. "Hell no. I love it and I'm happy you guys invited me. And I'm also pretty sure Sal is the one who brings the crazy."

Sal spun around with a gasp of pretend offense. "I bring the *fun*. There's a difference."

"No, no," Basil said. "I think Calvin had it right the first time."

Sal huffed and walked toward Calvin. "Witchy Poo loves my

kind of crazy. Don't you?"

Grinning, Calvin reached a hand out to him. "Since it was part of the packaged deal with getting the rest of you and I love all that you are, we'll go with that."

Sal took Calvin's face in both hands, smiling as he gave him a rough kiss.

"As sweet as that is," Valentin said, "Could you please let Calvin have his mouth back long enough to eat? His, yours, and Nathan's steaks are done."

Nathan moved to Valentin's side. "What about Sebastian, and you and Basil? Aren't you eating?" He paused, his green eyes widening as if he'd made a horrible faux pas. "Or, I'm sorry, do you not eat regular food?"

Valentin laughed softly. "No apologies needed. We vampires can and do eat typical food, but it's more of a pleasure for us than needing the sustenance."

"And they just throw their steaks on the grill long enough to get a little brown on the outside," Sal added.

Sebastian hopped up and walked toward Valentin. "I've been taking mine a little rarer these days." He stopped behind Valentin and wrapped his arms around him, resting his head on Valentin's as he spoke to Nathan. "Vampire in training, that's me."

Valentin laid one hand over Sebastian's arms. "You're going to make a brilliant vampire, prior training or not." He extended a plate with a steak on it to Nathan. "And if you have any questions about vampires, feel welcome to ask."

Nathan took the plate and walked toward the table. "I appreciate that. I have a ton of questions, the problem is sorting them all out. I think I'm still trying to wrap my head around everything that's happened."

Already sitting at the table, Basil said, "Understandable. You went through quite a shock, between having your trust betrayed by who you thought was a new friend, to finding out about our kind, to…well, Sal. He's enough of a shock for anyone."

Sal let out a fake laugh. "You're hilarious tonight! And I think meeting you long fangs was more of one."

Nathan smiled at Sal. "Actually, I think Basil's a little more right."

Sal laid his hand on his chest. "You shouldn't say such things and hurt your demon-in-law."

Calvin glanced back at him as he collected his plate from Valentin. "Demon-in-law? Where was I when we got married?"

Sal joined him at the grill. "I gave you immortal life. That's pretty much the same thing."

Calvin gave him a light kiss on the lips before turning toward the table. "Glad you let me know that now." He sat beside Nathan and clapped a hand onto his brother's shoulder. "I'm just happy I'll get to have you around for a long time now."

Nathan laid his hand over Calvin's. "The worst of it was, I almost brought about my own demise faster than anything else." He shook his head. "There's still a part of me that can't believe I didn't see that demon for what he was."

Sal dropped down into a chair on Calvin's other side. "Don't be so hard on yourself about it. We demons are tricky bastards."

"Yeah, but I was even warned about him, right after I met him. I didn't understand it at the time, but now I see it so clearly."

Sebastian looked at him in curiosity as he sat down with his plate. "Who warned you?"

"I don't know who he was. He appeared out of nowhere, in the rain, and gave me his umbrella." Nathan looked up at Valentin, who approached the table to set Basil's plate before him and carrying another for himself. "Thinking about him now, he reminds me a bit of you two, but maybe that's because he was from England, too. At least, he had the same accent as you both, with that sophisticated roll to his words." He picked up his knife and fork. "All I know is he told me not to trust the priest and his name was Malcolm."

Valentin paused in pulling out his chair, his gaze on Nathan.

He shook his head, sighed, and finished dragging his chair out from under the table. "Well, there's that mystery solved."

Basil took his knife across the steak, slicing it with more force than needed. "I don't understand why that little shit is still here. He certainly gained more than enough money from his antics for him to go back to England."

Nathan looked back and forth between them. "You know him?"

"Too well," Valentin mumbled into his snifter of brandy.

Sebastian took Valentin's hand. "Malcolm is Valentin's ex, who Valentin had turned into a vampire. There's kind of bad blood between Basil, Valentin, and Malcolm, but the guy saved my life, so I don't think he's all bad."

"Your life needed saved because he put it in danger," Valentin growled.

"There were a lot of factors involved that day." Sebastian kissed Valentin on the cheek. "The important thing is, we're all still here, from that day and what happened a just a few days ago."

Basil held up his wine glass. "Cheers to that."

"And," Nathan said, lifting his glass, "here's to new life and new friends." His gaze went to Sal, a warm smile on his lips.

Sal touched his glass to Nathan's. "I'll definitely drink to that."

Everyone touched their glasses together.

Calvin bumped Nathan playfully on the shoulder with his shoulder. "I'm proud of you."

"I'm proud of you, too." Nathan reached over and swiped his hand over Calvin's hair, making the already tousled strands messier. "My little brother teaching me about life. I think I need to catch up to you on some things."

"Like getting a job now that you're healthy," Calvin snickered.

Nathan gave him a shove. "Yeah. That too."

"Will you not return to seminary school to finish your studies and become ordained?" Valentin asked.

Taking a deep breath, Nathan shook his head. "I'm not sure that's my calling, anymore. All of this has left me with a lot of… questions."

Basil tipped his glass toward Nathan. "Well, if you're looking for work, I happen to know a place that's hiring."

"And there he goes into business mode," Valentin said.

Sebastian nodded. "But Ambrosia can't be anything but a success with that attitude of his."

Nathan turned to Basil. "What's the job and the place?"

"This may take a while to explain," Basil began. "Now, put aside your morals for a moment and hear me out…"

With Basil explaining about the soon-to-be blood house to Nathan, Calvin glanced at Sal and found his demon's lavender gaze was already on him. He'd caught Sal looking at him a lot in the past few days and he always liked was he saw in his eyes — warmth, affection, love.

He laid his hand on Sal's, and Sal curled his fingers around Calvin's. He lifted Calvin's hand to his lips, placing a kiss on the back of it. He lowered his head toward him, resting his forehead on Calvin's, and whispered, "I was looking at you and thinking of everything. And you know what?"

Calvin rested his other hand on Sal's cheek. "What?"

"It feels good, knowing I'm going to have you forever."

Calvin smiled. "Feels good to me, too." He brought their lips closer. "I love you."

"I love you too, witchy poo."

Calvin touched their lips together. Around them, their friends, who he now considered family, continued talking. Warmth flowed through him, loving energy Sal was passing to him, and he opened his mind and emotions for Sal to feel the same from him. The years would pass, new adventures would come to them, but he knew no matter what they faced, nothing would ever be truer than his and Sal's love for each other.

About the Author

S.J. Frost resides in Ohio with her family and pets. Her short stories have been featured in several romance and erotica anthologies, and her gay erotic romance novels are published at MLR Press. To learn more about her writing, please feel welcomed to visit www.sjfrost.com and http://sj-frost.blogspot.com/

Trademarks Acknowledgment

The author acknowledges the trademark status and trademark owners of the following wordmarks mentioned in this work of fiction:

Craigslist: 1010 Cole Street, Inc.

Armstrong State University: University System of Georgia

Range Rover: Jaguar Land Rover North America, LLC

Viper ACR: FCA US LLC

Honda Civic: The Honda Motor Company

Lightning Source UK Ltd.
Milton Keynes UK
UKHW010622180419
341238UK00001B/44/P

9 781944 770235